Down to Earth

Parker Moose

Down to Earth

ISBN: 978-1-7361781-0-2

Also by Parker Moose:

Bucky the Sweet-Toothed Beaver
(written as Papa Moose, with illustrations by Yusup Mediyan)

In this delightful children's book, a beaver named
Bucky comes upon a mysterious crate of candy.
Can he overcome his sugar habit
before the rainy season begins?
Available on Amazon.com.

To Mike Rigg, for his input and inspiration.

CONTENTS

CHAPTER ONE

In a misguided moment of inspiration, they named their child Shirt. Not that Shirt was a funny name or a bad one for a caveboy. It was just that no Neanderthal had been named Shirt before.

Rock, Shirt's mother and aptly named, was taken by the name Rain. Ugh leaned more toward Peanut, but knew there was no use fighting his wife. The only time he had won an argument was when he courted her. Ugh had bashed Rock over the head and dragged her to his cave, and before she knew it Rock woke up married. But Rock made Ugh rue that day. She wore the pants in the family. Except there were no pants back then.

At first cavemen wore togas, wooly off-the-shoulder numbers. But then someone came up with sleeves, and shirts were all the rage. They were warmer in the wintertime and prevented sunburned shoulders and could be slipped over the head instead of having to fuss with knots. Otherwise they were like togas, stretching from neck to ankle, both comfortable and functional, though easily snagged on twigs.

So Ugh and Rock, which is to say, Rock, had decided on the name Rain. But when Ugh came to the birthing hut and saw his son for the first time, he looked down at the wrinkly infant and said,

"Him look like Shirt."

Rock, overcome by childbirth, which alas did not involve drugs, actually thought her husband had come up with a good idea. Everyone loved shirts. Her son would be ahead of his time. It was...Rock's head swum for the right word, and she coined the term right there. It was a *trendy* name, Rock thought. Then she passed out for a week.

Shirt was a fine student at what passed for caveman school. He learned how to hunt, how to swing a club, what leaves he shouldn't eat (most of them). He had an uncanny aim with a rock and could run as fast as the wind. But Shirt was taunted nonetheless. His classmates envied his name.

"Shirt think him am so smart," they'd say.

"Shirt am too good for old names."

"Shirt belong in laundry."

Which was actually quite good.

By now Shirt was eight and used to insults. There had never been a Shirt before. He wished he could be plain old What or Fire or, heck, even Smell. Now, there was a name just begging for taunting. But Shirt got all the grief.

And so, Shirt kept to himself in class, no friends at the boulders beside him. He watched his instructor point at what vaguely resembled a dinosaur. (Artists had poor survival skills and were generally eaten first). "Big lizard bad," his teacher said. "What do when see big lizard?"

Shirt knew the answer, but did not want to show off. Why add sticks to the fire?

"Me ask Shirt," said Fight, the class bully, turning to his friend What. Fight grabbed his shirt and spoke into it. "What am answer, Shirt?" Even the teacher had a laugh. That Fight was rather clever.

Shirt just fidgeted on his seat, which was uncomfortable to begin with. He knew he could knock Fight unconscious with a well-thrown rock, but Fight was the son of Chief Dog and therefore untouchable. So, instead, Shirt bowed his head and stared at his...well, shirt.

Head was born on a thunderous night full of sound and fury. His tribe, a superstitious lot, looked to the sky in fear. They did not know why the gods were not pleased on this night of all nights. Mud, their greatest warrior, was about to be a father. And the child's mother was Puddle, the finest cook in the swamp.

The Swamp People's diet was big on frog, an easily caught meal. Frog soup. Frog sandwich. Frog pot pie. On Friday's, frog on a stick. When swamp children asked what was for dinner, the answer started with "frog".

But Puddle knew ways to prepare a frog that no other swampwife could. She was a visionary, really. An amphibian artiste. The way she ground up leaves just so to flavor her frog souffle. Or that certain playfulness evoked by her signature frog scampi. Mud had certainly done well when he dragged Puddle to his hut.

At the onset of childbirth, however, Mud regarded his wife with fear. She was screaming like his best friend did when Big Teeth swallowed him.

"What am wrong?" Mud asked the midwife.

"Son of Mud am stuck."

Mud dared a look, and the next thing he knew he woke up on the floor.

"What happen?"

"Mud faint," the doctor told him.

"Am Son of Mud out yet?"

Puddle was wailing, expanding the caveman language by a few choice words. Bash, the doctor, glanced at the midwife, then reached for his trusty club.

Prehistoric anesthetic rendered its victims either unconscious or dead. Luckily Bash had stumbled upon nonlethal pressure points. He bonked Puddle with a surgical whack, and the screaming abruptly stopped. Puddle would live through the ordeal, although Mud never touched her again.

It took three cavemen to yank the newborn out of his comatose mother. Mud gasped when he beheld his son. He had a whopping noggin. A little less sloped than the typical skull, but still.

"Him have big head."

It was more of a statement than a boast. But the name worked, so it stuck.

Head was a precocious infant. He said his first word, mud, at five months. A cavebaby who said more than "ugh" his first year was considered a prodigy. But Head was doing more than that. He was actually making words up.

Puddle first noticed it at nine months, when Head spotted a squirrel. Cavemen called squirrels "fuzzy tails," but Head smiled and pointed.

"Squirrel!"

At first Puddle thought it was gibberish, just random baby talk. But the next week, they were out for a walk when Head did it again.

"Squirrel!" Head squealed from his knapsack.

Puddle froze when she saw the fuzzy tail.

Soon she realized Head was coining new words left and right. He called the pretty bug a "butterfly" and the stupid moo a "cow." Nose holes were "nostrils" and pointy sticks "spears" and he loved calling smelly sounds "farts." And when Head saw his first big lizard he named it a "dinosaur," clearly preferring the Latin derivation, *terrible lizard*.

Puddle thought Head was a genius and made him perform for his father. The three came upon a fuzzy tail and Puddle asked Head,

"What am that?"

"Squirrel!" Head said.

"What am squirrel?" Mud asked.

"Fuzzy tail. Head call it squirrel."

"Why him call it squirrel?" Mud said. "It am fuzzy tail."

"Squirrel am special word," Puddle said. "Head call fuzzy tail squirrel."

Mud's thoughtful stare ran from the squirrel to his son before resting on his wife.

"Head no learn him words so good. That am fuzzy tail."

But Puddle was determined to prove her son was a genius. She had Head point out butterflies and nostrils, cows and spears. Mud humored her until the day she brought the big lizard home. It took all of the men of the swamp to fell the bewildered rex, who was only looking for the chef behind the tasty trail of frog. As the tyrannosaur, covered in spears, collapsed at the door to Mud's hut, Puddle walked out the front door calmly, holding their son in her arms.

"What am that, Head?"

"Dinosaur!"

Puddle leered at her husband.

"Ha!"

Mud's reputation for being quick to club stifled any remarks about Head, as well as the Swamp People's craving for frog and Puddle's continued good will. But she had no visitors the rest of that week except for her best friend Robin.

"Me try frog recipe," Robin said as Head crawled about the hut. "It turn out pretty bad."

"You add cup of berries?" Puddle asked.

"No."

"Pinch of fungus plant?"

"Forget that too."

"Fungus important," Puddle said. "Otherwise frog am bland."

"Too hard remember," Robin huffed. "Me go back to frog on stick."

Puddle sighed as Head poked at a spear Mud retrieved from the dinosaur.

"Head!" Puddle said. "No touch spear! Spear BAD!"

"Bad!" Head aped gleefully.

"Puddle, what am spear?" Robin said.

"It am pointy stick."

"Then how come you say spear?"

"Head call it spear. Am new word for it. Spear am pointy stick."

"Spear!" Head said excitedly as Puddle snatched it away.

"That am amazing!" Robin said, a bit jealous of Head's development. Her own son Break's only inclination was headbutting foreign objects. And Break was four years old.

"Yes, him know more words than me," Puddle said matter-of-factly.

Robin's initial amazement took a right onto skeptical street.

"But why Head no use caveman words?"

"Because..." Puddle thought for a moment. "Because them not good enough."

"So Head too good for Swamp People."

"Me no say that," Puddle sighed.

Their conversation would have grown uglier had Head not drawn their attention.

"Spear!" he said, reaching for the object on his mother's lap. When he saw the prize just out of his range, Head stood up. Erect.

"Puddle," Robin gasped as Head took his first few awkward steps toward them. His cherubic smile seemed demonic now, and she flinched when he held out his hand.

"Me have to go now," Robin said. She bolted out the door.

"Robin go?" Head asked his mother, still standing straight as an arrow.

"Yes," Puddle said. "But no be sad. Robin am just dumb."

Whenever cavemen encountered something they did not understand, they either destroyed it or built it a temple and worshiped it as a god. But neither seemed appropriate in Head's case, so they called a tribal council.

Puddle sat with Head on her lap at the front of the Great Hut. She looked at the clansmen gathered before them as Fire, the Swamp Chief, spoke.

"Where am boy's father?"

"Here," Mud said, standing amid the crowd.

"Why am Mud not with family?" Fire asked.

"Because me scared of boy."

The crowd murmured. Fire raised his club, bringing the room to order.

"Mud am great warrior. But scared of boy?"

"Yes," Mud said, ashamed.

"Why Mud scared?"

"Him different," Mud said, raising his eyes to his son.

"Big lizard different from caveman," Fire said. "Fuzzy tail different from tree." There was another round of murmurings as the crowd digested Fire's wisdom.

"But Head come from Mud's loins," Mud said. "No am son of tree or big lizard."

"Head am devil!" the priest, Sun, said. "Him no walk like man!" The third wave of murmurings covered the best techniques to drive a demon out. Boiling and clubbing seemed best.

"Head am different." Puddle clutched her son. "But him am still caveman."

"What Puddle mean?" Chief Fire said.

"Him just smarter than us."

Mud bowed his head amid the laughter.

"Him smarter, huh?" Fire said. "Then let me speak with boy." Fire covered the few steps between them and knelt in front of Head. "What you have to say, son of Mud?"

"Fire!" the infant squealed.

"Him am smart!" Fire said to the crowd. "Him know my name!"

"Fire!" Head said, but he looked worried now.

"Yes, me know name," Fire said.

That's when Puddle looked through the door and saw the cloud of smoke.

"Fire!" she said.

"What?"

"FIRE!" She pointed. The Swamp People turned and panicked.

It was not the Great Hut which was ablaze, but rather Fire's home. Its thatch roof was billowing so much smoke Shirt's tribe saw it across the lake.

The Swamp People formed a bucket brigade but it was too late for Fire's hut. At least they had contained the blaze before it spread any further.

"Head start fire! Am devil!" Sun the priest said from the crowd. But the Swamp People parted to let Fire through. He stooped and looked Head in the eye.

"Him okay," Fire pronounced at the foot of his former home. "Boy save village." Puddle beamed.

"Fire!" Head grabbed his leader's nose.

"Yes, fire," the Swamp Chief chuckled. He patted the infant's head.

Mud kept his suspicions to himself. He was already sleeping outside.

CHAPTER TWO

Thomas slithered along the palace hall on his way to see the king, hoping that the emperor would be more coherent today.

"Ah, Thomas, my anxious advisor!" King Stanley called from his throne. "Come! I'll lend you an eager ear!"

So much for that idea. Thomas tugged at his tunic, a short-sleeved number whose skirt rode up his tentacles. It was hard finding sensible clothing for someone with two arms and a quartet of legs.

"Good morning, your grace," Thomas said. His words, a mixture of shrieks, trills and clicks, echoed in the room. King Stanley was mostly alone these days. He had a habit of babbling.

"Is that a data pad I spy huddled in your harried hands?"

"It is, your grace."

"Any news of our stagnant Steranko?"

Thomas fought the urge to wrap his tentacles around his king's throat.

"I'm afraid nothing has changed, your grace."

"That's too bad," King Stanley said. He rubbed the eyeballs at the end of his antenna. "You'll have to excuse me, old friend. I feel a nagging need for a nap."

"Well spoken, your grace." Thomas bowed and glided away.

Hover cars whizzed in orderly patterns outside the palace glass. Smooth-faced buildings stretched to the sky, poking through processed air. The global weather satellites guaranteed a perfect day, only sending rain when needed.

Thomas hated it all.

He was born in an age of automation, fertilized in a lab. His parents had browsed through a gene catalogue and bought their perfect son, though they later regretted not upgrading to the behavioral implant chip. Children were raised by robot nannies until they were six, when they were deemed to be more interesting, stopped leaking and ceased crying. By then they had learned to read and write and speak fluent Sterankon. There was nothing more they needed to know. The machines did all the rest.

The only careers available were in government and computer repair. Most Sterankons were happy to be unproductive and unemployed. They lay like slugs watching holovids or surfing the CableNet, eating their paste intravenously while pulleys worked their limbs. Their eyes had evolved into antenna so they wouldn't have to turn their heads, and they got at least twelve hours of sleep each night. There wasn't much else to do.

As a young squid, Thomas had an annoying habit of asking his parents questions. A medidroid diagnosed him with an acute case of curiosity. It was, by then, a rare disease on an apathetic world, and Thomas' parents responded by sending him to stay with his grandpa. Grandpa Shuster was two-hundred and fifty, preserved through gene therapy, and the last known example of a dying breed, the crotchety old squid.

"In my day, we didn't have holovids," Grandpa told the 10-year-old youth. "We watched our shows on flat little screens. And we didn't have hover cars, either. Why, we had to drive on the ground. Do you know what that was like?"

"No," Thomas said. He didn't. He had never imagined that things were different from the way that they were now. His parents' plan was backfiring. He thought Grandpa was cool.

Then Grandpa Shuster told him about a place they called the library. The library, so Grandpa claimed, was full of something called "books," which were some kind of story dispenser units that only contained words.

"But what about the pictures?" Thomas asked.

"In my day," Grandpa narrowed his eyes. "We made the pictures up."

Thomas shrank away from him.

"It's frightening, eh, boy?"

"Yes," Thomas said, but as he did he wrestled with his thoughts. It dawned on him that he wasn't repulsed by squidkind's primitive past. He was sad they had given up so much. They'd lost their imagination.

"Grandpa? Do you have any books?"

"Why yes, I believe I do."

Thomas followed him down the hall. Grandpa stopped outside a doorway. Grandma Siegel sat in her recliner holding her knitting needles. Her hands moved only occasionally as she watched a holovid.

"It's tragic, really," Grandpa said. "She's been working on the same pairs of socks since the year your father was born."

At the end of the hall Grandpa searched his pockets and pulled out a metal ring.

"Here we are."

Thomas saw a blank wall. "Here?"

"That's right," Grandpa said.

Thomas looked at the wall again. "But Grandpa, there's nothing here."

"You youngsters think you know so much." Grandpa cleared his throat. "Open."

The hologram of the blank wall blinked, revealing a secret door. It was wooden and hinged, unlike any door Thomas had ever seen.

"But..."

"I'm not used to having kids in the house. Didn't want you mucking around." Grandpa tried a number of the peculiar-looking keys before he found a fit. Dusty light poured through the doorway.

"Well?"

Thomas followed him in.

It was as close to a museum as there was on Steranko. A cluttered room of artifacts, each one a mystery. There was a square black box with a glass screen and two metal antenna. A grooved disc on a spindle with a pivoting arm to the side.

"What's this?" Thomas said, standing by a contraption that was almost as tall as he.

"That's called a stove," Grandpa Shuster said. "It was the first thing your grandmother threw out."

And beside the stove, the holy grail. An entire shelf lined with

"Books?"

Grandpa Shuster nodded.

Thomas reached up with a shy tentacle and took one in his hands. It was smaller than he imagined, with a colorful painting on front, a man embracing a woman squid whose clothes were falling off. Thomas mouthed the cover copy. "*She was trapped in a loveless marriage. He was a squid with a dark past. Together, they found their passion bound by Tentacles Of--*"

Grandpa snatched it away. "That's one of your grandmother's romance novels." He replaced it on the shelf. "They're better left extinct."

"But Grandpa, I liked that one."

"Here's one I enjoyed at your age." Grandpa handed him the book.

"*Showdown in Kane County,*" Thomas read. The other book swam in his mind.

"Have a seat." Thomas sat in a chair and Grandpa pulled a lever. Thomas jumped as the foot of the chair elevated his legs. "I envy you, my boy," Grandpa said. "You have a whole new world to explore."

Thomas turned the book in his hands, anxious to begin. He felt along the front and back covers.

"Grandpa?"

"Yes?"

"How does it work?"

"Just turn to the first page and read," Grandpa said.

"That's it?"

"That's it."

"Sounds easy."

"Then I'll leave you alone for a while."

Grandpa checked on Grandma Siegel while Thomas cracked his book. It was the story of a squid named Conway who was something called a sheriff. Apparently the sheriff's job was to punish criminals, either by putting them behind metal bars or slaying them in the middle of town. It was an interesting concept, but it didn't make much sense. Why was Sheriff Conway such a fan of capital punishment? Why didn't the town abolish its outdated monetary system? And why use lead projectiles instead of a matter displacement ray?

Thomas gave up about halfway through and browsed the rest of the shelf. He poked his antennae outside to see if Grandpa was coming, then he curled up in the recliner with *Tentacles of Lust*.

Romita's tentacles quivered as Perez brushed up against her. She felt the muscles in his arms and admired his emerald tan. "I've travelled all over Steranko,' he said, 'but I've never seen a body like yours." Her antenna twitched in anticipation as he

"Good heavens, boy! Put that down!"

Thomas had not seen Grandpa enter. Grandpa whipped the book out of his hands. "Maybe you're still too young for books."

"But Grandpa..."

"Mind your manners. Hmm," he pondered, "what else is there? Ah!" He slithered across the room. He flipped a switch on the small black box and the flat screen glowed with static. Grandpa turned on another component below it. This one kept flashing 12:00. He put a cassette into its slot. An image filled the screen.

"Good evening, my fellow Sterankons."

"That's King Stanley," Thomas said.

"Many of you may be mystified by my amazingly alert appearance. After all, a month ago I was declared decidedly dead."

"What?" Thomas said.

"Keep watching."

"Well, never fear fellow citizens, I've been saved by sensational science! I'm ready to rule regardless of my postmortem predicament!"

King Stanley's face was replaced by a screen of the Sterankon royal seal.

"Did he always talk like that?" Thomas said.

"Before he was cloned, he didn't."

"You mean," Thomas said, turning slowly to Grandpa, "that's not the real King Stanley?"

"I'm afraid not, m'boy," Grandpa Shuster said. "Old Stanley is a clone."

Thomas turned a pale shade of green.

"Didn't your parents tell you?"

"No," Thomas said with drooped antennae. "They don't tell me anything."

"I don't suppose they would."

Grandpa turned the antiques off.

"A few years before you were born, King Stanley died in a hover car crash. Apparently his fool driver didn't notice the needle on 'E.' At any rate, Steranko didn't know what to do at the time. Stanley was a popular king, and no one else wanted the job. So instead of selecting a new king, we replaced him with himself."

"But I thought cloning was illegal," Thomas said.

"It is. And with good reason."

"What's so bad about it?"

"For one thing, it's a lazy way to go about making a squid. You do know how squid are made, don't you?"

"Sort of," Thomas said. His parents had been hazy on that one, something about eggs and frozen tadpoles.

"Well, back in my day...how old are you, boy?"

"I'm almost eleven," Thomas said.

"Hmm, I guess that's old enough. Now then, where was I?"

"Back in your day."

"Ah, yes. Back in my day squid decided that they couldn't be bothered with procreation. Too much work. Too messy. Varicose veins. That sort of thing. So most of them had their eggs and such frozen and fertilized in the lab, but others thought Steranko would be better off stocked with clones."

"But why would they think that?"

"They thought clones would be more predictable. The problem was, they were right."

"What do you mean, Grandpa? Did the clones try to rebel?" Thomas envisioned a squid armada with zombie eyes and laser beams.

"Something like that," Grandpa said. "The first clone was named Liefeld. He was our chief scientist back then. Liefeld wanted to clone himself but he didn't want to raise a son. So he made a clone and accelerated its growth until it was as old as him."

"Cool," Thomas said.

"Until the clone was disintegrated."

"But why?"

"He was after Liefeld's girlfriend. He should have known the clone would have the same taste in women as him. Besides, having his growth accelerated did something to the clone's mind."

"You mean like he was evil?"

Grandpa Shuster smiled. "You've got quite the imagination. No, the clone wasn't evil. He just wasn't altogether there."

"But couldn't you make a nice clone if it didn't grow up so fast?"

"That didn't work out, either."

"Why?"

"How would you like to learn that you're going to grow up to be your father?"

"I see what you mean," Thomas said.

They partook of a much-needed lull.

"Grandpa?"

"Yes."

"King Stanley's clone wasn't accelerated, was he?"

"Yes, I'm afraid he was."

"But I thought you said that was bad."

"Well," Grandpa Shuster said, "you can't have an infant for a king."

The hover bus flashed its landing lights as it eased down in front of the terminal. Grandpa Shuster raised his shoulder harness and fumbled with his seat belt.

"Dag blast it, I'm stuck."

One seat down, Thomas stared into space.

"What's the matter with you?"

"I don't want to go home," Thomas said.

"Well, I can't keep you forever. I have to look after your grandmother."

"It's too boring at home."

Grandpa freed himself from his seat belt and raised Thomas' harness. "A boy your age should have plenty to do."

"Yeah, like sit around all day."

"Listen to yourself. When I was your age, I played outside until the suns went down."

Thomas tugged at his seat belt strap. "I wish things were like back then."

A stewardroid rolled up to them. Her gears clicked when she blinked.

"Hi! Do you need a hand, little boy?"

"No thanks," Grandpa said. "We're fine." He watched her send off the other passengers with the same robotic chirp, then he thought of the old days and patted Thomas' head.

"So do I."

Stanley International was the largest teleport on Steranko, beaming over 25,000 squid around the world each day. It was a small number compared to the crowds that passed through Stanley when it was an airport, but a plane carried hundreds of passengers. Teleports had to be done one at a time. Otherwise you never knew what would come out the other end.

Grandpa glanced at the arrival board as he rode the conveyor with Thomas, alarmed at all the passengers it listed as 'delayed.'

"Maybe you should have taken the bullet plane home."

"Don't worry, Grandpa," Thomas said, "I've done this before."

"Don't worry. Heh. That's what they said about microwaves."

The conveyor stopped at the baggage check. They moved their way to the front of the line.

"Hi there! Can I check your bags?" a perky android said.

"Great scott! She followed us from the bus!"

"Grandpa, they all look like that."

"Hmm," Grandpa Shuster said.

"Come on, Grandpa," Thomas said. They headed for their gate. Thomas had his atoms scanned and input in a computer. They watched a stewardroid help the next passenger up to the teleport pad. The tourist stood on a lighted circle, shimmered, and was gone.

"What does that feel like?" Grandpa said.

"I don't know, tingly," Thomas said. "Kind of like you have to pee."

"Now serving Thomas, Watterson City," the stewardroid announced.

"That's me."

"Give me a call to let me know you got there in one piece."

"I will." Thomas gave him a hug. He took his place on the teleport grid while the android worked the controls.

"Please keep your arms and tentacles inside the pad at all times."

"'Bye Grandpa!' Thomas said.

"And don't worry about your parents, you'll be--"

Thomas didn't hear the rest. The next thing he knew, he was standing in front of another stewardroid.

"Welcome to Watterson City! You may feel some disorientation after your molecular reassembly. But these should help you readjust."

It was a lousy bag of peanuts.

Thomas sat in an air car beside his father, who met him at the teleport. Thomas was impressed he had come in person instead of sending a droid.

"How was your trip?"

"Okay."

That was it for the father-son chat.

"Did you know we used to fly through space?" Thomas said shortly thereafter. "And that King Stanley's really a clone? And baby squids just used to fall right out of their momies?"

"Who told you that?" his father blanched.

"Grandpa," Thomas said.

"Look, son, don't believe everything my father may have told you. He means well, but he's old."

"But I saw videos and everything. We had this spaceship, and it flew to Starlin but the Starlins thought we were invading, so they shot it down with this laser beam and ate the captain's brains, and..."

"That's enough. I knew this was a bad idea. You already had too many thoughts in your head."

The hover car flew on cruise control. Young Thomas stewed in his seat.

Thomas' mother was glued to the holovid, watching her favorite soap. Thomas passed by in the hall.

"Hi, mom. I'm home."

She drooled.

The door to his bedroom slid open. Thomas stared out the window. His grandpa had given him a new perspective, but here his view was the same. He called Grandpa Shuster on his computer then realized he was bored already. He turned his computer back on and logged on to the CableNet.

"Computer," Thomas told the screen, "search for Sterankon history."

There was no reference to King Stanley's cloning, and the only mention of space travel was how Steranko's flagship, the *Eisner*, had become a restaurant. Thomas sat back and stared at the screen. What the heck, he thought as he searched *Sterankon conspiracies*. He never imagined his computer would come back with so many results.

He scrolled down the list, which ranged from entertaining to outrageous. Then Thomas stumbled upon a chat room. There were others just like him.

gruenwald187: my `rents don't even know Stanley's a clone

downwithrobots: yeah

gruenwald187: they just sit around watching holovids all day

downwithrobots: while the bots take control of their brains

thomas308 has entered the chat room.

downwithrobots: i think we should scrap all the bloody machines

thomas308: what about the one you're on now?

gruenwald187: who R U?

thomas308: just logged on

thomas308: just wanted to say I agree with you

gruenwald187: yeah

thomas308: things are out of control

downwithrobots: he's kewl

gruenwald187 do you have a job?

thomas308: no

downwithrobots: im a computer tech

thomas308: but I thought you hated machines

downwithrobots: yeah but it gets me perks

thomas308: like what?

downwithrobots: you don't know?

thomas308: know what?

gruenwald187: computer techs live longer

thomas308: what?

downwithrobots: civilians get gene therapy but techs get brand new organs

gruenwald187: dude he just got a new heart and hes only a teen.

downwithrobots: yeah and since i joined the union i only work three hours a week

thomas308: I don't believe it

gruenwald187: its true

downwithrobots: i know this tech who lost a tentacle and they replaced it with bionics

gruenwald187: now he's like a robosquid

downwithrobots: the stanley clone oked it all

gruenwald187: king clone is buggin out

Thomas stayed in the chat room another hour. He'd made his first two friends.

Downwithrobots' real name was Morrison. He had an appetite for anarchy and the principles of a Swiss banker. He was only too happy to fix the machines he claimed had dominion in mind. He was a mercenary engineer in an age of specialists, one of the few squids on Steranko who could fix most anything, and though he turned thirty when Thomas did he had the heart of a twelve-year old. Plus the liver of a ten-year old and a new pair of lungs on backorder.

Gruenwald was a computer tech who let Morrison steal the spotlight, content to play second fiddle as long as he stayed in the loop. His level-headed thinking offset Morrison's fanciful rants, but Gruenwald's input was still weighed by the fact he was thirty-three and living at home.

As an adult Thomas decided to grab hold of his own destiny, so he got a job in government as a member of Parliament. Though Steranko had moved toward automation and self-sufficiency, it still looked to its politicians to make things complicated.

Parliament was divided into two branches, Congress and Progress. Congress governed the city councils and wished they were in Progress. Progress ran the computer tech union and hogged the best parking spots. They didn't draft any legislation but had power over it, since Congress was at Progress' mercy if they wanted anything fixed. "How many Congressman does it take to change a light bulb?" the riddle went. Actually, it was a trick question. All the bulb techs were in Progress.

Thomas started out in Congress but moved to the other side, thanks to some freelance hacking by Morrison, who fancied a new spleen. Thomas had his qualms about the methods he'd used to get the assignment, but he wanted to be where the action was.

And his people were facing a crisis.

Sterankons had never given much thought to conservation. They had a vague notion that their natural resources were going to run out some day, but the general consensus was to let the next generation deal with it. When gene therapy doubled, then tripled, the average life span on Steranko, they realized they were the next generation, and they uttered a planetwide whoops.

Steranko had different species than Earth, none of which produced milk. Their primary source of calcium was derived from the Busiek plant. Unfortunately no one realized this until the last Busiek plant was endangered, about to be plowed under to make way for a hover car plant.

As the Busiek plant accounted for less and less of the Sterankon diet, elder squid started noticing an ache in their tentacles. A member of Progress broke his arm by bumping into a table. And King Stanley tripped in the throne room and had to have his hip replaced. A computer diagnosis came back with bad news.

The planet had osteoporosis.

Parliament responded like any concerned government would. They denied the problem existed while they hoarded the Busiek plants. But the few sprouts saved from the hover car site weren't enough to go around. Accelerated growth worked fine on clones but not at all on plants, and the seeds would take decades to pollinate enough to feed the planet. The answer became obvious. It was time for an old-fashioned panic.

The CableNet swarmed with reports of a government conspiracy. (The first rumor was posted by someone using the screen name downwithrobots.) But the public wasn't enraged until King Stanley preempted their shows.

"Good evening, my fellow Sterankons!" the King's regal hologram said. "I'd just like to talk to you about some recent rampant rumors! Some of you may have heard about a dietary disaster. Well, good news, my paranoid people! These reports are factually false. It was merely a salacious story spread by sinister Starlin spies! So return to your programs, my stagnant squid. And remember, carpe diem!"

Thomas slithered over as King Stanley signed off the air. "An excellent performance, your highness."

"Thank you, Thomas. Did you tape my soap?"

"Of course, your grace."

"I'm grateful you left your post in Progress to come and work for me."

"If I may say so, sir," Thomas said, "I don't know if it was wise of us to blame the Starlins like that."

"Don't fret, my faithful friend. Our nimble negotiator just returned from Starlin."

"Really?" Thomas said. "Are they willing to trade for their Busiek plants?"

"No, although they did appear apologetic for our disemboweled diplomat."

"Oh."

"What about Project Alchemy?"

"It doesn't look good," Thomas said. "So far all they've been able to do is turn lead into that useless yellow metal."

"Then there's no other choice," King Stanley said. "We need to proceed with your project posthaste."

CHAPTER THREE

Head sat off to the corner in Professor Duck's survival class. He was twelve now and his first few years in school had not been happy ones. Head learned the lessons right away, but his classmates were imbeciles. They had spent most of second grade learning to count to two. By the sixth grade, Head felt he knew more than any of his teachers did, but his theories met with scorn and laughter. Either that, or confusion. Most of the time his teachers couldn't follow what Head said.

"Big lizard bad." Professor Duck said, pointing to a scribble. "What do when see big lizard?"

"Run," Head's classmates said on cue.

"Good." Duck turned back to the drawing. He saw Head's hand go up.

"Ugh," Duck sighed, butting heads with the wall. "Yes, Head. What am it now?"

"I don't think that dino...big lizards are bad."

There was a collective groan from the class.

"Head, no say such stupid thing. Of course big lizard bad."

"It's just..." Head scanned his classmates' faces, but his intellect urged him on. "I think the dinosaurs are just acting upon their natural instincts. I don't think you can assign a moral value to what they do. Their eating cavemen is comparable to, say, our eating plants or frogs. When a caveman eats a frog, we don't say that caveman's 'bad.'"

Duck stared blankly at his student. His glazed eyes finally blinked.

"Big lizard bad," Duck told the class. "Tomorrow learn not touch fire."

Head sat under his favorite tree as the other kids enjoyed recess. He had never been coordinated, but as he watched his classmates play dodge rock, Head was gripped not with a longing to fit in but amazement at their stupidity.

Snack, a particularly brainless lout, didn't have the sense to duck, and Head winced as Snack took a good-sized boulder right between the eyes.

"You should really find a safer game," Head told two of Snack's friends as they dragged him to the nurse.

"Shut up, Big Words," one of them said.

"Humph." Head leaned back on his tree.

He scanned the horizon of Swamp Village and wondered what lay beyond it. There had to be someone out there who could hold a conversation.

"Hello, Head?"

Head snapped to his senses. His classmate Daisy stepped out of the sun.

"Me join you?"

Head processed the question, making sure he'd heard her right.

"Sure," he said. His mouth turned dry as Daisy sat beside him.

Daisy was the first girl Head noticed when his hormones kicked in. She had long flowing hair and didn't slouch as much as the other cavegirls. She further distinguished herself by the fact that she actually liked to bathe.

"Me like what you say about big lizards."

Her voice was sweet as honey. Head's primal self thought how her waist-length hair was tailor-made for dragging.

"Really?" He dared to look in her eyes. "Do you think I was right?"

"Me no understand your talk. Me just like big words."

Appalled by Daisy's atrocious grammar, Head vacantly turned away.

"Maybe you be teacher some day?" she blurted, sensing her window was closing.

"I don't think so," Head said. "I think I'm going to leave the swamp."

Head was surprised when Daisy's smile melted into despair. He had spent so much time being teased by the boys and frustrated by his teachers that he had never noticed the cavegirls giving him extra attention. He was, in caveman terms at least, becoming quite a catch, with his excellent posture, cultured ways and knack for forward thinking.

"Maybe," Daisy said quietly, "maybe Head take Daisy with you?"

Head looked past her sad, doe eyes.

"I don't think so," he said.

His home smelled of spices when Head walked in. Puddle turned from the fire to greet him.

"Hello, Head. How am school?"

"The usual," Head said. He looked to his side, where Mud was busy sharpening a spear.

"Hi, Dad."

"Ugh." Mud returned to his work.

"What's for dinner? Smells good."

"Me am trying new recipe. Call it frog flambé."

Mud sneezed, and the follow-through made him poke his head on the spear.

"Mud!" Puddle said. "What me say about putting spear down before sneeze?"

"It your fault me am always sick."

"You no have to sleep outside."

"Really?" Mud showed the first signs of hope in the twelve years since Head was born. "Mud share bed with mate tonight?"

"Mud sleep on floor. Plenty room."

Mud rubbed the spear on the sharpening rock. His dull eyes fixed on his son.

Puddle outwitted her husband for another four years, and the next thing

Head knew he was being unwillingly jostled from his sleep.

"Head, wake up. Am time for hunt."

Head's bleary eyes focused on Mud. His father was holding his favorite spear. An axe was strapped to his waist.

"What time is it?"

"Am sun time. Come. Am time for boy become man."

"Oh," Head grimaced, rubbing his eyes. "The initiation's today?"

"No confuse father with big words. Come. Big lizard wait."

Head propped himself up on his cot. Mud's arms were as cross as his face.

"I don't feel like going," Head said. "The rite of passage is stupid."

"Boy am twelve now. School end soon. Must learn provide for village."

Actually, Head was sixteen, but Mud couldn't count that high.

"How is tempting death with a dinosaur going to help provide for the village?"

Mud steeled his mind against Head's verbal magic. He leveled his spear. "Come."

"Oww! Cut it out! I said I'm not going on your stupid hunt."

"Boy bring shame to family!"

"Whatever," Head said, lying back down. "Go point that somewhere else."

"Boy, me warn you."

"What going on?"

Puddle was in the doorway.

"Boy say him no go on hunt."

"Head, what Mud say true?"

"Yes," Head said, expecting his mother to rally to his cause. Instead, her hands shot to her face.

"Boy bring shame to family!"

It was the first time Head saw her disappointed. He hated himself for it.

"All right, I'll go." He shoved back his blanket. "But I hope that I get eaten."

Mud stood motionless, took a deep breath, then held out his spear to his son.

"Take."

Head gazed at the weapon as Puddle fought back a proud tear.

"This belong to father. Now Mud give it to boy."

For a moment, their distance disappeared as Head took the gift in his hand.

There has been some debate over what is the smallest unit of measurement. Some would say an atom. Others, a millisecond. But there is one thing even smaller than these: a teenager's gratitude.

Head dragged his spear as he and Mud met the rest of the hunting party. His classmate Snack, his temple creased from another undodged rock, scrunched his face as he tried to muster his other foe, a thought.

"What am Head doing here?"

"I'm going with you, apparently."

The rest of the party responded with a barely suppressed ugh. There was Pointy, Snack's father; Head's classmate Leech and his father Grass. Rounding out the party was Professor Duck, who was sponsoring his student, Tadpole. Tadpole's biological father had wandered too close to a tar pit.

"Fire say that me lead party," Mud told the ragtag team, stifling the urge to bash some skulls. Only he could mock his boy. The others fell in line.

"Where us go?" Grass asked.

Mud squinted, pausing for effect. He planted his club on the ground.

"Today," he said. The group was rapt. "Today we hunt Big Teeth."

As far as gasps go, there was little doubt that this one was the biggest.

The tyrannosaur Mud called Big Teeth was actually named Rex. All the great lizards were named Rex, which was why they hunted alone. Every time they got together, they fought over the title.

But Rex, even among his peers, was worthy of being called king. For one, he was fierce, slaying pointy-top lizards or fellow rex left and right. For another, although his brain was pea-sized, Rex was a wily beast.

A t-rex couldn't chew. He had to swallow his food whole, and Rex learned from experience to maintain a sensible diet. He had seen many a Rex wannabe eat nothing but red meat, but Rex mixed it up with plants and grubs. He didn't want to get gout. That's what too much raw meat got you, joints as useless as arms. Which on a Rex were short and stubby, a bit of a practical joke.

So while his peers were aching along, Rex was different. He was a meat and potatoes man. And now it was time for lunch.

Head sat on a branch two-thirds up a tree and stuck his spear in the trunk. He would have climbed higher, but the view was sufficient, a sight line measured in miles. It was, in fact, quite dizzying. The forest started to swoon. He leaned back, squeezing his eyes shut. *Acrophobia.* Fear of heights. Another of his "made-up" words. At least his hives had gone down.

He had broken out touching some sap-filled reeds. Mud made him climb the tree. He mistook Head's allergies for a curse, a bad omen for the hunt, and forced Head to play lookout while the party forged ahead.

Head had lost track of the band but was glad to be rid of them. He was a thinker, not a fighter.

He thought he heard a scream.

The Head-less party pushed on through the choking sea of reeds. Mud was silent, grimly focused. They reached another clearing. This one was expansive, sparsely dotted by tall grass and trees. The others were glad to see flat terrain, but Mud raised his hand.

"What am it?" Professor Duck said.

Mud stared at a clump of head-high grass a few yards away. He had had a cold since Head was born, but his instincts were sharp.

"Stay by me, boy," Duck told Tadpole. The lad huddled close to his guardian. The tall grass rustled, parting in ripples. Mud rested his hand on his club.

Eight dinosaurs about Head's height poked their heads out of the grass.

Mud had never seen this type of lizard before. He thought they were kind of cute. Their appearance was like a slim, dwarfish rex with fins pressed flat on their cheeks.

The dinos must never have heard of Mud, for they were unafraid. They approached the cavemen, circling round, bobbing as they walked. The others stepped back, but Mud held his ground, staring the pack leader down.

"Why you fear small lizard?" Mud said, disgusted with his crew. The dino was close enough to strike but hissed at Mud instead.

With one swift whack the leader's head made like a coconut, and Mud stood over its cute little corpse. He turned to his tribesmen.

"See?"

It seemed like a bright idea until the other dinos charged. The fins which seemed pointless a moment ago flared up to frame their faces, drawing attention to their teeth. Of which there were a lot.

Head sat up and strained his ears. Had he imagined the scream? He calmed himself by thinking of a word for his condition. *Nous.* That was the Greek word for mind. *Para nous.* Of the mind. Head smiled at his new word's perfection. He was paranoid.

But then he thought he heard several screams. Head leaned out over his branch. It was like the screams were phantoms. He could not see anything.

Except for the tyrannosaurus rex directly underneath him.

Head jumped to his feet and grabbed his spear as Rex followed Mud's trail. "AUGGGHHH!" Head screamed, just as his foot slipped, sending him horizontal. To his credit, he picked the softest branches to bounce off on the way down.

His grandfather's spear hit the ground beside him. Unlike Head, it was broken. Head's mind swam stupidly before he passed out. *Barophobia*, he thought.

Fear of gravity.

There was nothing Mud loved more in life than a good, clean whack. He had become a connoisseur of the sounds of a well-clubbed skull, and he liked the whump these dinos made, their heads like hollow melons. Besides the leader, he had already felled another of the beasts, which weren't all that much trouble if you kept them at club's length.

Snack, Pointy's boy, the unruly one, had redeemed himself in battle, slaying his foe with a brutish fury which made Mud warm inside. Grass' son Leech, on the other hand, was being gnawed upon. Around him was chaos, clubs and teeth, but Mud strolled through it all. He raised his axe, aiming at the head of the dinosaur wrestling Leech. It was going to be a tricky shot, the way they were rolling around, but Mud hadn't missed a moving target since his mother-in-law had ducked. He cocked his arm and lined up his target.

The dino looked at him and spit.

Rex observed the battle from behind a group of trees. The old Rex would have charged right in, all roars and attitude, and limped away victorious but battered. That was for the birds. Let them wean each other, he thought. He was sick of all these creatures who fought each other until he showed up. Then suddenly, it's him versus everyone. Like that was really fair.

He watched one of the hairy creatures slay two of the small lizards, and thought he recognized his smell. Maybe he ate one of his friends. The hairy man was the fiercest warrior, so Rex thought he'd pick him off first. Besides, he had good meat on his bones. Rex leaned closer in to the trees.

One of the pesky spitters hit the hairy man in the eyes. It was the perfect time to strike. Rex cleared his throat and stretched. A good roar, he found, went a long way towards panicking his prey. It was all about first impressions.

Hit 'em hard, grab a snack, then leave.

As he rubbed the venom in his eyes, Mud sorted out the screams. Duck's was like a little girl's. Snack's, a warrior's howl. He placed each player in his mind, but there was something else. A faint cry carried on the wind.

It sounded like his boy.

Mud rubbed his eyes furiously, his vision reduced to a blur. There was a large blob bearing down on him. Mud froze for a second.

"Ugh."

It was one of Rex's best entrances, some really deep bass in his roar. The dino snacking on Professor Duck turned to see what the fuss was about, but his vision was blocked by the end of a club.

Snack was having a ball. All his young life he was taught that hitting his fellow cavemen was "bad," and now that he had an acceptable target he was going to town. The spitter flopped off Professor Duck as Snack charged toward Rex. The remaining spitters knew their place on the food chain, fleeing the way they came.

Duck found Tadpole intact but in shock. He grabbed the boy by the arms.

"What do when see Big Lizard?" Duck screamed.

Tadpole came to his senses.

"Run?"

Professor Duck nodded, let go of Tadpole and dashed for the horizon. He was gone before Tadpole realized what his teacher had failed to cover.

"Where?"

Mud heard the thunderous roar and recognized it as Big Teeth's. He said a prayer to his ancestors and aimed at the fuzzy shape.

Rex got up to charging speed and lowered his head for the kill. Then he saw a shiny object spinning toward him. *Wait,* Rex thought, *I've seen those before.* He was too big to pull up. The object sailed over his sight and landed with a thunk.

That's strange, Rex thought, *did something bite me?* He stood up and looked around. His brain finally heard from his nervous system.

You've got an axe in your head.

Rex felt around with his stubby arms, which couldn't reach past his chin. Then he received another message.

Hey genius, look down.

A hairy creature was riding his foot and bashing his toes with a club.

Oh, for crying out loud, it's a hairy man-cub, Rex thought. Snack swung away. Such was the boy's mania that he ignored Rex's roar. Though he didn't avoid Rex's teeth. *Not bad,* Rex thought as he felt his lunch kick. *Now where'd the other one go?*

Mud's vision cleared as Rex ate Snack. Grass sidled up beside him.

"What do now?" Grass asked his leader, hoping the answer was "run."

"Give me spear." Mud held out his hand. Grass gave him his weapon.

Rex charged the creature who had given him the headache. Mud held deathly still. Grass watched Mud out of the corner of his eye and shuffled to the side.

Rex gave Mud a toothy grin before he opened wide. Then his brain flashed, *wait a minute, what's that coming at me? Swerve!*

The spear hit Rex in the head with a thunk, splitting the axe's handle. It stayed there, wedged in Mud's first weapon. Now Rex had a horn.

Rex reared up and studied Mud, who'd stayed his ground throughout. The hairy creature looked unarmed, but Rex thought that before. Who knew what weapon his stubby foe would produce if Rex charged him again? So Rex did what he had never done.

He turned and ran away.

Mud watched, dumbfounded, expecting the battle to end in one of their deaths. His mood settled on disappointment.

He'd really loved that axe.

Mud knelt down beside his boy, who lay at the foot of the tree. He inspected a piece of Head's broken spear.

"Am boy dead?" Grass said.

Mud turned Head over, put his head on his chest, and listened.

"Me not sure."

"Him make noise?" Grass asked Mud.

"Yes."

"What sound like?"

"Like small drum."

"See if wind come out boy's nose."

Mud's hand hovered over Head's face.

"Me feel nothing."

"That am bad," Grass said. "Mean wind am stuck in boy."

Mud looked at his motionless son.

"You know how to get wind out?"

"Yes," Grass said. "Must pray to gods, then smash boy's head with club."

Mud stood up, raising his club. He mulled over Grass' prescription. Mud was no doctor, but neither was Grass. Mud's large brow knitted with thought. He put a hand on his chest. He lowered his weapon. Inhaled and exhaled. Than he realized,

"Wind come from chest."

Mud laid down his weapon, knelt beside Head, and pushed him in the sternum. He waited. Nothing. Mud placed one hand over the other and pumped Head's chest three times. When Head did not stir, Mud propped him up, put his mouth on Head's and blew.

"Uh," Grass said, repulsed but intrigued, "why you do that?"

Mud ignored him. If Head died, it would be Mud's fault. Besides, Head was his son. A son who had often caused him to question his favor with the gods, but one whom Mud loved in his own way. And Puddle would never forgive him.

He pumped his boy's chest and blew in his mouth, but Head did not respond. Mud pulled back and looked at Pointy, who had lost his own son, Snack. Pointy stepped forward, picked up Mud's club, and put it in Mud's hands, closing his leader's fingers around it with a calm, sad nod. Mud thought that if Head's wind was trapped he could give him his own, but now it was time to try Grass' way. He raised his club over his boy. A heartbeat away from catastrophe, Mud checked his swing.

Head coughed.

His chest hitched as he sucked in air. Head opened his eyes. And there was his father holding a club a few inches over his face.

"Boy am alive!" Mud said, beaming, as Head scrambled away. Head cowered against the base of the tree. Mud lowered his club.

"Where boy go now?"

"You're trying to kill me!"

"Mud save boy," Grass said.

The cloud over Head's thoughts slowly parted.

"I fell out of the tree."

"Yes, me know," Mud smiled.

"How?"

"Am bark marks all over face."

Head counted the rest of the party.

"Where's Snack?"

"Him in Big Teeth," Mud said.

A lump welled up. "Did you kill Big Teeth?"

"No. Kill small ones, though."

"What about Professor Duck?"

"Oh, him?" Mud said. "Him lost." He tousled Head's hair and helped him up. They started the long journey home.

CHAPTER FOUR

The *Eisner* had a line of squid waiting to get into the restaurant. It was one of the few things on Steranko that could get them to leave their homes: the chance to sit in a former spaceship while being served a four-course meal. Morrison's team of computer techs pushed their way to the maitre d'roid.

"Excuse me, sir, do you have reservations?" the robot asked Morrison.

"We're with the government."

The droid ran a finger down its book.

"I don't see that name on the list."

"Look, you sodding scrap heap. Do you want to get disconnected?"

"I'm sorry, sir, but that kind of language won't get you seated any faster."

"Excuse me," Thomas said, making his way up front. "I've been authorized by King Stanley himself to commandeer this spaceship...er, bistro." He handed the droid a data card confirming his credentials.

"You'll have to excuse me," the maitre d'roid said, handing Thomas his card. "How may I be of assistance?"

Morrison said, "Hand me the intercom."

The robot turned to Thomas, who nodded. Morrison took the microphone.

"Good evening, fellow citizens. Your government speaking here. I hereby claim this restaurant in the name of good King Stanley. You have precisely five minutes to finish your dessert."

The maitre d'roid whirled as the patrons panicked and headed for the exit hatches, nervously eyeing Morrison's men, who all were dressed in black.

"Right," Morrison said, observing the anarchy with cool detachment. "Let's go."

"Excuse me, sir," the maitre d'roid said, "but I must disagree with your methods."

"I think you have a wire loose."

"Your rather crude humor aside--"

"No, I mean it," Morrison said. "Let me have a look."

"Well, I," the maitre d'roid blushed.

"Put your head down." He circled the droid.

"I must apologize for my conduct, sir. It's my programming, you know."

"Yeah, I know," Morrison said. He flipped a plate on the robot's neck and yanked out a fistful of wires. The maitre d'roids facial features went dark. It collapsed on its podium.

"This one's my payment," Morrison told Thomas. "I always wanted my own waiter."

They fanned out through the spaceship-turned-restaurant and passed the souvenir shop. Morrison grimaced at the T-shirts that read, "I ate aboard the *Eisner.*"

"What do you think?" Thomas said.

"I like the paintings," Morrison told him.

"You know what I mean. Can you do it?"

"Make a restaurant fly through space?" Morrison grinned. "Why not?"

The neon sign outside the *Eisner* was changed the following morning, with three cryptic words added to it: *closed for remodeling.* Morrison and his hand-picked squid worked 24-hour shifts, retrofitting the tourist attraction with the latest Sterankon technology. Four months later the *Eisner* resembled its former space-faring self, and its newly-christened officers were lined up on the bridge. They were a motley crew of engineers with no time spent in space, although they had all logged countless hours vomiting in a simulator. Gruenwald was one of them. Thomas needed a squid he could trust on the bridge. He had his qualms about the captain.

Thomas stood in front of the crew, his hands on the captain's chair, and thought Grandpa would have been proud and amused to see how far he'd come. "Good evening, gentlemen," he said, "I'm Thomas, King Stanley's chief of staff. On behalf of King Stanley, I'd like to welcome you all to tonight's momentous event. For the first time in a generation, squidkind is heading into space."

The men applauded politely, though their faces said *we're doomed*.

"King Stanley wishes he could be here tonight to thank all of you in person, but unfortunately he's been called away by a diplomatic emergency. But he's given me this message which I'll play for you men now." Thomas inserted a data disc in a nearby terminal. The front viewport turned into a screen, a closeup of King Stanley.

"Greetings, my intrepid explorers! Your kindhearted King Stanley here! I'd just like to take a moment to express my grateful gratitude and to wish you auspicious astronauts lots of luck on your titanic task. I'm sure your expedition will be a sensational success!"

The screen turned back into a window.

"Well," Thomas said, glad to be rid of the ambassador of alliteration, "I'm sure we all found that inspirational. Now I'd like to introduce you to the captain of this ship."

"Excuse me, but if I buy it in space, will I be gettin' cloned?"

"First of all, McFarlane, you're not going to die in space. And secondly, as you all know, we don't clone squid anymore."

"But King Stanley's a clone."

Exactly, Thomas thought. But what he said was, "He's an exception."

"And what about this Commander Kirby?"

"What about him?" Thomas said.

"Is this the same Commander Kirby who used to fly the *Eisner*?"

"He is."

"So wouldn't that make him somethin' like three hundred and fifty, then?"

"I assure you, gentlemen, Commander Kirby is in full control of his faculties. There's no one better to fly this ship. Is that understood?"

Thomas looked at the officers, and their gazes wandered off. It was their first shot at insurrectino, and they were dabblers at best.

"Then it's my privilege to introduce your captain, Commander Kirby."

The door to the bridge slid open, and a lone figure slithered through. The officers stood at attention as Commander Kirby inspected their ranks. Any doubts they had were dispelled by his presence, his aura of confidence. He had yet to speak but his stare spoke volumes. And he looked good for his age. At the end of the line, he turned to Thomas.

"Is this the best you could do?"

Thomas had met the Commander before, but he was taken aback by his power. For a moment, he forgot about the circumstances behind Kirby's return.

"You there," Kirby told Gruenwald before Thomas could gather his wits. "How many missions have you flown?"

"This will be my seventh, sir."

"Seven, eh? What's the toughest quadrant you've travelled through?"

"Well the Negative Zone was frightening. But I got the high score."

"So your superiors held you in high regard."

"I guess so," Gruenwald said, wondering why Thomas was making a throat-slashing motion behind Kirby's back. "The program designer's a friend of mine."

"Program?" Kirby said. "This wasn't an actual mission?"

"Not actually," Gruenwald stammered, "but we did simulate--"

"Simulations? Bloody hell!" Commander Kirby bellowed. "This 'Negative Zone' was nothing but a bloody simulation?"

Gruenwald's antennae hit the floor, an action which dominoed.

"All right," Kirby breathed hotly. "Raise your hand if you've never actually been on a mission in space."

The officers sheepishly raised their hands. The First Mate, Ditko was the last to do so. He was planning on pretending until Sprang shot him a look.

"Good lord."

"Commander Kirby," Thomas said. "I can assure you that these men are the best Steranko has to offer."

Kirby stroked his chin as he regarded the novice crew. "Yes, I'm afraid you're right." He strode dramatically to the head of the bridge and looked out over Steranko, his hands clasped stiffly behind his back.

"Very well, then. Let's be off."

Thomas joined Morrison in the launch center across from the *Eisner.* Morrison studied a panel of readouts tied to the spaceship's systems. A large screen above the panels served as a video link to the bridge.

"How's it look?" Thomas said, making his way through a group of technicians.

"Brilliant," Morrison said. He smacked a defective readout and its lights blinked on again. "I'd say we're a go."

"Then let's get this show on the road." Thomas flipped a switch and the videoscreen showed Kirby larger than life.

"*Eisner*, this is Grummet control. All systems are go."

"Understood, Grummet control."

"Good luck, Commander."

"Harrumph," Kirby said. "Luck has nothing to do with it."

"Commander Kirby," Morrison said as the screen switched to outside the ship. "Where'd you dig him up?"

Thomas spun around.

"Who told you?"

"Told me what?"

"Never mind."

The *Eisner* fired its engines.

"You wish you were aboard?"

"I've got too much going on down here," Morrison said. "We just found the *Giffen*."

"You're kidding me. Where was it?"

"At the bottom of Levitz bay."

"Is it spaceworthy?" Thomas asked.

"It will be when I'm through."

They watched the screen as the *Eisner* rose in a cloud of lights and steam. It rotated majestically, then disappeared from view, its warp engines' energy signature leaving a fleeting, star-shaped blink.

"Well that's that, then," Morrison said. No one saw him uncross his fingers.

CHAPTER FIVE

Chief Fire walked through the Swamp Village, patting the heads of all the children who ran up and gave him flowers. He had defied the laws of demographics by living well into his forties, and his old age had bestowed upon him a deep respect for nature. He had a strange rapport with animals, whether they walked, crawled, swam or flew, and Fire had taken to addressing every creature he met as brother.

"Ah, brother monkey," he said as one emerged from the edge of the brush. The monkey shied away as Fire approached with a neighborly smile.

"Am brother monkey lost?" Fire said. The monkey bared his teeth. "No be scared. Am friend." Fire went to pat the critter's head. The monkey hissed and bit the chief's finger, then ran back into the swamp.

Fire watched it go, his feelings hurt. He held his bleeding finger. He didn't think about it much until the fever hit.

Head paused at the door to Fire's hut, recalling a faint memory of how the previous one burned down. He checked the tools in his medicine bag but knew they'd see no use. He was only an assistant. "Doctor" Leech was in charge.

The previous doctor, Bash, had been stepped on by a mammoth. Leech was Bash's intern and received a quick promotion. Head was sixteen and unemployed, a bit of an embarrassment. His father was a great warrior, but all Head killed were conversations. So Fire put him where he could do the least harm. He made him Leech's assistant.

Head spent two years watching Leech drive health care into the ground. His answer to any ailment was a parasite or a whack. Head tried working around him, sneaking back to their patients alone, administering his own special herbs. Leech found out and snapped. From that point on, he made Head's job as useless as a vice president.

It was a humid day, but Fire was shivering when Head entered his hut. Chief Fire lay on his back on a cot, engulfed in fevered dream. Fire's wife Drizzle watched nervously as Doctor Leech ran his tests.

"What are you doing here?" Head asked Puddle, who was on her way out.

"Leader ask for bowl of soup but now him not so hungry." Head touched his mother's shoulder and smiled. She left with her half-eaten offering.

"Head am late," Leech said, not bothering to look up. Head had learned to pick his fights. He opened his kit in silence. Leech put his head on Fire's chest and peered up the old chief's nostrils. Fire wheezed.

"Him no sound so good," Leech said.

Head laid his tools beside Leech's club. "He seems to have a fever."

"Oh? Then why him cold?"

"A fever means you're hot or cold."

"Which am it?" Leech said.

"Never mind." Head turned to Fire's wife, Drizzle. "How long has he been like this?"

"Like what?"

"Like this."

"You mean, hairy?" Drizzle said.

"No." Head looked to the ceiling for strength. "How long has he been sick?"

"No hurt Fire. Am friend," Fire moaned, bunching up his blanket.

"Stand away," Leech told Drizzle. "Him may be dangerous."

"He's hallucinating," Head said. Leech turned back to his patient.

"Brother monkey demon monkey," Fire said, thrashing about.

"Him get worse." Leech reached for his club.

"Wait!" Head shielded their leader. "What did he say?"

"Monkey...fingerrrrr."

"Monkey finger?" Head thought, then he noticed the cut on Chief Fire's hand. "What did this?" he asked Drizzle. She stumbled back, overwhelmed by the spirits swirling around her husband. Head focused on the more rational spouse.

"Fire, can you hear me?"

Fire's tortured features relaxed for a moment. His voice floated up. "Brother Head?"

"Yes, it's me." Head smiled. "Listen very carefully. I want you to tell me about this cut on your finger. Did a monkey give this to you?"

"Brother monkey," Fire said, twitching.

"Yes, a monkey. Good. Did a monkey bite your finger?"

Fire lurched forward, opened his eyes, and grabbed Head by the collar. "DEMON MONKEY! FIRE AM FRIEND!"

Leech inched toward the door. Head stared into Fire's wild eyes, unable to free himself.

"Chief Fire friend to animals! Why am monkey BLAAAARRRGGG." It was a most unhealthy sound. Fire's eyes rolled back, as did the rest of him. His arms fell to his side. Head turned to Drizzle.

"He's dead."

Drizzle took a step in the sudden calm. She glanced at her mate.

"Am sure?"

Puddle sat by the fire finishing her bowl of soup. She heard Mud snore from their room. After years of nocturnal exile he could sleep on any surface, but his thirties were causing his back to stiffen. Puddle took pity on him. She let him move from the floor to the bed as long as he stayed on his half, a rule Mud tried to break the first night with a bogus yawn-and-arm stretch.

Puddle reached for her birth control, Mud heard a rush of air, then she leaned the club back against the wall. Mud kept to his side after that.

Puddle set the empty bowl on the floor as Head returned from work.

"Hello, mother." He kissed her forehead.

"Am Fire okay?"

"No." Head sat on a boulder beside the fire and bowed his head. "Fire's dead."

Puddle was stunned, but then she remembered the story of Bear the elder. Bear was the only caveman to ever die of natural causes. He outlived his wife, their three children, and seven of nine grandkids. He was a man of few words and ran out of them at sixty. After that he never moved out of his favorite chair, spending every waking hour staring into space. His people moved him into a throne they carved out of respect and also to draw tourists. Cavemen traveled from faraway tribes to see the living legend. They offered their finest goods for the right to try to make Bear blink.

One day Bear didn't blink at all. The crowd got their admission back. Bear was laid out according to custom, then buried three days later. The next morning he was back on his throne, much to his clansmen's dismay.

"Grandpa!" his grandson Tree exclaimed. "You am back from dead!"

"No," Bear said. "Me just decide me like it more in chair."

Bear died in his sleep a year later but stayed in his throne a month longer, his people only daring a burial after he decomposed. His legend passed into folklore, frightening children for ages to come, one of whom grew up to be Puddle. So she asked Head,

"Am sure?"

"Yes, I'm sure," Head told his mother. "It's hard to be wrong about these things." Puddle was about to tell him the legend of Bear when Doctor Leech knocked on the door.

"Head, grab things. Must go back to Fire's." Head exchanged looks with Puddle.

"Don't tell me Fire's alive."

Leech thought it was a strange thing to say. "No," he said, "Him still dead.

But now Drizzle am sick."

When they got to Fire's, Drizzle had taken her husband's place in his bed.

"How am feeling?" Leech asked Drizzle, who was soaking her sheets.

"Feel on fire."

"When did this start?" Head asked.

"When me clean mate."

Head looked at the Chief and saw that Fire had been dressed in a burial gown. Leech reached into his medicine bag and pulled out a jar of worms.

"Drizzle catch evil spirit from Fire. Good bloodletting fix."

Head thought that Leech was right for once, except for the bloodletting part. His suspicions were confirmed a few days later when Drizzle's last words were "BLAAAARRRGGG."

But before Drizzle died there was the matter of naming Chief Fire's replacement. Since Fire and Drizzle had no children, tradition called for the new leader to be the oldest male in the swamp. The winner, by two weeks, was Mud. Head didn't know what to think about having his father assume the role. Then again, none of Head's fellow tribesmen were overqualified, so equating age to ability was as good an approach as any.

Head prepared for Mud's inauguration, pausing on his way out. He followed a moan to his parents' room. Puddle was turning in bed.

"Mother?" Head said. She was asleep, but her forehead was hot to his touch. Head was about to fetch her water when Puddle opened her eyes.

"Head?" she said. He brushed back her hair.

"Yes, mother. How do you feel?"

"Room turn in big circle."

"How long have you felt this way?"

"Am hard to think. Since sun time."

"Aren't you going to dad's ceremony?"

"No," Puddle said. "Me try get up but room turn dark." She propped herself up and looked out the window. "Am Mud chief now?"

"Actually, the ceremony's just about to start."

"Then go. Mud need son there."

"I don't want to leave you alone like this. I'll send word I'm not coming."

"No, must go. No worry for me. Me think am stomach ache."

"But what if you need medical attention?"

She gave him a stern look. "Go!"

Head saw there was no use arguing until after he got back. Then something Leech had said about Drizzle made him turn around.

"Mother? You know that bowl of soup you made for Fire last night? What did you do with the rest of it?"

"Me eat it," Puddle said. She saw the color drain from Head's face. "Me sorry. You want some?"

Head worked his way to the front of the crowd and took his place beside Leech. Mud was seated on stage with the elders, with Chief Fire laid out before them. A leopard skin, the symbol of leadership, was draped over Mud's shoulders. He rose from his throne and shot Head a look to let him know he was late, then raised his club in dramatic fashion. The shawl snaked to the floor.

Mud froze, deciding whether he should try to play it off. He kept his eyes locked on the crowd as he stooped and picked up the skin. *Act cool*, Mud thought, adjusting his vestment. He raised his arms again. The room waited. Mud parted his lips. His fur fell to the ground.

He kept his arms up, looked over his shoulder. The leopard skin coiled at his feet. Mud's eyes darted over the audience, seeing who would dare to laugh first.

"Brothers and sisters. Fire am dead. Me am new leader," Mud said. He decided to keep it at that. He nodded, and two of the elders rose and flanked him on each side. They put the shawl back on his shoulders. Mud stepped to Fire's altar and took the cup that was placed by his body. Mud raised the glass. The elders held their palms up in prayer.

"This am Fire's cup. Me drink from it so me share leader's spirit." The rim was perilously close to his lips when someone cleared their throat. When the goblet cleared his field of vision, Mud rolled his eyes. It was Head.

"Excuse me," Head said, standing up and feeling the heat of the village. "I don't think that's a good idea." Mud's leopard skin fell off his shoulders.

"What am wrong?" said the elder, Tarpit. "Think father no make good chief?"

"No," Head said. "I mean, yes, I think he'll make an excellent chief. I just don't think that he should drink out of Fire's cup, that's all."

"And why do Head think that?" scoffed the elder, Snake. He and Tarpit had never cared for Head's shenanigans.

"I think if my father drinks from Fire's cup, he may catch Fire's bad spirits."

Snake liked that idea. He had missed making chief by two weeks. If Mud died and his son were disgraced...

"Chief always drink from cup."

"I know it's tradition," Head said. "But Fire gave his bad spirits to his mate, and he made my mother sick, too."

A gasp rose from the audience. Mud snapped out of his daze.

"Do boy think Fire--"

"Snake!" Mud said. "Me am leader. Me speak to boy." Snake bowed with a smirk. Mud turned to his son. "Boy think spirits make Fire sick?"

"No." Head paused. "I mean, yes. Actually, it was a monkey." The elders joined the crowd in a laugh.

"A...monkey?" Mud said.

"Fire told me a monkey bit him. I think that's what made him sick."

"Then," Mud tried to follow the logic. "Monkey bite mate, too?"

"No, it only bit Fire. But Drizzle caught the monkey fever from Fire and Puddle got sick from his food."

Mud didn't feel regal anymore. In fact, he was getting warm. "Food...make Puddle...sick?"

"Yes, I believe Fire was contagious."

A cricket chirped outside.

"That is, I think the monkey gave Fire his bad spirits and Fire put them in his soup."

"But Drizzle no have Fire's soup."

"No, but..." Head regrouped. "Fire could give his bad spirits to anything he touched."

A well of panic spread through the crowd. Mud felt strangely relieved. He finally knew the reason he could never touch his wife. "Am way can stop bad spirits?"

"I think so," Head said, unused to the rush of being taken seriously. "I don't think we can do anything for those who have already caught the disease, but I think we can stop it from spreading further if we just wash our hands."

Mud echoed the thoughts of the congregation. "Me no like getting wet."

"That's the thing," Head said craftily. "The bad spirits don't, either."

Mud picked up Fire's cup. "But cup have water in it. So how can cup have bad spirits?"

Head stumbled. "Well, that is..."

"So, boy no am as smart as chief." Mud raised the glass.

"Don't do it!"

Mud belched and wiped his mouth with his sleeve. The crowd hushed. "Me feel fine."

Head sank to his seat and buried his face. Doctor Leech turned to him. "Me no want you see patients tomorrow. Me think you am nuts."

So by the time Drizzle died, three days after Fire, half of the village was sick. Leech had not caught the fever but was an ideal carrier, managing to infect his wife and upgrade his patients from sick to dead. Then the disease unleashed its deadliest plague: bureaucracy.

At Tarpit's behest, Chief Mud headed a crisis management team, which spent their first two meetings debating whether to wash their hands. By the time Tarpit was done filibustering and Mud called for a vote, a two-thirds majority was hard to reach. Half the committee's lives had been vetoed.

As for Head, he had his hands full tending to his mother. Puddle lay in bed, delirious. He feared she was reaching the end. He propped her head up with his arm and tipped a glass to her lips.

"Head," she whispered hoarsely. Head helped her take a drink.

"Shh," Head said. "Don't try to speak. You have to get your rest."

"Me must talk." Her face was angelic. "Am time me say good-bye."

There was something in her voice Head knew to be true. He let the room be still.

"Me have dream. Am beautiful." Puddle stared toward the sky. "In dream me no am sick, like here. Me am on walk with you. And me say time for you find mate."

"But mother, you know I'm different. What if I never find someone?"

"That am what you say in dream."

Head smiled. "Then what happened?"

"Then am when the bears attack. But that am scary part. Now me tell you what me tell you after that in dream. I say Head am different here." Puddle touched her son's forehead. "But he am same in here." She moved her hand over his heart. "Problem him use head too much. Should try use other part."

Head put his hand over hers. "How did your dream end?"

"That am the best part. You find mate and--"

"Someone from the swamp?"

"Nice cavegirl. Me no ask her where her from."

"But what did she look like? Did you know her?"

Puddle closed her eyes. "Me tired."

"Wait! What happened to you?"

"Me walk through tunnel." She started to drift. "Am light at other side."

"I don't understand."

"Me follow light. Tunnel go to big field. Am full of squirrels and butterflies. And that where I see Bear."

Head snapped out of her spell. "You fought another bear?"

"No, not bear like animal. Bear am ancestor."

"Oh."

"At first me think Bear back from dead and me should go and hide. But then him say, 'No be afraid. This here am land of dead.'"

Puddle was resting easily now, her hands draped on her chest. Head was at the opposite end of the emotional spectrum. "But that means..."

"Yes, me know. So me look at Bear and me ask him, me ask him..."

"What?"

"...Am sure?"

Head laughed despite himself. "Mom, listen to me. It was only a dream. It's just the fever, that's all."

"No," Puddle said distantly. "Tell Mud me am sorry. Him have whole bed now if him want."

"You're the only one who listens to me."

"Boy am thirteen now."

"Twenty." A tear rolled down his cheek.

"You no need me anymore." Puddle's head listed to the side, her breath coming in sighs. "Oh, hello, Fire. Am dinnertime? Me try...new..recipe..."

Head continued to hold her hand long after it turned cold.

Mud rested his head on his hand as Tarpit recited the minutes. "Last meeting timekeeper die," Tarpit said. He took his seat. Mud stirred, looking up from the table to let Snake know he was on. As Snake spoke, Mud returned to his trance. He needed a nice long nap.

Snake reported that the death count had risen to twenty, and urged the crisis management team to respond with a mission statement. Every group needs a goal, he said, as long as it's not specific. He turned to Mud for a reaction. Mud plopped into Tarpit's lap. His resistance had been overcome. Mud died of politics.

All told, the monkey fever claimed two-thirds of the Swamp People. Which is how the land became known by its present-day name, Germany.

Kirby stood at the door to the bridge and waited for the hiss, the soft sound of hydraulics as the panel slid away. His antennae drooped as the door stayed shut. He opened it manually. He had not cleared the entrance when he heard the familiar *sssss*. He felt the pinch of the tentacle that was caught in the door. His first mate Ditko glided over, his clam-shaped face all atwitter.

"Do you need a hand, Commander?"

"No thank you," Kirby said. "At least the other three are free." He liberated his trapped appendage and took his seat up front.

The *Eisner* was hovering over Sol 3, the latest stop on their quest. The planet looked pretty from out in space, a blue-and-green swirled marble. Up close it merely looked undeveloped. Not a shopping mall in sight.

Kirby looked out the wraparound viewport which enclosed the top of his ship. He turned his antennae to his right. "Ensign Gruenwald, why aren't we cloaked?"

Gruenwald fretted over his terminal, his skin greener than usual after their close call on Sol 4. "Sorry, Commander. The system crashed again."

Kirby sighed, strumming his fingers on his armrest. He tapped his chest communicator, a triangular pin. "Ensign Lightle?"

"Yes, sir," a voice said.

"I find myself wondering why my ship is visible. Do we want the natives to see us?"

"No, sir," the intercom squeaked.

"And who's in charge of door maintenance?"

"That would be Gibbons, sir."

"Have him come up here at once." Kirby nursed his throbbing tentacle. "You there, Gruenwald." He looked to his left.

"Sorry, sir. I'm Sprang."

"Well you look like Gruenwald. A clone, are you?"

"I don't believe so, sir."

"Let's jolly well hope not," Kirby said. "I don't cotton to clones."

"If I recall, Commander, clones were outlawed three cycles ago."

"Harrumph. Hard to tell if a squid's a clone when we bloody all look the same."

Kirby slumped in his chair and gazed at the stars, too many for him to count. Their latest attempt at finding calcium was nearly a disaster. A most inhospitable planet, Sol 4. When Sprang picked up a pebble, he didn't know he was manhandling an egg. Until the landscape stood up and roared. They had beamed out just in time.

He'd guided the *Eisner* through three solar systems, beamed squid down to 17 planets. Weaved his ship through asteroid fields and skirted a black hole. He had command of a group of officers as green as a Busiek plant, took orders from a bureaucrat whose king was a lunatic clone, and piloted a spacecraft that recently had its own salad bar. All for the sake of a mineral which seemed native to his home system.

Ah well, Kirby thought. Maybe this time would be different.

Head sat in his lonely home adjusting to the change. He had been an orphan a day now, his parents laid out at the Great Hut. He turned his father's club in his hands and stared at the fireplace. His solitude was interrupted by a knock on the door.

"Snake," Head said. "Come in." Snake stepped in through the moonlit rain. He was wearing Mud's leopard skin shawl. Head rested Mud's club against the wall. "Can I get you anything?"

"No, am fine," Snake said.

"What can I do for you?"

Snake shifted on his rock. "Us have to talk about new chief now that father am dead."

"Actually, I was wondering when that would come up. I mean, I am Mud's only son, after all, so naturally--"

"Village want me to be chief."

Head recoiled, his mind handcuffed. "But you can't do this," he said.

"Am sorry," Snake said. "Council vote today and them make me new chief."

"But the chief's not elected. He's appointed."

"Me no understand big words. But if them mean Head think him new chief, than big words am wrong."

"But I'm Mud's son."

"New chief no am old chief's son no more."

"Why not?" Head said.

"Am change in law. Besides, Mud am bad chief."

"What? He was only chief for a week."

"That my point," Snake said. "Bad chief."

"This is insane." Head paced the room. "I'm the best man for the job."

"Village no say so. Them say if Head so smart, why him let parents die?"

Head realized, then, why Snake was so smug. He muttered, "I've been set up."

Snake slapped his legs and got to his feet. "Me start job at sun time," he said. "Me hope you am there."

Head watched Snake depart in the rain. He reached for his father's club. Be he was a thinker, not a fighter. He closed the door and screamed. A strange calm overcame him and he felt his mother's spirit. He sat by the fire and gathered his thoughts, then stood and went to his room. He spread a blanket on the floor and filled it with clothes and tools. He tied the blanket at the ends and hooked it over Mud's club. On the living room wall, Head recorded man's first written words:

I QUIT.

The rain was cold but Head did not want to wait until morning to leave. His exit had to go unnoticed. That had more panache. *Where am Head*, the village would say come morning. Simpletons. He hoped Big Teeth ate the lot of them. All except for one.

Daisy had never married. Head thought he was the reason why. His mother's last words made him realize that he dismissed Daisy too quickly, and his heart skipped as he picked up his step toward Daisy's hut. They would make their future together somewhere far beyond the swamp.

The lightning flashed and Head saw a figure outside Daisy's home. Her parents were in the doorway, waving. The figure moved slowly away. Head strained to see who it was. Another bolt obliged. Doctor Leech dragged Daisy through the mud. He was a widow no longer.

Head watched from a distance, enraged. His hair dripped. His shirt itched. The rain became a baptism. He tore the shirt off his chest.

He left the village without looking back and followed the lakeshore. His life had been a miserable failure, one long disappointment. *But that was Head*, his anger whispered. *A genius among Neanderthals. You are a Cro-Magnon man.*

Head was dead.

Long live Cro.

Shirt skipped a rock across the water, his aim as uncanny as ever. He liked coming to the lake at night. It helped him clear his thoughts.

It had been another long day at school, full of the usual taunts. But here his world was his alone, no Fight or his dimwitted thugs. Shirt lay on his back along the shore. The twinkly lights danced for him. Shirt never knew where they went in the daylight (and Ugh wasn't any help), but he knew they'd reappear at night, like friends who had come out to play.

Shirt let his eight-year-old mind roam free, imagining constellations. These four lights looked like a rock. And over there, a stick. He picked out a spoon, then a bigger spoon. And look, a UFO.

Children accept the fantastic, so Shirt didn't doubt his eyes. He stared in wonder, and a little fear, at the circle with all the lights. These lights didn't twinkle like the ones in the sky. They ran around in an arc, illuminating what looked like a bowl. A big green bowl that could fly. It hovered like a hummingbird and buzzed like a mosquito, and for a second Shirt thought that it was looking right at him. He wondered if Big Lizards flew the ship and trawled the lake for children. Little kids who were all alone. Shirt reached for a rock.

He cocked his arm, lying flat in the sand. The big bowl held in place. Then the stars around it rippled and the craft faded away. Shirt breathed fast and probed the sky, relieved and disappointed. He sat up, got to his feet, and froze.

Something was coming his way.

Head's first full day as Cro had been a bit of a disappointment. He was wet, tired and hungry, and was down to one wearable shirt. He spied smoke in the daylight as he walked along the lake, but now the stars obscured the trail. He figured he'd stick to the shore. Any tribe with half a brain would live close to the water. He stopped to rest, took a drink from his deerskin,

And saw a UFO.

The water dribbled down Cro's chin as he gaped at the luminous craft. It was the most magnificent thing he had ever seen. A chariot of the gods. But then the image shimmered, leaving him alone once more.

Cro did not consider that he had imagined the craft. He was smart, but not creative enough to conjure something like that, an engineering marvel that could fly without using wings. Instead his Cro-Magnon mind worked at the object's origins. What type of beings could build such a ship? And what was their intent? Perhaps the gods had, at long last, recognized him as a peer, acknowledging his intellect by giving him this sign.

"Show me another," Cro asked the sky.

It was quite the coincidence when he looked down the shore and saw Shirt's silhouette.

Shirt's fight-or-flight instinct was stuck on pause. He squinted at the figure. It looked vaguely human, but something was off. The shadow did not stoop like a man. Shirt knew of no creature that walked that way. It had to be a trick.

Cro smiled at the caveboy. Enthusiasm quickened his step. The gods themselves had delivered a child to guide him to his new home.

So the part where the kid hurled a rock at his head came as a surprise.

Kirby's view out the *Eisner's* viewport took on a light blue tint, which meant the ship was cloaked again. At least something was going right. "Gruenwald."

"Yes, Commander?"

"Give me a view of the planet below. I'd like to see the terrain."

The viewport fluttered, changing to a view below the ship. A lake, a shore, indigenous shrubbery. Two aliens.

"What's that?"

"What's what, Commander?"

Kirby studied the figures, two small silhouettes on the screen.

"Gruenwald, enlarge sector seven."

The viewscreen stayed the same.

"I'm sorry, sir. I'm not licensed to do that. That would be Ensign Sprang."

"Bloody union," Kirby muttered. "Sprang--"

The screen zoomed in. The crew reared back when they saw the two life forms.

"Enlarge again. Full screen."

They were humanoids, two arms and two legs, but no catalogued race held such horror. One walked erect, but the small one was stooped and even more deformed. Their eyes were misplaced. Hair covered their skin. Kirby gripped his seat.

"Good lord."

The small alien threw a rock at the big one. The big alien fell in the sand. The young one sniffed and poked its victim. At least the rock wasn't alive.

"Do you think they're the dominant species?" the youngest officer, Bagley, asked.

Kirby stared at the barbarians.

"I certainly hope not."

CHAPTER SIX

Rock let Dog and Smash in her hut and showed them to the prisoner, who was lying in a sweat-drenched bed with her husband Ugh standing guard. She joined Shirt in the next room. This was a matter for the elders.

"This am him?" Dog asked Ugh, studying the foreigner, who was covered in blood and bruises and had thrown up on his shirt. Aside from that, the stranger was the most handsome man in the room.

"Am him," Ugh told his chief.

"Where boy find him?"

"By shore," Ugh said.

"Shirt bring man here alone?"

"No. Me help boy drag him here."

"Ugh." Dog stood and pondered. Ugh wasn't sure if Dog was addressing him or just making a general statement.

"Where him come from?" Smash asked Ugh.

"Boy say him come from sky."

"From sky?" Smash said.

"From flying bowl."

Dog found that amusing. "Boy have big imagination. Me think stranger am spy."

The men considered Chief Dog's words.

"Am spy from swamp village," Ugh said.

"Me take care of spy right now," Smash said. He raised his club.

"Wait," Dog said. "Before you bash, me want ask questions first. See if there am other spies."

"That good plan," Ugh said. Dog poked the stranger's chest with his club. The stranger writhed in his sleep.

Consciousness returned cruelly to Cro. His head throbbed from Shirt's rock. His eyes stung with sweat as his vision focused on the hostile forms around him.

"Where am I?"

"So, spy awake," Dog said.

Cro propped himself up on his arms. "Spy? Who are you men?"

"Me ask questions here." Dog shoved him flat with his weapon. "What am name?"

"Head," Cro said. "I mean, Cro."

"Like bird?" Dog asked

Cro looked at his captors. "Okay."

"Where you from?"

"The swamp."

Dog nodded. "Why you spy on boy?"

"I wasn't sent to spy on you. I came to join your tribe."

"Why you want to leave Swamp People?" Dog's posture relaxed a bit. Cro jumped at the opening.

"Because you're smarter than them."

"Am true," Dog said, relaxing his club. Ugh seemed taken in. Smash was the one who didn't buy it.

"Am trick! Him come from bowl!"

"Me say there am no bowl," Dog said. Cro didn't catch the reference until Smash pointed at him and said,

"Him come from sky!"

Then the pieces fell together. There really was a ship.

"I need to speak to the boy," Cro said. He swung his feet to the floor. He forgot these cavemen were strangers. When he stood erect, they gasped. Cro saw their reactions through a blackening tunnel.

He swooned and hit the floor.

The advance team stood in the teleport bay checking their equipment, four anxious Sterankons ready to beam to the planet below.

"All right, men," Commander Kirby said. "This is a simple reconnaissance mission. No interacting with the natives. Do I make myself clear, Ensign Sprang?"

"Yes, sir."

"And be careful with that scanner, Englehart. It's the only one we've got."

"Aye, sir."

"The atmosphere seems breathable, but that's what we thought on Sol 4. If you feel your heads imploding, give the sign and we'll beam you up."

The advance team exchanged uneasy glances.

"Very well, then. Carry on."

Rex sniffed his way around the forest, looking for a meal. His stunted horn was a constant reminder of his run-in with Mud. He had snapped the spear handle off on a tree, but the axe was still dug in. It only hurt when it was about to rain. He stopped and sampled the air. A strange aroma appeared out of nowhere, a vaguely animal scent. Rex was in the mood for something new. He lumbered along the trail.

He stopped short of a cluster of trees, bent down, and took a look. His beady eyes focused on a creature he'd never seen before.

It was about the size of a hairy creature but had skin more like his, with stubby arms and four curious legs. Each one looked like a snake. Rex hated snakes, but he figured he would bite the creature in two, eating the soft-looking torso and leaving the snakes for someone else.

He was about to make his entrance when another snake-legs appeared. It didn't step from a hiding place. It literally appeared. *What the heck?* Rex thought. He'd never seen a creature do that. The second snake-legs' scent filled the air.

Rex's stomach growled.

Mignola's antennae perked up.

"You hear that?"

"Aye," McFarlane said.

"Scan the area for life forms."

"I'm not licensed for scannin'. That's Sprang."

Mignola gripped his phaser. Sprang beamed down beside the squid.

"You have the life form detector?"

"Uh-huh," Sprang said, looking queasy.

"Give me a sweep of the area."

"Hold on."

Sprang made a bee-line for a pond.

"Will ya be on yer hunkers the whole mission, then?" McFarlane shouted Sprang's way. Mignola's eyes went wide.

"Look out!"

He knocked McFarlane down. Englehart materialized where McFarlane had been standing.

"Watch where yer beamin'," McFarlane said, dusting himself off with his tentacles.

"Sorry," Englehart said. "Where's Sprang?"

"He's heavin' over yonder."

"You need a hand with that mineral detector?"

"I'm fine," Englehart told Mignola.

"Then let's get it set up and get back to the ship. I have a bad feeling about this."

The mineral detector was a modified laser canon. Englehart pressed a button and a tripod sprang from its housing. He planted the tripod legs in the grass and turned the scanner on. He pivoted it in a slow, steady arc, watching the readout screen.

"Hey! I've got something! A big one!"

"A calcium deposit?" Mignola said.

"Looks like it."

"Where?"

"Over there."

The scanner was aimed at the cluster of trees Rex was hiding behind.

"You sure?" Mignola asked Englehart. He could swear those trees had growled.

"That's what this little thingie says."

"All right. Let's take a look." Mignola set his phaser on stun and inched toward the trees.

Sprang knelt over the edge of the pond, revisiting his lunch. He didn't see how the others stomached teleportation so well. He knew this wasn't going to help his standing on the ship. He already had the rock incident on Sol 4 to live down. As Sprang resolved to have no more screw-ups, his chest pin splashed in the pond.

Some kind of alien aquatic life forms swarmed to the glittering prize. "Oh no you don't," Sprang told the creatures, fishing around with a tentacle.

"Oww!"

Sprang beat his leg on the ground until the tenacious fish let go. Even then, it flopped toward Sprang, its razor jaws snapping away. He trained his phaser on the beast and left a fish-shaped crater.

"Shots fired!" Englehart yelled nearby, jerking the mineral detector.

"Sorry. I was just, ah, calibrating my weapon," Sprang called to the others. He glanced at the fish guarding his communicator and decided they could have it.

He took out his hand-held life form detector and extended the antenna. The stationary blip was Englehart, a few clicks ahead of him. McFarlane's blip was trailing Mignola's, which left one other blip.

"Englehart?"

"What is it?"

"I'm getting an unknown life sign here."

"Where?"

"One click in front of Mignola."

Englehart consulted his mineral scanner.

"That's the calcium deposit."

"I don't think so," Sprang said. "It's pretty big."

"You must not be reading it right."

"Look, I'm reading mine right, okay? Maybe you're the one who's wrong."

"I know my minerals from my life forms," Englehart said. "It can't be both."

"Why not?"

"Because in order to have that much calcium, its bone mass would outweigh that tree."

Sprang eyeballed the mystery blip.

"I'd say that sounds about right."

"Let me see that." Englehart looked at Sprang's screen. "There's only four blips."

"It isn't counting you."

"See, now the big one's moving. Maybe it's some kind of interference."

"I don't think so," Sprang said, checking the mineral detector.

"Why not?" Englehart said.

"The blip on your screen's moving, too."

The caveman formerly known as Head was having a fitful dream when something told him to open his eyes. He woke up just in time. "Hey!" he said as he ducked Rock's club, rolling over the side of his bed. She overturned a lantern as Ugh burst into the room. Cro kept his head low until he saw the oil from the torch. It spilled toward the outer wall with the flame trail right behind.

"Excuse me," Cro said as Ugh held onto Rock's neck for dear life. It looked like she'd have her shot at Cro yet.

Until the wall went up like a match.

"Fire!" Cro shouted, snapping the contestants to their senses. By the time they cleared the front door with Shirt, half the village was out of their huts. Cro's presence resulted in a far more organized bucket brigade than usual, and Ugh and Rock's hut was spared with only a few minor burns. Cro set his bucket down by the others while Ugh accosted his wife.

"Why you try bash Crow?" he asked. "Chief Dog say him okay."

"Me no believe him," Rock said. "Am afraid Crow try hurt boy."

"But Crow am friend. Him help fight fire."

"Me guess him not so bad."

Rock went to apologize to Cro, who flinched when he saw her coming.

"Me am sorry me try crush skull."

"That's...okay," Cro said. But for his safety and the village's, Cro was moved to Chief Dog's hut.

Rex felt reasonably confident no more snake-legs would grow from the air. But he had no idea why they were heading right for him. Maybe snake-legs were dumb. He drew himself up from his crouch and made his way stealthily through the trees, getting within snacking distance.

The two farthest snake-legs were shouting.

"Mignola!"

"What?"

"There's a life form behind those trees," Englehart yelled.

"What?"

"There's an unknown life form behind those trees. We just saw it move," Sprang said.

"Did you hear what they said?" Mignola asked McFarlane, who was standing between him and their shipmates.

"I got some kind of alien buzzin' me ear. I can't hear a bloody thing."

So once again, Mignola yelled, "What?"

And Rex burst out of the trees.

Now to Rex, the Sterankon dialect was a mishmash of shrieks, trills and clicks. All except for their word for "what?"

That sounded like a dinosaur whistle.

So his actions were somewhat justified when he swallowed Mignola whole. *Delicious*, Rex thought. The snake part was squirmy, but the top half tasted like chicken.

"Mignola!" McFarlane screamed. He fired at the beast. Rex felt an oddly pleasant tingle. His right arm disappeared.

Sterankon rayguns had three settings: daze, displace and disintegrate. The higher the setting, the longer it took for the weapon to recharge. So though the beast's arm had been vaporized, McFarlane was a sitting duck.

Rex roared his outrage at the sudden loss of an otherwise useless appendage. McFarlane used the opening. He ran under the alien's legs.

"*Eisner*, this is McFarlane!" he screamed into his chest pin. "We have hostiles! Beam me up!"

"McFarlane, this is Commander Kirby. I thought Mignola was field commander."

The giant alien roared.

"I'm sorry, McFarlane. How's that again?"

Rex turned and saw the snake-legs.

"Mignola's been eaten, ya tosser. Now come on and beam me up!"

And when Rex lunged, he came up with dirt. But there were two other snake-legs left.

Englehart's hands gripped the mineral scanner. He couldn't make them let go.

To his side, Sprang frantically tapped his shirt.

"*Eisner!* This is Sprang!"

He patted his chest and remembered his pin was swimming with the fish.

Commander Kirby whirled in his chair.

"What do you mean, you can't give me a visual?"

"The foliage is blocking our cameras, sir," Ensign Gruenwald said.

"Preposterous! Is McFarlane alive?"

"He's in the teleport bay," Ditko said.

"Get a lock on Sprang and Englehart and get them out of there."

"I'm afraid the mineral scanner is interfering with our frequencies, sir."

"Then raise them on their communicators."

"Right away, Commander."

"Ensign Sprang, this is Commander Kirby."

Kirby listened to the transmission.

"What is this I'm hearing?"

"I think it's water, sir," Bagley said.

"What in the world is he doing in water?"

"Maybe he's...bathing, sir?"

"Close this channel," Kirby bellowed. "Get me Englehart. Englehart, this is Commander Kirby. What is your situation?"

The reply was a mixture of static soup, screams and an alien roar.

Englehart's communicator squawked to Sprang's side as the giant alien charged. Sprang fumbled with his raygun and got off a shot. Rex's right leg took a nap. The last thing Englehart ever saw was a closeup of Rex's tonsils. Sprang barely dodged the toppling beast.

His phaser had been set on "daze."

Sprang switched the weapon to "disintegrate" but a message flashed *battery low.* Rex had broken some molars on the mineral scanner and was not happy about it. His leg still numb, Rex crawled toward Sprang using his remaining arm. One of Englehart's tentacles was squirming in his teeth.

Sprang slithered away for dear life.

Cro's stomach was making the tough transition to bunking with Chief Dog and Fight.

"So, friend Crow, tell boy why you come here," Dog said as they sat down to lunch.

"I was hoping you'd be more civilized. I come from a village of savages."

"Ugh," Dog said, slurping his gruel and wiping his mouth with his arm.

"Father, am done," Fight said.

"But boy no touch him gruel," Dog growled.

"Am sick of gruel. Me want go eat at Bug's hut. Him mother make roast bird."

Dog simmered, than sighed. "Okay."

Fight leapt from his chair and ran out the door. Cro was glad to see him go.

"Me am sorry for boy," Dog said. "Him not so smart sometime. Doctor no catch Fight so good when him fall out of wife."

Cro glanced at his lumpy meal. Its smell intimidated.

"Can I ask what happened to your wife?"

"Her turn blue and cold."

Cro was touched by Dog's eloquence. "I'm sorry," he said.

"You no have to be sorry. Her am one get stuck in ice."

Sprang stopped by the side of a distant creek and took out his lifeform detector. The jungle was full of unknown blips, but the giant one was gone. He emptied his survival kit and rifled through its supplies, ignoring the rations, his translator and the Chameleon 3000. Then he found it. His homing beacon. He set the metal egg on a log and flipped the beacon's switch. Nothing happened. He checked the device.

It didn't have batteries in it.

Sprang turned a wary antenna toward the lifeform detector. Its screen went dark as he removed its cell and placed it in the beacon. So when the bushes behind him rustled, it was his first sign of company.

Sprang leapt to his feet as something shrieked and moved past him in a blur. As quickly as he could aim his phaser, the alien crouched by the beacon.

It was small and hairy, with two legs and two arms and a long, prehensile tail. Unlike the two other aliens Sprang had seen, this one was kind of cute. It turned the beacon in its hand, poking it with a finger. A quizzical look crossed the alien's face as it sniffed it. Sprang lowered his weapon.

"Hey, there. Easy now." He dug in his pack and unwrapped a protein bar. He laid a piece on the log by the monkey.

"There you go."

The alien turned and bared its fangs. It hissed, then went back to the beacon. It turned it a few more times in his hand, then popped it in his mouth.

"Hey!" Sprang said. The alien yelped and scampered up a tree. It showed itself on a limb halfway up, jumping and screeching its triumph. This was Peanuts, after all, who had bitten the Swamp Chief's finger. He wouldn't show fear to a snake-legs, either. Or whatever the green creature was.

Sprang trained his phaser at the tree but faced a predicament. He couldn't displace or disintegrate. That would ruin the homing beacon. And if the critter was dazed and fell from that height, it might damage the beacon, too. What if he tried to catch the alien, use his tentacles to cushion its fall? That's what I'll do, Sprang thought as he checked that the finicky switch was on stun. He blinked away a bead of sweat and aimed.

The creature was gone.

Aboard the *Eisner*, First Mate Ditko said, "Commander! I have a signal!" But back on the ground, Sprang was lost and alone.

He heard a distant roar.

Kirby came upon Gibbons, the portal tech, who was working on the door to the bridge.

"About bloody time. What kept you?"

"Union regulations, sir. I'm not allowed to work on Tuesdays." Gibbons studied the parts on the floor. He held one up to the circuit panel as the Commander looked over his shoulder.

"I don't suppose you could let me in."

"Oh! Sorry, sir," Gibbons said. He spliced two dangling wires together and the portal slid away.

"Status report!" Kirby bellowed as he glided to his chair.

"We've got a lock on the beacon, sir," Ensign Bagley said. "We're almost in range."

Kirby looked at the blip on the screen.

"Good lord. Look at him go."

"Perhaps he's running from something, sir."

"Give me floodlights. I want a visual."

"Commander, if we use the floods we'll have to drop our cloak."

"I'm aware of that, Ensign Gruenwald. But I'm not going to lose any more squid."

The viewport blinked. It showed the treetops below, the darkness awash in lights.

"There!" Bagley pointed. Through the gap in the trees, they saw Peanuts the monkey.

"Is that Sprang?" Gruenwald said. Peanuts' location matched the beacon's blip.

"He must be traveling incognito," First Mate Ditko told the Commander.

"Of course. Sprang's undercover. He's more resourceful than I thought."

"But why doesn't he drop his disguise? We've seen him."

"Deep cover, Ensign Bagley. The lad's immersed himself in the role."

"We've got a lock, sir," Ditko said.

"Very well, then. Beam him aboard."

The beacon in Peanuts' stomach blipped as he felt himself disappear.

CHAPTER SEVEN

"Where is he?" Commander Kirby said, barging into the quarantine bay.

"Here, sir," a technician said.

Peanuts cowered in the strange room he had suddenly found himself in.

"Why is this man in a status field?"

"It's standard procedure, Commander. We don't know what kind of contagions he may have brought aboard."

"Good heavens, man. It's Sprang!"

"Not according to my bioscan, sir."

"Naturally. He's undercover."

"Yes, well," the technician said, "the Chameleon 3000 would explain his appearance, but it can't simulate biofields. The closest I've found to this creature's scan is the howler tails on Gaiman 9."

"That may be your opinion, Ensign, but you don't have my years in the field. Now drop this status field, would you? I'd like to have a word with this squid."

The technician shrugged at his coworker, who turned off the transparent shield. Kirby slithered onto the platform. Peanuts cringed at his approach.

"There now, soldier. A bit traumatized, are we?"

Peanuts shrieked.

"Yes, I know. So tell me, lad, how did you fool that bioscan? Cobbled a scrambler together, eh? That's thinking on your feet."

Kirby was a tentacle away when Peanuts bared his teeth.

"See here. Even a soldier who's undercover must show his commander respect. Now tell me, Ensign, how did you come upon choosing this curious form?"

Peanuts scampered to the far end of the cell. Kirby cornered him.

"Look here, Sprang. I admit you have a gift for espionage. But now's not the time for this nonsense. Be a good lad and drop the disguise."

The supposed Sprang hissed.

"Gone native, have we? Very well, then. I'll do it myself."

Kirby reached for the rather convincing monkey, thinking he'd turn off his crewman's disguise, but Peanuts was having none of that. He bit the Commander's finger.

"Good heavens, man. You're mad!"

Peanuts shrieked and leapt off the platform.

"Ensigns! Arrest that squid!"

"Uh, I don't think he's a squid, Commander."

"I've never seen a squid jump like that."

"Cut the prattle! He's getting away!"

Peanuts leapt across the room. He landed at the foot of the door. Naturally, it was stuck.

"Aha! We've got him!" Kirby said. "Make sure you're set on stun!"

The door slid away, and there was Ditko, facing two phaser barrels.

"Oh there you are. I thought I heard--AUGHH!"

Ditko slumped to the floor. Peanuts scampered over him and fled into the ship.

"He got away, sir."

"Yes, I see that," Kirby said. "Get this man to his quarters and let me know when he comes to. I believe he's earned a commendation for taking friendly fire."

"What about your finger, sir?"

"Nothing to worry about," Kirby said. "I'm sure it's just a scratch."

Thomas roamed the empty throne room, studying his data pad. Kirby's latest report was muddled. He had lost at least two of his men. The data pad blinked and its tiny screen flashed *incoming transmission*. It was on Gruenwald's private channel. Thomas put his friend on-screen.

"Thomas, can you hear me?" Gruenwald whispered in his quarters.

"I can hear you," Thomas said. "You're a little fuzzy, though."

"We've been having some problems with interference. I'll try to make this quick. Did you see the Commander's report?"

"I just read it this morning."

"Than you know about Mignola and Englehart. And Sprang is MIA."

"But Kirby said Sprang was on the ship."

"The Commander's a little confused," Gruenwald said. "A native swallowed Sprang's homing beacon and Kirby thought it was Sprang."

"Have you captured this creature yet?"

"No. We were tracking him using the beacon but he passed it this afternoon."

"What do you mean?" Thomas said.

"The beacon was in a pile of droppings we found in engineering."

"What about Sprang?"

"We don't have any way to track him. He could be anywhere on Sol 3."

"How's the Commander doing? Have you spotted any signs?"

"Nothing so far," Gruenwald said. "But it might get ugly soon. Kirby wants to send some men after Sprang but no one wants to go."

"All right," Thomas said. "I've got to go. But keep me informed. And good luck."

King Stanley wandered out of his bedroom, still wearing the royal pajamas.

"Good morning, your grace."

"Good morning! Any word from our far-flung friends?"

"Yes, I'm afraid that two of our men have been eaten," Thomas said.

"Great galaxies! Cannibalism?"

"No, they encountered a hostile alien."

"A carnivorous creature!" King Stanley exclaimed.

"Exactly," Thomas said.

"Have they found any of that..."

"Calcium, sir?"

King Stanley snapped back to his senses.

"Calcium, yes! That miraculous metal!"

"It's actually a mineral, sir."

"You'll have to excuse me, Thomas. I'm not feeling quite myself."

"An ironic insight, sir."

"I appreciate your due diligence in divulging these deaths by digestion."

"I'll be sure to keep you updated."

"Thank you, Thomas," the king said. "Now I feel the need for a nap."

His mental maladies multiplied. The king spent the week in bed.

Shirt sat under a tree during recess watching the other kids play. His classmates parted for the upright man they'd seen around the village. Some had heard he was a demon, or a big lizard in disguise. Shirt saw him and grabbed a rock. It was the bad man, Crow.

Cro had taken to carrying a club for his own protection. Not that he was good with it. The idea was deterrence. Maybe Rock would be more civil if she saw that he was armed, too.

As he neared Shirt, Cro saw another kind of rock approaching. The small, round, hard type aimed at his head.

"Mister, look out!" someone said.

Without thinking, Cro swung his club and hit Shirt's rock dead-on, careening the pellet off the sweet spot. The rock sailed out of sight.

"Wow," the kids said, that long, drawn-out wow that showed they were impressed, and a light bulb went off in one of their heads. A new game was about to be born.

Cro stared at his club, surprised. Shirt dropped his other rock. He shied away as the Bad Man approached, but then Cro spoke.

"Hello."

The Bad Man's voice wasn't deep and scary like Shirt imagined it. It didn't make the ground shake or the noisy lights flash in the sky. In fact, judging on voice alone, the Bad Man was a wimp.

"You're Shirt, right?" Cro sat beside him. Shirt warily shook his head. "Do you know who I am?"

"Am Crow, like bird."

"That's close enough."

"Rock say you bad man."

"Yes, well, I think your mother's charming when she's not trying to crush my skull."

"You no look like bad man," Shirt said.

"Why thank you."

"Me think you look like runt."

"Uh-huh." Cro thought, *this is going well*. "Why aren't you with your friends?"

"Me no have friends," Shirt said.

"Why not?"

"Them all make fun of me."

"Yeah," Cro said, thinking back to his youth. "Kids can be pretty mean."

"You stay with Fight?"

"Unfortunately."

"Then me no talk to you."

"Why?" Cro said.

"You am friend of Fight."

"I'm just staying at his home. Between you and me," Cro said to Shirt, "I think Fight's pretty dumb."

Shirt cracked a smile.

"You think so, too."

"Me hate him guts," Shirt said.

"I don't know if hate is the proper term..."

"Me want hit Fight with rock."

"Okay, then. Hate it is."

A horn blew. The kids started heading inside.

"Me have go now," Shirt said.

"Wait! Have you seen a bright bowl in the sky? A big, green bowl with lights?"

"Chief Dog say there no bowl," Shirt said.

"I know he did," Cro said. "But I'll believe you. Tell me what you saw."

Shirt stood up. "Me have to go now."

"I won't tell anyone," Cro said.

Shirt looked at Cro and realized he wasn't like the other adults. He wasn't dull-eyed, slow, or brutish. He was something else.

"Do you come from bowl?" Shirt asked quietly.

"No, but I'm looking for it."

"Why?"

"Because I have friends who come from there. At least, I hope I do."

Shirt thought hard as he watched the last of his classmates leave the yard. "Me see bowl, but only one time. Am time me hit you with rock."

"Thank you, Shirt," Cro said.

Shirt ran toward school, then turned around.

"No tell no one, okay?"

"I won't," Cro said with a smile. "It'll be our little secret."

Sprang listened outside Shirt's classroom window, disguised as a mobile rock. He had come upon the school just as the upright alien did, but he could not get close enough to hear what the hairy man said.

But he seemed to be more advanced than the others. Perhaps he was their leader.

Sprang's universal translator soaked up the class discussion, but it seemed he kept hearing the same words over and over again. Maybe his translator couldn't pick up on the nuances of these primitives' language.

Or maybe they were as dumb as they looked. Their young ones hurled rocks at each other in what appeared to be part of a game. Who knew what kind of barbaric customs they practiced behind closed doors?

But the young one he had seen under the tree seemed different than his peers. He didn't partake of the rock ritual. He shunned the ones who did. And he seemed to have the favor of the one who walked erect.

Sprang kept his antenna trained on Shirt. He decided to follow him home.

"Straighten up, men," the Commander said. "I'm calling this meeting to order. "Bagley," Kirby bellowed, looking down the conference table. "Why haven't we captured this stowaway yet? I don't cotton to having aliens running amuck on my ship."

"We're trying to track it down, sir. I've got men on every floor."

"Good show. Now as for Sprang, I'm looking for a few good squid to bring him back. Volunteers?"

The men looked in every direction but Kirby's.

"McFarlane. You'll lead the mission."

"I would, if I were mad."

"See here, soldier," Kirby said. "Sprang's your responsibility."

"Sprang's the one who bolloxed it up," McFarlane said. "You want him, go get him yerself."

"Mind yourself, soldier. I won't tolerate dissension in the ranks. Now pick two squid and report to the teleport bay within the hour."

"Ach, there's the problem, cap'n. I hear the teleport bay's on the blink."

"Gruenwald, what have you heard about this?"

"I can't say that I have, Commander."

"That reminds me," McFarlane said. "I want Gruenwald on me team." He crossed his arms and stared Gruenwald down, flashing a wicked smirk.

"Come to think of it, Commander, I do recall seeing something about the bay malfunctioning."

Kirby's antenna panned from McFarlane to Gruenwald. "Am I to believe this report, Ensign Gruenwald?"

"I'm sorry, sir. It slipped my mind." Gruenwald weathered the Commander's stare.

"Very well, then," Kirby said after a long deliberation. "Ensign Bagley, I want a full report on the state of the teleport bay. I trust you'll let me know as soon as it's operational."

Bagley dared a glance at his shipmates before answering, "Aye, sir."

"Jolly good," Kirby said. "Moving on. Who's building the new mineral detector?"

"That would be Lightle from engineering," Ensign Bagley said.

"Excellent. I'm sure a squid of his calibre can guarantee results?"

"He said that it might take a while since he has to rebuild it from scratch."

The door to the conference room slid open. Ditko slithered in.

"Ditko!" the Commander said. "On your feet again, I see."

"Aye, sir," his first mate said, frog-throated. He sat down gingerly.

"Sorry about the cross-fire, lad."

"I understand, Commander."

"Gruenwald! Make sure this man gets an extra busiek plant in his rations."

"Aye, sir."

"Can't have you breaking anything in your weakened condition."

"Thank you, sir," Ditko said.

"McFarlane, pay attention. That's how you deal with adversity."

"Let him have a go with that beastie, then."

"Ah yes," Kirby said. "The one who ate Mignola and Englehart. Our scanner picked up some calcium, eh?"

"If I may, sir," Ditko said, "apparently, the calcium deposit was mistaken for the lifeform."

"My understanding was that the two were shown to be one and the same," Kirby said.

"Ah, that may be so, sir, but I don't see how that benefits us."

"That's because you lack vision," Kirby said. "What if we harvest these beasts?"

"Harvest, sir?" Bagley said.

"We do have a science lab aboard this ship, don't we?"

"I believe so, sir," Bagley said.

"Then I would think it would be a simple matter. We merely clone a herd of these creatures and extract their calcium."

"I'm not sure about your science, sir."

"Nonsense! It's child's play."

"Excuse me, Commander?"

"What is it, Ditko?"

"Even if this were possible, I have to remind you of clause 203 of the Interplanetary Conduct Code."

"Rubbish. What does it say?"

Ditko cleared his throat. "I quote: *Any third party wishing to remove a lifeform from a planet must first obtain a written waiver from that planet's governing species.*"

"Written waiver?" Kirby said.

"A permission slip, Commander."

"Harrumph. We're Sterankons, Ditko. I say we make our own bloody rules."

"That's not such a good idea, sir. The Starlins wouldn't be pleased."

"Starlins!" Kirby said. "Good lord! Don't tell me those savages have their hands in this."

"I'm afraid they do, Commander. If we violate the ICC, the Starlins may invade."

"Those brain-eating mongrels. All right, Ditko. How should we proceed?"

"Well, ah, I believe the charter calls for a standardized aptitude test of a cross-section of the native species to determine the dominant class."

"Cut the gibberish, Ditko."

"We have to give them an I.Q. test, sir."

"Very well, then. Make it so." Kirby winced and flexed his injured finger.

"Are you feeling all right, sir?"

"It's nothing, Ditko," Kirby said. "Merely a dentally damaged digit."

Gruenwald's antenna perked up. He had drifted off after Ditko's arrival, but Kirby raised his alarm.

"What did you say?" he said.

"Nothing that concerns you, Ensign. Now try to stay awake."

Gruenwald settled back into his haze. He must have imagined it.

Sprang stood at the door to Rock and Ugh's hut and waited for it to slide open. He looked down and held his arms out, but they looked like caveman arms. The Chameleon 3000 had turned him into an average Neanderthal, or as close to one as a holographic projector would allow.

He had followed the boy to this primitive home and watched him go inside. But now Sprang couldn't figure out how to gain entrance himself. There was no control panel or intercom. He peeked in the front window.

Shirt was sitting on the floor playing with carved wooden toys. "Roar!" He made the dinosaur say. "Big lizard eat you, Fight!"

"Oh, please, big lizard, no eat Fight," Shirt pantomimed with the smaller stick figure.

Rock watched her son play while she visited with Petal. Their husbands were out on the hunt.

"Shirt, clean toys when you am done."

"Okay," Shirt said.

"*Shirt.*"

"Who say that?" Rock said.

"Say what?" Petal said, looking up.

"Say boy's name."

"Me no say Shirt."

"*Shirt.*"

"There it am again," Rock said.

Then she saw Sprang in the window. Only instead of seeing a squid with antennae, she saw a strange caveboy.

"Shirt," Sprang said, hoping his translator got the boy's name right.

"Am him friend, Shirt?" Rock asked her boy.

"Me no see him before."

"What am name?" Rock said. Sprang panicked, his translator lagging behind. He answered with the word he had heard the most.

"It."

"Where am parents, It?"

Sprang improvised.

"In fight."

"Him voice sound funny," Petal said.

Sprang tried smiling his way through.

"Maybe him no have mother," Rock said. "Him am not so smart."

Shirt left his toys and approached the caveboy. "Am you lost?" he said.

"Lost. Am it!" Sprang sweated bullets. His translator was useless. It interpreted Shirt's last question as "Why are your teeth so loud?"

"Him do talk funny," Rock told Petal. "Maybe him know Crow."

"I don't know about this," Gruenwald said. He was in the teleport bay. McFarlane was removing the panel from a circuit board on the wall.

"What's not to know?" he said.

Gruenwald darted his eyes to Bagley, who, like himself, had a wrench in his hands and a pretzeled conscience. "I don't know," Gruenwald said. "Isn't this mutiny?"

"This is survival, boyo." McFarlane set the panel aside. "Now which a ye's gonna do it?"

"Why can't you?" Ensign Bagley said, his stare-down with Gruenwald a draw.

"I can't be the only one who gets me hands dirty."

"But what if the Commander finds out?"

"Who's gonna tell 'em? Now come on, Gruenwald. Why don't ya give it a go?"

Gruenwald stared at the dangling wires, an intricate web of spaghetti. "But what if we need to teleport later?"

"We'll fix it, then." McFarlane said.

"Do you know the schematics?"

"No, but someone aboard will."

"I don't know about that," Gruenwald said. "I think Morrison wired this. And he's back on Steranko."

"Look, man, don't be daft. We either make a hash o' this or we tussle with the beast."

Gruenwald weighed his options. He swung his wrench toward the board.

"Stop!"

The weapon stopped shy of its target.

"What are ye thinkin'?" McFarlane snapped.

"You told me to take out the system."

"But not with that, ya muppet. Ye have ta make this job look like it went an' done itself."

Bagley looked around nervously as Gruenwald stripped two wires. He touched the ends, winced, and jumped back, avoiding the greasespit shower of sparks. The room's climate system slowed to a groan. The teleport bay went dark.

McFarlane replaced the circuit board panel as the emergency systems kicked in.

"I say we bolt for the mess tent, lads. I'm gummin' for a pint."

Sprang sat at the dinner table, watching the others for cues. The hunk of meat on his plate smelled delicious, but he didn't have silverware. Maybe Rock had forgotten to set the table. He wished he knew their word for fork.

Rock placed a bowl of figs on the table and took her place next to Ugh. "Ugh, you want say prayer?" she said.

"Ugh." Ugh bowed his head. "Us thank gods for roast oink and hunt and funny new caveboy."

"Ugh," the others responded. Sprang gaped in horror as his hosts tore into their meat with their bare hands.

"It, you no like oink?" Rock asked the alien in disguise.

Sprang flashed his usual clueless smile. He was saved by a knock on the door.

"Dog," Ugh said. "Why am you here?"

"Me want see caveboy." Sprang straightened up when he saw the upright man walk in behind the chief. But Cro was too entranced to notice. He gazed longingly at the roast pig. Dog was not just a woeful cook, but also a lousy hunter.

"Crow, am hungry?" Ugh said. "Want eat some roast oink?"

"Yes, I'd like that very much." Cro eagerly took a seat. Sprang noticed that even the upright man ate his food using his hands. He reached for his pork shank warily, but Dog stopped him from taking a bite.

"So, you am caveboy Shirt and Rock find."

Sprang tried a beguiling grin.

"Why him smile so much?" Dog said.

"Us think him am slow," Rock said.

"Where are your parents? Do you live around here?" the upright man asked Sprang.

"Am lost."

"Crow, am him from Swamp?" Dog said.

"No, I've never seen him before." Cro's language was throwing Sprang's translator. He used more than one verb tense.

"Perhaps him spy," Dog speculated.

"You said the same thing about me." Cro turned to the covert alien. "What's your name?"

"I'd like that VERY MUCH!" Sprang blurted.

"Him name am It," Rock said. "Sometime him no speak so good."

"Hmm," Dog thought. "No can have caveboy grow up without family. Crow, you no have son. Me think give boy to you."

"Me want take boy," Ugh said. "Shirt like him."

Chief Dog sat back to think.

"Okay, It now am son of Ugh unless real father show up."

Rock, overwhelmed to the point of tears, crushed the hapless squid in a hug. "Why you feel funny?" she said, feeling through his disguise.

"I'd like that VERY MUCH!" Sprang beamed. Rock placed her hand on his forehead. She barely missed his antennae.

"Him feel clammy," she said. "Like frog."

"It may just be a fever," Cro said. "He should get some rest."

Sprang wrapped his tentacles around his seat. He had a feeling he was in over his head.

Gruenwald's antennae drooped over the bar. His head spun merrily.

"Crikey, lad. Ye're a lightweight," McFarlane said, holding a glass.

"Whash ish this?" Gruenwald studied his drink.

"Me own family recipe. Barkeep! Another for me n' me friends."

Gruenwald tipped off his stool.

"I'm sorry, sir," the bartendroid said. "Your friend appears to be drunk."

"Aye," McFarlane said. Bagley got Gruenwald back on his perch. "Make his coffee, then."

"We shouldn't have come here. We're still on duty."

"Ah, lighten up, Bagley."

"Yeah, lighten up, Bayshley. McFarlung's right. Wesha haf some fun."

"Careful, there, laddie. Ye spilled me ale."

"Yer funny," Gruenwald said.

"What if the Commander wants to talk to him?" Bagley asked McFarlane.

"Relax. Kirby's thick as a plank."

"Yeah," Gruenwald said, hugging the table. "An' everyone knowsh he's a--"

"Gruenwald!"

Gruenwald flopped his head over.

"What's the meaning of this?" Kirby said.

"We wush firsty."

"Good heavens, man."

"Beggin' yer pardon, cap'n. We didna know he couldn't handle his drink."

"That's enough, McFarlane. And you, Ensign Bagley. I thought I told you to check on that teleport bay."

"I'm afraid it's worse then we thought, Commander."

Gruenwald had a giggling fit.

"What's so funny, Ensign?"

McFarlane jumped in.

"He's a wee bit polluted, that's all."

"Gruenwald, I thought you'd have better judgment than carousing with this ruffian."

"Aye, aye, cap'n." Gruenwald saluted. His head hit the bar with a thunk.

"McFarlane, make sure he's breathing, will you? Now how bad is that teleport bay?"

"The circuits are fried," Bagley said, straight-faced. "It could be down for a while."

"Harrumph," Kirby said, stroking his chin. "Then we'll have to use tractor beams."

Gruenwald mumbled unintelligibly.

"Good lord. Get that squid to his room."

Pointy had never gotten over the death of his son, Snack. He still saw Big Teeth in his dreams. Then the monkey fever claimed his mate, River. All Pointy had left was his cow.

Pointy thought of his wife and son as he went to check on Betty. She was out of her barn, grazing in the moonlight. "Moo," she called to her owner. He knew she missed them, too. Their melancholy was interrupted when someone called his name.

"Oh, hello Snake," Pointy said, making out the form of his chief.

"Hello, Pointy. How am Betty?"

"Me think her am sad."

"That am why me come tonight. Me come here to take Betty."

"Moooo," Betty said mournfully, echoing Pointy's dismay.

"Come in hut," Pointy told Chief Snake. "Me no want Betty to hear."

They sat in the kitchen. Pointy was still in shock. His beloved cow grazed through the window.

"Am sorry," Snake said, "but village hungry. Moo feed many men."

Pointy turned toward the window. Betty was so angelic, he swore he saw a spotlight around her.

"Can me let village milk Betty?"

"Us have plenty milk," Snake said.

"But there am plenty frog to eat."

"Village am sick of frog. Puddle am only one cook them good but now Puddle am gone."

Betty mooed nervously. Had either man turned, they would have seen her hooves leaving the ground.

"Me know Snake new leader," Pointy said. "But no can take Betty away."

"Am good for village," Snake said. Meaning he planned to eat Betty himself.

"But Betty am family."

"Mooo," Betty said, a good twenty feet off the ground.

"What am buzzing noise?" Chief Snake asked.

"Maybe am flies," Pointy said.

"Maybe should cover window. No let bugs in hut," Snake said.

"Am good idea," Pointy agreed. "But then hut get too hot."

"Hmm, am true," Snake mused. "Maybe put frog in window."

"Why frog?" Pointy said.

"So frog can eat the flies."

"But how make frog stay in window?"

The two men pondered mightily while Betty sailed away.

Sprang lay in bed, clutching his blanket, his fake caveboy eyes wide awake. He shared the room with Shirt, Rock and Ugh, who roared through his nose as he slept. Sprang turned on his side. He was face-to-face with Shirt.

"No be scared," Shirt whispered, having crept across the room. "Am still sick?"

"Am tired," Sprang said. His new language sounded foreign to him. But his translator had made strides after an evening spent with Cro.

"Here." Shirt handed him some pebbles.

"What these for?"

"Put in ears. Help make Ugh's noise go away."

"Okay," Sprang smiled.

"Me go sleep now." Shirt crawled back to his bed. "Good night, It."

"Good night."

Sprang tried to dream of Steranko but all he thought of were large, pointy teeth.

Professor Duck ventured out of his cave to gather some grubs and berries. That had been the bulk of his diet since he had run away from Big Teeth. He had spent years looking for the Swamp Village only to realize he was lost.

He looked at the stars and tried to remember the constellations he'd taught, regretting he'd paid so little attention to his own survival class. He walked toward the sun when it came up and then followed it when it went down, only to find it led him to the same spot he started from.

Duck bent down to gather some grubs. He wished it wasn't so dark. Suddenly, he was accommodated by a brilliant light. Duck shielded his eyes and looked to the sky. Then he found himself headed that way, floating up toward a fuzzy shape, a green glowing circle that hummed.

Professor Duck tried to find the words to describe his awe.

"Pretty lights."

CHAPTER EIGHT

Professor Duck gripped the strange gray bars. A gorilla was caged beside him. Betty mooed from her cell on the end. The door to the room slid away.

"So these are the first three candidates, eh?"

"Yes, sir," Ditko said, holding a bowl.

The strange creatures slithered toward the cages. The ape beat its chest. Duck backed away.

"The first two look identical," Commander Kirby said.

"I'm certain they're different species, sir. Look at the second one's hair."

"Ah, yes. Quite right," the Commander said in his Sterankon trill. The ape rattled its cage. Duck covered his ears. Betty looked for something to graze.

"See here," Kirby said. "I don't have time for this translation business, but I trust you'll get the idea." He took a key from the bowl Ditko held and showed it to the subjects. "This is a key. It opens your cages. Quite simple, men. Like so." Kirby's tentacle snaked toward the door on Duck's cell. The lock turned with a click. The door squealed, but the caveman stayed in the corner. Kirby swiveled the door back and forth.

"Open. Closed. Open. Closed. I'm sure you get the point. You in the corner, stop cowering. I assure you, I mean you no harm." Kirby locked Professor Duck's cell and slid the key between the bars. Ditko did the same, offering the means of escape to Betty and the gorilla.

"Now then," Kirby said, stepping back. "Show me what you've learned."

Duck eyed his key suspiciously. He took it to the back of his cell. He bit it, used it to scratch his leg, then hid it in his shirt. Betty stared at hers, wishing she had opposable thumbs. That was all that ever held cows in check. They couldn't hold a weapon.

The ape sniffed his prize, turned it in his hand, then ate it.

"Oh, good lord."

"Perhaps they're bluffing, sir," Ditko said.

"Harrumph. How long do we wait?"

"I'm not sure. No one's ever failed the first part of the test before."

"I pictured the primitive primate passing."

"What did you say, sir?"

"Nothing, Ditko," Kirby said. "Keep me informed."

A hiss signaled the Commander's exit.

Betty ate her key, too.

"It, wake up. Must go school now," Shirt said, nudging Sprang's shoulder.

"Am doctor coming?" Sprang said, checking the state of his disguise. He worried he may have accidentally switched the projector off in his sleep.

"Doctor am busy. Him come after school."

"What am school?" Sprang said.

"Am place where elders talk a lot."

"Me no want to go to school."

"It must go to school," Shirt said.

"How come?"

"All caveboys must go to school."

"But me no am caveboy."

"Yes you am."

And then Sprang understood. The Chameleon 3000 had botched his disguise. It made him look like a kid.

"Us have new boy in class today," Professor Hide told his students. "What am name?"

"It," Sprang said. A rock careened off his head.

"Now him it," Fight said from his seat. His classmates laughed dutifully.

"Am head okay?" Shirt asked his friend.

"Ib realby hurcz," Sprang said. To the class, it looked like he was hit in the forehead. But actually, it was his nose.

"That am Fight."

"I figurb thad oud."

Sprang rubbed his throbbing nose. Between Sol 4, Shirt's hairtrigger mother and now this, he had a thing about rocks.

Ditko snacked on the stalk of a Busiek plant while he watched the test subjects. The four-legged horned one remained complacent, mooing now and then. The hairy primate grunted and paced. The clothed one had soiled himself. Ditko slouched and wondered if this planet had any leader at all.

The gorilla got all worked up over something, roaring and pounding his chest. Ditko was used to his antics by now. He reached in his pocket again. *That's funny,* he thought, *I could swear I had another Busiek plant.* Then he saw something on top of the gorilla's cage. It was the small alien with the long tail. It shrieked and cavorted, showing Ditko its fangs and his missing snack.

"Hey!" Ditko said, as Peanuts jumped and landed in front of the cage. He hunkered down, took a bite of the plant, then whipped it at the ape. The hairy alien picked up the stalk, sniffed it, and took a nibble.

"Security, this is First Mate Ditko," Ditko said into his badge, but all he heard was static. He trained his phaser on Peanuts. "All right, now. This won't hurt a bit." Peanuts stared like a deer in headlights. But as Ditko fired, he leapt away. The gorilla slumped to the floor.

"Oh, dear," Ditko said, searching the room. He swept his gun over the ceiling. He heard a hiss, turned, and saw the door closing. The small one had gotten away.

"Commander Kirby, this is First Mate Ditko." He eyed the unconscious ape. Ditko took a spare key off his belt and inched towards the cage. He unlocked it, bent beside the beast, and felt its neck for a pulse. "Thank goodness," he said a moment before he heard the door clang shut behind him. He whirled and saw the long-tailed alien outside the cage with his key.

As Ditko rattled the bars to his cage and fumbled with his weapon, Peanuts unlocked Duck and Betty's cells and screeched that they were free. Betty took the cue and strolled out of hers. Duck wasn't so bright. *Oh well,* Peanuts thought, leading Betty to the exit.

Ditko cursed his phaser. Or more accurately, his aim. The ape was stirring at his feet. He tapped his intercom. "Commander Kirby, this is First Mate Ditko. Is anybody there?" He felt hot breath on his tentacles. The large alien was almost awake. "Oh dear, oh dear," Ditko fretted, watching his raygun's status screen. He clanked it against the bars in frustration. Something yanked it out of his hand.

"Put that down!" Ditko chided Duck, who was drawn to the shiny object. Professor Duck poked and prodded the weapon, switching it to disintegrate. He pointed the gun at Ditko, the way he'd seen the snake-legs do it.

"Stun!" Ditko screamed. "Switch the setting to stun!" He fainted when Duck pulled the trigger. Huh, Duck thought. The shiny toy wasn't as loud as before. But it made the snake-legs go to sleep.

He stored the gun next to his key.

"Uh-oh," Rock said, opening her door to the small delegation. Shirt and It were home from school early, with Dog and Cro in tow. Rock appraised the situation and asked Dog, "What am wrong?"

"Boy in trouble," Chief Dog said. "Him hit Fight with pointy stick."

"Shirt!" Rock said. "Me tell you hundred time no can hit Fight!"

"Not Shirt," the chief said. "Other boy."

"It?"

Sprang stared at his feet.

"Am accident," Shirt said. "Him throw pointy stick but miss."

"By about twenty feet," Cro said.

"When Ugh come home," Chief Dog told Rock, "me help him punish boy."

"But It am sick," Rock said. "Maybe fever make him miss."

"It, cough in hand," Shirt whispered to Sprang. They had worked out the signal beforehand. Sprang hacked away, then recited his line.

"Me no feel so good."

"See? Him need doctor," Rock told Dog.

"Doctor am with Fight."

"I'm a doctor," Cro said. "I could take a look at It."

Sprang flinched as Cro reached for his hand. His instinct was to run. Surely Cro would wonder why Sprang felt different than he looked.

A moment away from catastrophe, Rock stepped between Cro and her ward.

"No, us wait for real doctor," she said. She still had her qualms about Crow.

"I am a real doctor," Cro told her. "I practiced in the Swamp Village."

"Am good doctor?" Rock said.

"The best."

"So you save many men in Swamp?"

"Actually, most of them died."

The other cavemen stared at Cro.

"It wasn't my fault," he said.

"Me think him should leave village," Rock said. Cro took Chief Dog's arm.

"Surely a man like you doesn't believe in superstition."

"Ah!" Dog said. "Take hand off arm! No want to catch bad spirits!"

"That's it," Cro said. "I'm out of here."

It was time to try a different race.

Commander Kirby took the model spaceship out of its display case. It was a replica of the *Ordway*, the first ship he served aboard. He was a young ensign in those halcyon days and the universe was his oyster, which was ironic since the *Ordway* was destroyed by a giant clam. Kirby survived that incident only to find himself on the *Kesel*, which defied convention as well as physics by actually sinking in space. Then came the *Portacio*, where he was promoted to First Mate. But the warp engines overloaded, plunging it into a parallel universe ruled by flesh-eating ducks.

"Fanatical fowls on feeding frenzies," Kirby said to himself. He felt another spell coming on and grabbed the display case. The door to his quarters beeped.

Kirby steadied himself.

"Come in."

"Excuse me, sir," Gruenwald said as he slithered. "We have a situation."

"What? Why wasn't I informed?"

"Our communicators are down."

"Rot. What is it now?"

"I think you'll want to see for yourself."

Kirby followed Gruenwald out the door. The hallway was blocked by a cow.

"What's the meaning of this?" Kirby said.

"Moo."

"Well, we found one of them," Gruenwald said.

"One of them?" the Commander roared. "Get me First Mate Ditko at once!"

Betty looked up and mooed nonchalantly.

"I wasn't talking to you."

The gorilla sat in the corner of his cage, still groggy from being stunned. It stared at Ditko's unconscious form and wondered what he'd missed. The last thing he remembered the snake-legs shot him. Now he was his roommate.

Two more snake-legs entered the room. The gorilla tried to act casual. Kirby took in the two empty cages and then the one in the middle.

"Ensign, set your phaser on stun."

"Is that wise, sir?" Gruenwald said. "I don't think I can hit the alien without stunning Ditko, too."

"Tut-tut, Gruenwald. He's been shot before."

"All right, sir," Gruenwald said. One zap later, the ape was out.

"Good show," Kirby said. "Now be a good lad and get Ditko out."

Gruenwald approached the cage. He tugged at the door, then turned around.

"Commander? Do you have the key?"

Thomas sat in King Stanley's throne to see how it would fit. It was a bit too snug. Thomas tried to get up. A guard appeared.

"Oh, pardon me, sir."

"Ah, hello," Thomas said, struggling. "Say, could you give me a hand?"

"Squirming squids stuck in Stanley's seat?" the guard said, helping him out.

Thomas laughed. "That's very good."

"Don't you worry, sir. All of us boys were relieved when you took over for the king."

Thomas accompanied the guard to the back of the throne room.

"How's your project coming along?"

"What project would that be?" Thomas said.

"Operation: Osteoporosis."

"How did you know about that?"

"I've been surfing the CableNet," the guard said. "Err, off duty, of course."

"You learned about this on the CableNet?"

"Sure," the guard said. "Everyone knows."

"This is supposed to be a covert operation."

"The people have a right to know. That's what downwithrobots says."

"Who?" Thomas said.

"Downwithrobots. I don't think that's his real name, though."

"No," Thomas said. "It isn't."

"So tell me," the guard said. "Have they found any calcium yet?"

"No," Thomas said. "But I'm sure the Commander has everything under control."

Kirby watched Ditko snooze in his cell.

"Fetch me some explosive, will you?"

"Explosives?" Gruenwald said.

"We'll blow the bloody door open."

"Don't you think that may be a bit too much?"

"Preposterous. This is a battleship."

"We're supposed to be diplomats, sir."

"Tell that to Sprang," Kirby said.

"I could just use my phaser to disintegrate the door."

"Ah! Pip pip. Jolly good. We'll deliver Ditko from his dire dilemma!"

"Excuse me, sir?"

"Carry on."

Kirby's right antennae twitched.

"Sod it!" Morrison cursed, singeing a tentacle with his welder. He was below the deck of the *Giffen*, continuing its repairs.

"You should have that looked at," Thomas said, negotiating a mess of machinery.

"What brings you here, Thomas? You feel the urge to walk among common squid?"

"Just checking your progress," Thomas said. "How close are you to launch?"

"I don't know." Morrison put down his tools. "Two weeks. What's going on?"

"I was wondering if you could lower that estimate by about a week."

"Are you daft?"

"I'm just asking if you can do it."

"I'd like to know the reason why."

"I don't know," Thomas said. "You've never been very good at keeping secrets."

"So you've been surfing the CableNet," Morrison said.

"Not personally. But I hear you haven't changed your old screen name."

"A squid's gotta have a hobby."

"Maybe you've got too much time on your hands."

"I guess I could step up production, but..."

"Let me guess," Thomas said. "What's in it for you?"

Morrison smirked as he wrapped some cable.

"How'd you like to have command of this ship?"

"That would be deadly," Morrison said.

"Good. When can you be ready?"

"If you give me more men and equipment, four days."

"Make it two," Thomas said. "I'll get you everything you need."

"What's with the sense of urgency? The *Eisner* in a bind?"

"Their report sounds like they're close to something. I just want you there to help."

"Bugger that," Morrison said. "What's the real reason?"

Thomas put on his best poker face.

"If you don't want the assignment, I can give it to someone else."

"I thought I was the wily one," Morrison told his old friend.

"Thanks. Are you in?"

"Bloody right."

Cro dropped the armload of branches, then sat down to take a break. He had been at it since leaving Lake Village and finding his way back to the beach. But his hours of labor were paying off. The circle was almost complete. He piled the branches in the sand and looked hopefully to the sky.

Gruenwald slithered down the hallway after sending his report. He turned the corner, stopped, and yelped.

Duck was quite jumpy himself.

"Oh, there you are," Gruenwald said, backing up. "We've been wondering where you were."

Duck winced at the snake-legs' screeching noise. He dug the prize out of his shirt.

"You really shouldn't do that," Gruenwald said. The savage was holding a phaser. Duck pulled the trigger and slumped to the floor. He had forgotten which end was the front.

"Good lord!" Kirby said predictably as the door to the bridge slid away. Gruenwald's chest pin still wasn't working. He had dragged Duck there himself.

"I found him in the hallway, sir."

"Good show," Kirby said. "Is he dead?"

"Stunned," Gruenwald said. "Should I put him with the others?"

"Right. Ditko! Give him a hand. And what on Steranko is that smell?"

"I think it's his clothing, sir."

"Excuse me, Commander," Bagley said from his station. "I think you should look at this."

"What is it?"

"I've been scanning the surface for signs of Sprang."

"And you think that you've found something, eh? Good work, Ensign. Put it on-screen."

The viewport showed the beach.

"Blimey," Kirby said.

A circle of flame inscribed the shore, lighting the nighttime sky. Its circumference was easily wide enough to land a spaceship in. Four arrows blazed a path from the sides, pointing to the center.

"Zoom in," Kirby said.

A native was standing in the middle of the formation. It looked like the one Gruenwald just caught.

"It knows we have its friend," Bagley said.

Kirby knew better. "Sprang."

"Excuse me, Commander," Ditko said. "I think we've seen this native before. I believe he was there the night we arrived. He was with the smaller one."

Kirby stared at the full-screen image. "Then why is he signalling us?"

"Coincidence," First Mate Ditko said. "That doesn't mean he's Sprang."

"Of course he is," Kirby bellowed. "You think those savages could construct that?"

Ditko took another look at the fire.

"Maybe the long-tailed creature could."

"That the one that tricked you into the cage?"

"All right, Gruenwald," Kirby said. "Though you do raise an interesting point. These natives may be more cunning than we thought."

"So what do we do now?" Bagley asked.

"Beam the fellow up."

"The teleport bay is still off-line, sir."

"Blast it," Kirby said.

"If I may, sir," Ditko said. "We've already detained three natives in violation of the ICC."

"You can't reverse a tractor beam, Ditko. We'll return them unharmed when we can."

"You're twitching, sir."

"Beam him up, I say!"

"Once again, sir," Gruenwald interjected, "the teleport..."

"A tractor beam, then!" Kirby roared. "We must free this fellow from those fearsome flames!"

"Eye, sir."

"That's more like it, Gruenwald."

"I meant your antennae, sir."

Cro felt like something was watching him, but all he saw were stars. His eyes teared up from the billowing smoke. It was getting warm in the circle. He was about to faint from smoke inhalation when the *Eisner* uncloaked above him. He gazed at its splendor as it drew him in.

"It's about time."

CHAPTER NINE

An aperture opened at the base of the *Eisner* and the tractor beam pulled Cro through. He came to a stop, still blinded, but free of the beam's paralysis. His mind tried to process the flood of sensations. The rhythmic hum, the smooth floor, the lights. But his intellect was overmatched. He jumped when he heard the hiss.

Cro coughed, then choked, as an overhead nozzle doused him in a thick green gas. It was a universal disinfectant, standard practice for alien cargo. Cro struggled to blink back the spots in his eyes as the vapors were sucked through a vent. He began to make out fuzzy shapes. One of them looked like a door.

He took a few dazed steps, then bumped into an invisible wall. Cro felt it like a stone aged mime, defining its unseen shape. His vision was on the verge of clearing when he heard another hiss.

Two shapes moved through the open door. Cro gasped as they slithered toward him. He had always assumed a superior race would naturally look like him. He struggled to regain his composure. His entire life had led to this. As the two ambassadors stopped in front of him, Cro found his voice.

"Hello."

The bulkier alien turned to the other. They exchanged what looked like a shrug. The first creature parted his narrow green lips. Cro waited to make history.

The leader's voice was a banshee's wail with nails on a chalkboard thrown in.

"I'm sorry," Cro said as his eardrums winced. "I didn't understand you."

The leader shrieked something to his advisor, who screeched something back. Cro decided to start off simple. He placed his hands on his chest.

"Cro."

"What the devil is he doing?" Kirby said.

"I have no idea, sir."

"Cro," Cro said, in a long, slow drawl.

"He appears to be brain damaged, Ditko."

"I think he may be trying to communicate, sir."

"Well he's doing a sorry job of it."

"Croooooooo."

"Oh, shut up," Kirby snapped. The alien's body language was clear. Cro gave the whole name thing a rest.

"He's not giving the translators much to work with, sir."

"Never cared for the bloody things."

"So what will we do with him now?" Ditko said.

"Put him with the other one. We'll try again come morning."

Cro smiled and attempted to wave, but bumped his hand on the force field.

"I look forward to our next encounter," Kirby shrieked. "Welcome aboard the *Eisner*."

Ditko marched Cro down the hallway with his phaser drawn. He triggered a door and waved Cro in.

The only illumination came from the doorway's intercom panel. Cro felt his way along the wall and bumped into something knee-high. He figured it was a bed. Though he did not know what the fluffy object at the head of it was for. His eyes adjusted to the darkness and he saw another bed. This one was lumpy, and Cro stepped back when the lump began to snore.

It was human sounding, not alien. Cro inched forward and made out its head. It was another caveman, an older male. There was something familiar about him. Cro leaned over his roommate. He studied his face. Then it came to him.

"Professor Duck?"

Duck bolted awake in a hair-trigger panic. Cro put his hand on his shoulder and squeezed. "Professor Duck, it's me."

Duck studied Cro through the dimness of the light and memory. He managed to retrieve a name.

"Head?"

"Yes, it's me. Although actually I call myself Cro these days."

Duck stared blankly at him. "How come Head change name to bird?"

"Never mind that," Cro said. "I can't believe this. The tribe thought you were dead. And the whole time you were aboard this ship."

Which made things sticky for Duck. He couldn't admit his incompetence to a former student. He concocted a backstory.

"Snake-legs rescue from Big Teeth."

"So you've been here all these years? That's amazing! What's their culture like?"

Duck showed Cro his pillow.

"Them put these under head."

"Of course," Cro said, pausing to give the ingenious invention its due. "You must have seen some amazing things."

"Yesterday am in cage," Duck said.

"A cage? What were you doing there?"

"Am next to ape and moo."

"Are there other animals aboard the ship? Are there any other cavemen?"

Duck had gone years without conversation. It was hard to think of the words.

"Just monkey."

"So how are they treating you? What do you eat? Have you been to outer space?"

"Bed real nice," Duck said.

"That's it?" Cro said. "You're the first caveman in history to have contact with an alien race."

"Snake-legs' words make ears hurt."

"So they can't communicate?"

"Talk make head hurt. Me go to bed now." Duck laid back and pulled back his sheets.

"Wait! I've got a million questions."

Duck answered with a snore. Between that and his own excitement, Cro spent most of the night awake.

Fluorescent lights sprung to life in Cro's room, signaling a new day. Cro jumped to his feet. But the lights and soft hum of machinery did little to disturb Duck's sleep.

The door hissed and there was Ensign Gruenwald, signaling them to come outside. Cro jostled Professor Duck awake. Gruenwald ushered them down the hall. After another disinfecting they were led to the cafeteria. A mechanical arm on the tabletop swiveled and stopped over Cro's bowl.

"Excellent," Cro said. "I haven't had a good meal in weeks."

The food dispenser rattled and belched out a lump of paste.

"This is a joke, right?" Cro said in denial.

At least the aliens used silverware.

The two aliens who welcomed Cro aboard were at the head of the next room. Betty stood by three school desks and chairs. The gorilla was chained to his. Kirby gestured to the empty seats. The cavemen settled in.

"Good morning," Kirby said in Sterankon. His four captive students winced. "My name is Commander Kirby. I represent the planet Steranko." He turned to the strange green slate behind him. "Ditko, where's that chalk?"

"Sorry, sir." Ditko placed the piece he was holding in one of Kirby's tentacles.

"Ster-AN-ko," Kirby said, writing the name on the blackboard. His visual met with blank stares.

"Yes, well." Kirby cleared his throat. "I'll turn you over to Ditko."

"Thank you, Commander," Ditko said. A screen lowered in front of the chalkboard. "Computer, dim the lights, please." The ape panicked as the room went dark.

"You there! Show some discipline!"

The gorilla let go of his chains.

"Good man. On with the show."

"Yes, ah, thank you," Ditko said. "What I'd like to do today is to try to learn some of your language. So with that in mind...Computer. Start the projector, please."

Cro and Duck turned around to find the source of the bright light.

"Now I know you can't understand me, but we're ready to begin." Ditko clicked the remote control in his hand. A tyrannosaur filled the screen.

"AUGGGHHHH!" Duck screamed, drowning out the gorilla.

"It's not real," Cro assured them. It was the first time he had seen an illustration that was competently done. As far as advanced technology went, it was right up there with the pillow.

"I suggest you proceed," Kirby told Ditko. The screen changed to a slide of a tree. Ditko extended a pointer, looked to his audience, and prayed.

"Oh, I get it," Cro said, smiling. He straightened up and said, "Tree."

Ditko turned to Kirby, who nodded. The projector flashed again.

"Moo."

"Caveman."

"Where him come from?"

"It's just a drawing, Duck."

Click.

"Moooo."

"Grass."

Click.

"Gorilla."

"Moo."

The ape beat his chest.

"Go back to the first one," Kirby said.

"AUGHHHHH!"

Professor Duck curled in a ball.

"Dinosaur," Cro said.

"Leave me with this one," Kirby said.

"What about the horned one, sir?"

"Him? A brainless bovine. All he's had to say is 'moo.'"

"I believe he's a she, Commander. And my translator was picking up on quite an intricate language."

"Intricate?" Kirby said. "Rubbish. What's so intricate about 'moooo?'"

"Actually, it's quite fascinating," First Mate Ditko said. "The meaning of her moo's depend on length and intonation. It reminds me of the Claremonts, who have--"

"Good heavens, man. Enough!"

The gorilla, besieged by the snake-legs' shrieks, tore his desk off its pedestal.

"I suppose that savage is talking, too. An intelligent grunt, perhaps?"

"The hairy one, sir? I don't believe so."

"Good," Kirby said. "Take him away."

"What about the others, sir?"

"That will be all for now, Ditko. But I believe we'll focus on your horned friend and this chap with the excellent posture."

"Yes, sir," Ditko said.

Kirby surprised Cro by shaking his hand. "Well done," the Commander said. "I'll be keeping an eye on you."

If he could just keep it from twitching.

"Do you have to be so messy?" Cro said, back in his cell with Duck. Duck paused from shoveling into his bowl of tasteless protein paste.

"I mean, have you spent the last few years just learning to be a slob? Don't they pick up after themselves in space? Is that too much to ask?"

Duck set the bowl on his bed and wiped his fingers on his shirt.

"And you see this?" Cro held up his spoon. "It's called silverware."

Duck stood up and grabbed his club. Cro flinched as it whooshed past his face. The room got noticeably darker.

"What are you doing?"

"Light too bright."

"You can't just smash it," Cro said.

Duck ignored him and dug his fingers back into his paste.

"When we learn how to talk to the aliens, I'm asking for my own room."

"Can I help you, sir?" the bartendroid said as Gruenwald took a seat. He wasn't used to drinking in the afternoon, or at any time for that matter. But he needed a brief respite from his responsibilities.

"Yes, I was wondering if I could have a glass of what I had the last time I was here."

"I do have that drink in my memory banks," the robot said. "But as I recall, it seemed to severely impair your motor skills."

"Just give it to him, ya tosser," someone said. It was McFarlane. "An' gimme one too, ya bag o' bolts." He pulled up a stool beside Gruenwald.

"Awful early to have a pint, isn't it?"

"I'm off-duty," Gruenwald said.

"Relax, boyo. I'm just ridin' ya." The bartendroid served their ale. "So, I hear the cap'n's flipped," McFarlane said, hoisting his glass.

"What makes you say that?"

"Mistakin' the natives for Sprang and all."

"That was an honest mistake," Gruenwald said.

"Don't get your tentacles in a bind. This is friendly talk, is all. I'm just sayin' ta watch yerself. There's a want in the cap'n, for sure."

"I have some friends looking out for me."

"Aye," McFarlane said. "Some friends in mighty high places, I hear."

Gruenwald glared at the wily squid.

"I have to get back to work."

"Ye're the officer," McFarlane said. "I'm just a lowly grunt. But I'm tellin' ya there's somethin' afoot, and I'm aimin' to be in the know."

"This am boring," Sprang said, sitting under a tree with Shirt as they watched their classmates play.

"You no have to sit with me," Shirt said. "Can go and play if It want."

Sprang observed the new version of dodgerock on display in the field. Instead of throwing rocks, the caveboys were whacking them with their clubs. It was prehistoric baseball with human targets instead of mitts. If a fielder was able to catch the rock, that meant he got to bat. If he neither caught nor dodged, however, then he was the one who was out. Smell and Cricket had already taken line drives to the head.

"That okay," Sprang said. Smell's inert body was rolled over and used for a pitching mound. "Me think am more safe here."

The game stalled when there weren't enough players standing to take the field. Fight held a conference in the batter's box. Shirt saw them look his way.

"Uh-oh."

Fight and his pack of beady-eyed toadies closed in on their new recruits. "Me decide let you play game," Fight said.

"Am dumb game," Sprang's translator said.

"Maybe me use face for ball."

"Look like you try already."

An impartial judge would have scored that for Sprang, but Fight was the one with the mob. "You think It am funny?" Fight asked Shirt, catching him snickering. The tension was thick enough to cut with a knife. But Big Teeth's roar would do.

Rex had been cruising the neighborhood. He usually steered clear of the school. Even small hairy men could be trouble if there were enough of them. But he couldn't resist the easy pickings lying in the field.

"Am Big Teeth!" Sprang shouted.

"Am sure?" Fight said. "Him only have one arm."

Rex stood over Smell, whose sports career was about to come to an end.

"Run!" Shirt said, taking Sprang by the hand. But Sprang was paralyzed. Fight and his garg were too enthralled by the promise of carnage to leave. Rex tossed his head back and swallowed Smell. Fight watched his friend disappear.

"Cool."

Rex was satisfied with his meal and decided to make an exit. He turned to the small ones and roared for good measure as the first group of adults arrived. Ugh threw his spear but Big Teeth was already out of range. Sprang shook like the ground did under the beast. He flashed back to Mignola and Englehart.

"Am It okay?" Ugh asked Shirt, kneeling in front of his sons. Sprang turned, numb-brained, to his foster father.

"I'd like that VERY MUCH!"

Cro was led back to the alien classroom, but this time he was left there alone. The projection screen lowered from the ceiling. Kirby slithered through the door.

"Very well, let's try this again," the Commander said, taking the podium. The lights dimmed and the projector turned on. Kirby extended a pointer. "First slide, please." The projector clicked. Cro looked at the drawing.

"Tree."

"Very good," Kirby said, adjusting his earpiece, which translated 'tree' into Sterankon. "I'm going to speed these up a bit." Cro didn't understand a word he was saying.

"Hand," Cro said when the next slide came up. "Foot. Mouth. Nose. Ears. Eyes."

"Excellent," Kirby said. "Next series, please."

"Red. Green. Yellow. Black. Blue."

"Blue," Kirby said, but this time he said in it English, not Sterankon. Cro was startled by the change, but then grinned at the Commander.

"Sorry," Kirby said, fiddling with the voice modulator strapped around his throat. "Just trying to work this infernal contraption. Continue, please."

"Door," Cro said, watching the screen. "Chair. Bed. Table. Bowl. Window."

"All right, pay attention," Kirby screeched. "It's going to get a bit tricky." The next slide was a photograph, not a drawing like the rest. Cro stared at the image in wonder.

"It's me."

"It's me," Kirby said, aping Cro.

"No," Cro told him. "Cro."

"No, Kro," Kirby repeated.

Cro shook his head, smiled, and placed his hands on his chest.

"Cro."

"Kro," Kirby said in caveman. He spoke his own name in Sterankon. His modulator translated:

"Kirby."

"Cur-bee," Cro said. The Commander nodded.

"Kro."

"Curbee."

"Kro."

"Curbee."

"Kro."

They smiled and basked in their breakthrough. Ditko slithered through the door.

"I hate to interrupt, Commander. But the cow wants to speak to you."

"The cow?"

"The horned creature," Ditko said. "She asked me to be her interpreter."

"Can this wait? I'm speaking with Kro."

"Begging your pardon," Ditko nodded to Cro. "But I'm afraid Betty insists."

Cro was in a foul mood as he was escorted back to his room. His progress with the head alien was rudely interrupted, and he wasn't looking forward to another bowl of paste. So it didn't help matters when he arrived at his quarters and found the door ajar.

"What are you doing?" Cro screamed.

"Door too noisy," Duck said, sitting on the edge of his bed. The doorway's control panel showered sparks. Another light had been clubbed. And there was a pungent stench to the room.

"What's that smell?" Cro said. "Is that you?"

Duck looked sheepishly at his feet.

"That's the second time today! Why don't you use the toilet?"

"It scare me," Professor Duck said.

A snake-legs walked through the open door carrying a large toolbox. "Hello," Cro said. The alien ignored him.

"He made all the mess."

The alien removed what looked like a robotic basset hound. He reached back in the toolbox and pulled out a small remote. The snake-legs extended the remote's antenna and pushed its only button. The robot jerked, lowered its snout and headed for the mess, sucking the debris into its belly where it was atomized. Its brush tail swept behind it as it rolled on autopilot.

"You should apologize," Cro told Duck. "We're guests aboard this ship. And do you know how close I am to getting through to their leader?"

The squid packed up his cleaning droid and pulled a light bulb out.

"I mean, you've been up here for all this time and this is how you act? It's a wonder they even stuck around!"

"Hey buddy," the janitor said. "Give it a rest."

Cro's jaw dropped.

"You speak English."

"Yeah, well," the squid said, replacing the bulb, "you ain't that advanced."

Kirby entered his quarters and found Betty waiting.

"Moo."

"Indeed," the Commander said. "Now what is the meaning of this?"

"If I may, sir," Ditko said, adjusting his earpiece. "Why don't you have a seat?" Kirby eyed his first mate, then settled in behind his desk. Betty wagged her tail contentedly as Ditko stood beside her.

"Moooo."

"Yes, yes. You said that already."

"Actually, sir, she was talking to me."

"Oh," the Commander said. "Harrumph. What did she say?"

"She bids you welcome on behalf of all the oppressed creatures of Earth."

"Earth?" Kirby said. "What's that?"

"I believe it's her people's name for this planet."

"And what's her name?"

"Betty, sir."

"Betty, my name is Commander Kirby. Welcome aboard the *Eisner*."

"Mooo," Ditko said through his translator.

"Mooooo," Betty replied.

"She thanks you for your hospitality and for freeing her from her oppressor."

"Moooo."

"And she humbly implores you to use your power to free the rest of her people."

"What on earth is she talking about?"

"Mooo," Ditko asked Betty.

"Moooooo."

"Her people have been slaves to the hairy ones for countless generations."

"Hairy ones?"

"Cro's people, sir."

"He seems like a nice chap to me."

Ditko translated into bovine. Betty gave him an earful.

"The hairy ones round up her people and keep them trapped against their will."

"Moooooo."

"Some of them are used for food, others for their hides."

"Moooo."

"But most of them are subjected to the greatest cruelty, knowing that every morning..."

"Moooo."

"Oh, dear," Ditko said.

"Go on."

"...That every morning the hairy ones will come to take their milk."

"Their milk?" Kirby said. "Explain."

Betty, through Ditko, did. When it came to the part about how the milk was obtained, Kirby's eyes twitched even more.

"Savages!" Kirby pounded his desk. He tapped his intercom. "Gruenwald! This is Commander Kirby. Where are the test subjects now?"

"Which ones, Commander?" Gruenwald's voice said.

"The two half-naked beasts."

"I think they're in their room."

"Good. I need you to get down there and vaporize them at once."

"Your buddy done a real number in here," the squid janitor said.

"Yeah, he's funny that way," Cro said, still reeling. "What's your name?"

The snake-legs wiped his face on his shirt. "Well, my real name's pretty hard to pronounce, but you can call me Grell."

"I can't believe you speak English."

"It's like I said before. I always had an ear for language."

Duck cowered on his bed.

"Your friend's a dim bulb, ain't he?"

"I guess you could say that," Cro said. Grell stood on Cro's bed and removed another of the broken lights.

"Hey buddy, you wanna give me a hand?"

"My name's Cro."

"Like the bird?"

Cro sighed. "What do you want me to do?"

"Hand me that doohickey there. So what's your deal?"

"My deal?" Cro said.

"You know," Grell said. "Your story."

"Well, growing up I knew I was different..."

"Whoa there, I ain't got all day. What do you think of Commander Kirby?"

"Curbee? It's hard to tell. We're still working on the language barrier."

"I think the guy is nuts."

"Nuts?" Cro said. "I don't know that expression."

"Looney tunes. Insane."

"I hadn't gotten that impression."

"It's just my opinion," Grell said. Gruenwald interrupted as he arrived with his phaser drawn.

"Oh, hello," Cro told him. "Are we supposed to be somewhere?"

Gruenwald spoke to Grell in Sterankon.

"What did he say?" Cro said.

"Kirby wants you vaporized."

"What?" Cro screamed. "He's insane!"

"I told you so," Grell said. He chatted with Gruenwald, who had no intention of carrying out Kirby's orders. They both agreed on a course of action.

"Come on," Grell told Cro.

"Where are we going?"

"To go see Kirby."

"What about Duck?" Cro said.

"Your friend?" Grell looked the other caveman over. "You'd better leave him here."

Kirby's quarters played host to a summit as Grell, Gruenwald and Cro walked in. Ditko mooed something soothingly when he saw Betty flinch.

"Gruenwald!" Kirby bellowed. "What is this savage still doing here?"

"Sorry about that, Commander," Gruenwald said. "I guess I had some doubts."

"Doubts? This is the military. Soldiers don't have doubts. And who's this squid?"

"The name's Grell, captain."

"That's Commander to you. What's your rank?"

"Domestic engineer," Grell said.

"Good lord. A janitor."

"We're not called that anymore."

"Ask him why he wants me dead," Cro said, wishing someone would speak English.

"My friend here want to knows why you want him whacked," Grell told the Commander.

"You mean you can actually talk to this beast?"

"It's a gift," Grell said.

"Then tell him this. I will not tolerate savages who prey upon innocent beasts."

"He says you offended hornhead here," Grell translated for Cro.

"The cow?"

"If that's what you call it," Grell said.

"Ask him what the charges are."

"Ahem," Grell said after speaking with Kirby. "He said you manhandled the cow."

"What?"

"Not you personally. But your people did."

"That's outrageous!" Cro said. "Why would anyone...oh!" He had a good laugh.

"Does he find these accusations amusing?" Commander Kirby said.

"You're not helping your case," Grell told Cro.

"I'm sorry," Cro said. "This has all been a misunderstanding. My people don't abuse cows, we milk them."

"Milk? What's that?" Grell said.

"It's a white liquid that comes from their udder."

"What do you do with it?"

"We drink it."

"Gross," Grell said, eyeing Betty.

"Don't you have animals you milk on your planet?"

"If we did, I wouldn't drink it."

"See here, what's all the prattle about?" Commander Kirby asked Grell.

"Crow was just telling me how his people get some liquid called 'milk' from these cows."

"Yes, I know," Kirby said. "Betty here was just telling me about this barbaric practice."

Grell translated for Cro.

"Commander," Cro said. "If you let me, I can clear all of this up." Cro rolled up his sleeves and knelt beside Betty, who mooed her objections to Ditko.

"Sir, is this appropriate?"

"I doubt this creature's that modest, Ditko. She doesn't even wear pants."

"Actually, this is my first time doing this," Cro said nervously. He squeezed Betty's udder. Milk shot on the floor.

"Good heavens!" Kirby said.

"So, that's how it works," Cro said.

"And this, er, procedure doesn't harm the beast?" Commander Kirby asked.

"Crow doesn't think so," Grell said.

"Ditko, ask the cow, will you?"

"Betty says there's usually some discomfort, Commander," Ditko translated.

"Mooo."

"But she has to admit, having not been milked in some time, she's actually relieved."

"Well there you have it," Kirby said. "Grell, get this puddle mopped up. But first, apologize to Crow for this unfortunate misunderstanding."

"The Commander says he screwed up," Grell said.

"Screwed up? He wanted me shot!"

Cro waited for Grell to relay his complaint.

"He says he'll give you a medal."

"If he really wants to make it up to me," Cro said, "Tell him I want my own room."

Chief Dog peered at the distant treetop. The lookout waved his right arm. The chief blew a horn, and every available villager came running. They scattered, then reassembled in line, each with a bucket of water.

It was the latest test run of the Early Detection System, a communications feat inspired by Rex's morning attack. Ugh had had the bright idea of posting a chain of scouts, eagle-eyed cavemen in trees and on cliffs who could scan for signs of trouble. In those smog-free days, you could see a caveman wave a half-mile away. The problem came when the sentries were asked to remember more than one thing.

Much debate went into what a lookout should be on the look out for, and the general consensus was fire, big lizards and rival tribes with a grudge. Chief Dog thought that each threat should have its own individual sign, and another round of head-scratching resulted in the Three-Step Waving System. When the lookout waved his right arm, that meant a fire was headed towards town. His left arm meant a tribe of cavemen was coming to mix it up. A two-armed wave was the real whammy, though: a dinosaur coming for dinner.

The village had done two test runs, with Cricket acting as the threat. He started at the first lookout point and picked out his disguise, arriving in town with a torch, a club, or a homemade dinosaur head. The first try, Cricket chose the torch, but the first lookout waved his left arm, and the village expected a hostile tribe, not a forest fire. The second time, Cricket picked the club and posed as an angry clan, only to face an empty village hiding from Big Teeth.

Dog was hoping to get it right before the sun went down. He and his clansmen watched the lookout furiously signalling "fire." A half hour passed by. The townspeople clutched their buckets. A twig snapped, and the villagers tensed, ready to battle the flame. Cricket stumbled through the trees.

He was wearing a dinosaur head.

One of the villagers jumped the gun and doused him with her bucket.

"Ugh," Dog said, getting used to failure. Cricket took off the grass-covered head.

"Sorry. Me get lost."

"Us try again?" a villager asked.

"Am dark soon," Chief Dog said.

"How can us see guard when dark?" Ugh said.

An excellent point.

"I have an idea."

"Who say that?" Dog said.

"Am me." Sprang stepped from the crowd.

"Okay," Dog said skeptically. "What am boy's idea?"

"Torches," Sprang said as the villagers gasped. "Lookout can wave torch when dark."

Dog stroked his chin, but it was just for show. "Am good idea," he said. "Ugh, have guards all come get torch. Then us try again."

"Look at Fight," Shirt whispered to Sprang. "Him mad Chief Dog think you am smart."

Sprang ignored his human friend. He was thinking about Big Teeth. Any warning he could get was better than none at all. Rock, meanwhile, was swelling with pride over It's suggestion.

And to think that she had spent all that time getting worked up about aliens.

CHAPTER TEN

"I still have to object to this, sir," First Mate Ditko said as he and Kirby slithered down the *Eisner's* corridors.

"So noted," Kirby said.

"It's just that, ah, I don't understand this sudden turnaround. An hour ago you wanted Crow vaporized, but now you're doing him favors."

"That's because I've realized something, Ditko. Crow's in charge."

"In charge of what?"

"His planet, clearly."

"How do you know that?"

"Elementary, dear Ditko. It came to me when I realized his people actually milk these 'cows.'"

"I can't say I follow you, sir."

"Every civilization has an established chain of command," Kirby said. "If these 'cows' were in charge, the cavemen would provide beverages to them."

"I don't know, sir," Ditko said. "I'm still not convinced Crow's our man."

"Yes, but you lack my instincts."

"With all due respect, Commander..."

"Yes?" Kirby said. "Speak your mind."

"It's just that your instincts have been somewhat...questionable lately."

"Go on," Kirby said.

"Well first you think Sprang is an alien. Then you want Crow vaporized. Not to mention this whole 'dinosaur' business."

"Yes," Kirby said. "You're right. I must admit, I haven't been feeling quite myself lately."

"Are you ill, sir?"

"Nonsense." Kirby's eye twitched.

"I could send for a medical droid."

"There's no time for phony physicians," the Commander said. "Here we are." He triggered a door which opened to the engineering department, a crowded room with a handful of squid hunched over drafting tables.

"At ease, men," Kirby said as the technicians stood at attention. "Which one of you is Lightle?"

"I am, sir." A squid stepped forward.

"How is your project progressing?"

"The mineral detector? It's been giving me problems, sir."

"Perhaps you need to clear this clutter."

"It's a little chaotic, sir," Lightle said. "We had to move everything around to make room for our guest."

"Mooooo."

"Ah, there she is," Kirby said.

A corner of the workroom had been converted to Betty's quarters. There was a good-sized patch of grass to graze, a sturdy white picket fence, and holographic clouds on the wall.

"Good heavens," Kirby said. "She looks green."

"She says the clouds are making her ill," Ditko said after consulting Betty.

"Then turn the bloody things off." Ditko snagged a technician, and the nauseating scenery turned back into a wall.

"Mooo."

"Betty says thank you, but asks why she was moved to these smaller quarters."

"Tell her we had no choice," Kirby said. "We gave Crow her old room."

Ditko conferred with the cow.

"Betty appreciates the Commander's delicate position."

"Moooo."

"However, she understands you plan to barter with the hairy ones."

"Who told her that?" Kirby said.

"Well, ah, Commander," Ditko squirmed. "I may have mentioned it."

"Give me your translator."

Kirby held out his hand and relieved Ditko of his earpiece and voice modulator. Kirby put them on, turned to Betty, cleared his throat and said,

"Moo."

"It is an honor to speak to you directly," Kirby's translator said in his ear.

"The honor is mine," Kirby mooed back to Betty. "Now what's with this bartering business?"

"I understand this is a trading ship."

"This is a military operation."

"But you're prepared to trade with the hairy ones in exchange for the dinosaurs."

"See here," Kirby said. "I refuse to argue semantics with a cow."

"What if I were to propose a trade in exchange for my people's milk?"

"Milk?" Kirby said. "Why on earth would I trade for some biological waste?"

"But I'm sure your people would find our milk delightfully refreshing."

"And just what would you trade it for?"

"Perhaps some explosives," Betty said. "Or horn-mounted laser beams."

"Outrageous!" Kirby bellowed.

"What is she saying?" Ditko asked, bereft of his translator.

"This belligerent bovine wants our aid in wiping out Crow's race."

"Oh, dear."

"See here," Kirby said. "What your people need is backbone. Learn to stand on your own two feet."

"But we're quadrupeds," Betty said.

"Then you're not trying hard enough. Now if you'll excuse me, I have an appointment."

Betty mooed under her breath.

Kirby had his model spaceships out as he sat on the floor. The intercom on the doorway breeped.

"Commander?" Cro's voice said.

"Just a minute!" Kirby said, gathering the ships together. He got them in their display case, sat behind his desk, and said, "Enter."

"Good morning, Crow," Kirby said in caveman without using a translator.

"Good morning, Commander," Cro said, surprised.

"I trust you can understand me?"

"Yes. But how did you learn my language?"

"Grell made me this tape," Kirby said. "I listened to it in my sleep." The cassette's label was written in English: *Learn to Speak Caveman*. Cro sat down across from Kirby.

"One day I hope to learn your language," Cro said.

"How admirable," Kirby said. "But really, there's no need for that."

"But if I'm going to live on your planet..."

"Bravo!" Kirby slapped his desk. "What a wry sense of humor you have."

"But I wasn't kidding," Cro told the Commander.

"Another marvelous jest. Imagine, a savage like you on Steranko. Pip pip, I say. Good show."

Cro found himself scowling.

"Now enough of this comedy. Let's get on to business, shall we?"

"I wasn't kidding," Cro said bitterly. Kirby plowed ahead.

"As the duly-recognized leader of your planet's dominant species, I'd like to ask your permission to remove a few things from earth."

The legalese caught Cro off-guard.

"What are you talking about?"

"Ah," Kirby said. "I admire that. A cagey negotiator. Very well, in exchange for your cooperation, I'm authorized to advance your planet's technology by...oh, one hundred years."

"In exchange for what?"

"Why, your dinosaurs, of course."

"My dinosaurs?" Cro said. "I don't care what you do with them."

"Excellent." Kirby produced some forms. "Initial each copy, please."

The contract was written in English, but Cro barely followed it.

"The undersigned, having been judged both legally and mentally competent vis a vis the Interplanetary Conduct Code, clause 203, subparagraph 3.1, as ratified on the Universal Day and Year of 03.09.quid4, and being a native of the planet herein referred to as 'earth,' being the third planet from the primary star in the Sol system, hereby reneges on any and all territorial rights arising from his planetary coexistence with the subspecies known as the 'dinosaur,' herein referred to as 'the party'..."

"Would you care to have your lawyer peruse it?"

"Lawyer?" Cro said. "What's that?"

"By jove, there's hope for you yet. Initial here," Kirby said.

"Like this?" Cro marked an X.

"Marvelous. Now then, perhaps you can tell me the best place one can find a dinosaur?"

"What kind of dinosaur?" Cro said.

"They come in different sizes?"

"Oh, yeah."

"Let's start with the largest one," Kirby said.

"You mean the tyrannosaur?"

"Is that the chap who ate two of my crew?"

"I imagine so," Cro said.

"Very well, let's start with him. Now where can I find this creature?"

"I'm not sure," Cro said. "On my planet, the dinosaurs usually find you."

"Surely these beastly behemoths shouldn't be too hard to find."

"I don't know," Cro said. "The vegetation's pretty thick. Even from an aerial view..."

The Commander wasn't listening.

"Be perfectly still," Kirby said. He opened a drawer, removed a phaser and aimed it at the ceiling. Cro looked up. "Blast it all, he'll see you!" the

Commander scolded. His eye twitched, trained on the drooping tail he'd spied under one of the ducts. "I've got you now," Kirby muttered. He shot a divot in the ceiling.

"Blast!" Kirby said as Peanuts shrieked and landed on the floor.

"A monkey?" Cro said.

Kirby reached in his desk and pulled out a considerably larger weapon. He shut his twitching eye to aim and singed a hole in the carpet.

"Hey!" Cro said as the blast whizzed by him. He slid from his seat to the floor. "Don't you think it's--augh!" Cro squawked as Kirby produced a new weapon.

"Stand still, you stinking simian!" Peanuts leapt to the door. "Miscreant monkey!" Kirby roared, missing wildly. The control panel smoked as the door slid shut, covering Peanut's escape.

Cro smelled ozone and rose from the floor, which sparkled with dancing glass. Kirby's twitch had advanced to a tremor.

"Harrumph. Now where were we?"

"No civilians," Morrison said aboard the bridge of the *Giffen*.

"Very funny," Thomas said. "Is everything a go?"

"Neary's typing the jump coordinates. It's slowed us down a bit."

"Why don't you just scan them in?" Thomas said.

"I set my mug on the printout."

"Is this a 2 or a 3?" Neary asked, reading the coffee-stained string. Morrison squinted.

"A three."

"This mission's off to a great start," Thomas said.

"Relax. Want to talk to the men?"

"Oh, I suppose."

"Listen up," Morrison said. "This here's Thomas, our government man. He wants to say a few words."

"Thank you, Captain Morrison," Thomas said as the crew turned his way. "As most of you know, King Stanley has been ill for quite some time, but he still took a moment to make this disc to express his appreciation. So, if you'll take a look at the monitor..." Thomas slid the data disc in.

"Greetings, my intrepid explorers!" King Stanley's image beamed. "I'd just like to take a moment to express my grateful gratitude and to wish you auspicious astronauts lots of luck on your titanic task..."

"How'd you get him to make sense like that?" Morrison asked Thomas.

"I didn't," Thomas said, watching the disc. "We taped this for the *Eisner*."

"Brilliant."

"Hey listen," Thomas said. "Be careful out there."

"I'll bring you a souvenir."

Grell and Gruenwald slithered down the hall from opposite directions. They burst into Kirby's quarters. He was sitting quietly at his desk amid a room of debris.

"It's about bloody time," Kirby told them. "I'll remember this come your reviews."

"What happened here?" Grell asked Cro, finding him under a chair.

"The Commander went nuts," Cro said.

"I admit I may have overreacted."

"You fired these shots, Commander?" Gruenwald asked in Sterankon.

"Indeed. I spied a stealthy stowaway secreted in the ceiling."

"Stowaway?"

"The monkey."

"Did you hit him?"

"Regrettably, no. Now if you'll excuse me, Ensign, I'd like to finish my chat with Crow."

"What's he saying?" Cro asked Grell.

"He wants you to stick around."

"Ah, excuse me," Cro said hastily. "Can I take a rain check on that?"

"Are you hurt?" Kirby said.

"Just rattled. I'm more used to fending off clubs."

"Very well. We'll continue this conversation at Crow's convenience."

"I'll help him to his room," Grell said. He shooed Cro out the door.

"And where are you going?" Kirby asked Gruenwald, who looked eager to leave himself.

"Things look under control in here. I've, uh, got to go write my report."

"Carry on, Ensign. But be alert for that athletic alien!"

"Yeah," Gruenwald muttered as he left. "And crazy commanders."

Shirt and Sprang sat under the tree as another recess passed by. The shock of Rex's attack had faded, or at least dimmed, in Sprang's mind, and he hated to waste such a perfect day. He picked up a baseball-sized rock.

"Want to play catch?"

"What am catch?" Shirt said.

"It am game."

"Like dodgerock?"

"No. This game no hurt."

"Okay," Shirt said. "How play?"

"You stand here. Me go by bush. Then me throw you rock."

"And me dodge rock?"

"No, you catch rock," Sprang said.

"Then me keep rock?" Shirt said.

"No. Then you throw rock back to me."

"Then what am point?"

Sprang sighed. "It am just a game."

"But no try hit you with rock?"

"No, you just catch rock," Sprang said. "Am fun. Stay there." Sprang walked a few yards and turned. "No be afraid. Me no throw too hard."

"Okay," Shirt said.

Sprang lobbed the rock, but Shirt stepped aside. It bounced off of the tree.

"You have to catch," Sprang said.

"How about us take turns throw rock and let rock land on ground?"

"Because game called *catch*," Sprang said patiently. "Now you throw to me." Shirt cocked his arm and whipped the rock. Sprang ducked and chased it down.

"You no play right," Shirt complained.

"No throw so hard," Sprang said. "Now me throw rock. You catch this time." He tossed it underhand. Shirt traced its arc and spread his arms, catching the rock with a hug. The look in his eyes was magical.

"Me catch!"

"Now throw to me."

Shirt reared back and let the rock fly. Sprang gaped and hit the dirt.

After that Shirt got the idea, and the game was in full swing. Shirt laughed as they tossed the rock back and forth. The other kids headed their way. They weren't used to somebody throwing a rock without someone else getting beaned, and they followed the game like a tennis match as the ball lofted back and forth. Even Fight was caught up in the moment.

"Me want to play!" he said.

It was a bad time for him to interrupt, as the rock was heading Sprang's way. Sprang turned, distracted long enough. The rock plunked off his chest. The kids all winced in sympathy, then gasped in collective horror.

Where It had been standing a moment before, there was now a green man with four legs.

"Ohhhhhhhhh," Sprang said, deep-fried in fear. He was no longer disguised. The rock had hit the Chameleon 3000, busting his image inducer. Sprang stared at his former peers through inhuman antenna. His mind raced through scenarios of how they would react. Most of them ended in violence, with him on the receiving end.

The caveboys stood silent and motionless, all power routed to their brains. All but Shirt reached the same conclusion. They bowed down at Sprang's feet. Shirt turned to the bewildered deity.

"Me think me go get Mom."

CHAPTER ELEVEN

Liefeld toiled in his laboratory. There were some squid who dared call him mad. But Liefeld knew they were merely jealous.

"Jealous, I tell you!" he said.

He was King Stanley's chief scientist before he had to resign. So what if his first batch of clones were defective? He knew that the concept was sound. And who did they come running to when they needed their precious king cloned?

"Me!" Liefeld shouted aloud.

He was a clone himself, having transferred his brain to his first cloned body some fifty years before. He figured it was almost time to switch bodies again. His current one was starting to twitch. But he had a job to do first. Liefeld had taken it upon himself to save Steranko through science.

He tightened a nut on the giant raygun. So they thought he was useless, did they? He flipped a switch, and the domed roof of his laboratory retracted. He rubbed his hands as the behemoth machine began buzzing like a two-ton hornet, then reconsidered his preparations. He should have worn earplugs.

But all that would be academic once the collider powered up, folding a doorway in time and space. It was simple, really. He was going to go back in time to when there were plenty of Busiek plants, then toss them through the door in space until his lab was full.

Of course there were, theoretically, a few things that could go awry. He was drawing power directly from the planetary grid, and any surge in the collider would ricochet on down the line. And then there was the question of mucking around with time and space. But Liefeld couldn't be bothered with repercussions. He was a scientist.

The laboratory shuddered as the collider reached critical mass. Liefeld worked the joystick controller, turning the particle cannon. The collider's barrel glowed brilliant blue and emitted a luminous beam, which etched a doorway directly in front of him. Everything was perfect.

Then he saw himself fall through the door.

"Turn it off!" the new Liefeld shouted, drowned out by the machine.

"What?"

"Give me that!" Liefeld Two shouted, reaching for the controller.

"This is my invention," Liefeld said, yanking the joystick away. "I won't let you take credit for it."

"I am you," Liefeld yelled. "Five minutes from now, the collider will overload and black out the planet. I had just enough time to reset the door to come back in time and warn you."

"I don't believe you," Liefeld said.

"What?"

"What a ludicrous story. If that really happened, I would have reset the door to give myself more than five minutes."

"You have to believe me," Liefeld said. "We're running out of time!"

"Oh, right," the first Liefeld snickered. "I guess you'll just have to reset the door, then."

"Listen to me! Err, you. I have to--" The collider's buzz changed pitch. A hairline crack ran up its casing. The lights blinked on and off.

"Too late!" the second Liefeld yelled. The first Liefeld panicked, reset the door and dove through the portal headfirst, only to fall from it five minutes earlier.

Time is funny that way.

"Oh, drat," the second Liefeld said, alone again in his lab. The door closed behind his past self. Then the power went out for good.

"Why the long face?" Grell said as he walked Cro back to his room.

"I was hoping things would work out for me here."

"Who said they won't?"

"The Commander laughed when I told him I wanted to go back to your world."

"What, before he went nuts?"

"But he had a point," Cro said. "I'd feel just as different on your planet as I do on mine."

"I don't know," Grell said. "You're a pretty smart guy, and to be honest with you, your planet's kind of a dump."

"I appreciate what you're saying," Cro said. "But eventually, I'd want to settle down and find myself a mate."

"What for?" Grell said.

"To procreate, for one thing. Don't you want to have kids?"

"Who, me? I don't want no rugrats."

"Well, I do," Cro said. "Someday."

"Then just go down to the gene center. You don't need no wife for that."

"What?"

"The gene center," Grell said. "Isn't that how you do it on Earth?"

"No," Cro said. "We make our babies in person."

"Ah, cripes. I heard about that once."

"Well, I'm pretty convinced I'll never find the right girl anyway."

"Why?" Grell said. "What are you looking for?"

"Good looks, good posture, and brains."

"You're right," Grell said. "Where you come from, that might be pretty tough."

Ensign Gruenwald raced past McFarlane on the way to his quarters.

"An' just where are you dartin' off to?"

"I have to make a report," Gruenwald said.

"Oh, yeah? Then I'm taggin' along."

"Fine," Gruenwald said. "Come on." McFarlane tailed him to his room.

"Who's your friend?" Thomas said on-screen when Gruenwald dialed him up.

"He's okay," Gruenwald said. "He's harmless. But Kirby just shot up his room."

"What?" Thomas said. "Why'd he do that?"

"He spotted a monkey."

"A monkey?"

"A small extraterrestrial," Gruenwald said.

"Did the Commander kill it?"

"No, it was about the only thing he missed."

"Do you think he's deteriorating?" Thomas said.

"If not, he's certainly close."

"So he is mad," McFarlane said.

"What should we do?" Gruenwald asked Thomas. The viewscreen flickered.

"Sorry," Thomas said. "I lost you there. Now what--" The throne room went dark. "zZzkrtEAR ME?" Thomas' voice crackled. McFarlane stared at the blackened screen.

"He musta run out o' quarters."

Gruenwald worked the transmitter. "Nothing. The signal's dead."

"Well then, laddie," McFarlane said, "it looks like it's just you n' me."

Sprang fiddled with the Chameleon 3000. The image inducer was shot. "Enough with the bowing," he told his classmates. Their chanting was getting old. He saw two figures approaching but neither one of them was Shirt. Professor Hide, upon seeing the squid, had run off to fetch Dog. The caveboys got to their feet and parted to let the adults through.

"That am him," Hide said.

The chief approached warily, holding his club like a divining rod. He circled around the strange creature, which frankly made Sprang nervous.

"Dog," Sprang said, "am me."

"Green man speak," Dog said in wonder spiced with mortal fear.

"Him sound like It," the professor observed.

"It no have snake-legs."

"I am It," Sprang said helpfully.

"Maybe him am demon," Hide said.

"No, really. Me am It."

"Him could be snake god," Chief Dog theorized, checking out Sprang's legs and eyes.

"Oh, right. Am snake god," Sprang said, in what the cavemen would later realize was their first brush with sarcasm. Chief Dog and Professor Hide looked at each other and got down on their knees.

"Oh, for crying out loud," Sprang said.

"Snake god honor us with caveman tongue," Dog said, like a knight on one knee. Sprang was afraid that Dog would get his classmates bowing again.

"Snake god tired," Sprang told the chief. "Me want to go home now."

"No! Must stay," Dog said. "Us have big feast and then make sacrifice."

Sprang spotted Shirt with Rock in tow. "Excuse me," Sprang said. He slithered off to meet Shirt and Rock a few yards from the school.

"Where am It?" Rock asked her son. The alien approached.

"Me think that am him," Shirt said.

Rock saw the creature, jumped the gun, and charged at Sprang with her club.

Sprang's lizard brain kicked in in the face of Rock's maternal instinct. Before he knew what was happening, he pulled his phaser and squeezed. Rock's force of will kept her hurtling forward even after she'd been stunned. The schoolkids gasped when her face dug a trench that stopped at the snake god's feet.

"Oooooo," the class said. Sprang looked at Shirt.

"Sorry."

He nudged Rock's club away.

"Does anyone have any matches?"

"Thomas? Sir? Is that you?"

"Who is that?" Thomas said, his tentacles groping their way along the darkened throne room.

"It's me, sir. Raney."

"Raney?"

"The guard."

"Oh. Can you see anything?"

"Not really, sir. I--oww!"

"What is it?"

"I tripped."

"Are you okay?"

"Not really, sir. I think I broke a tentacle."

"Hold on, Raney. I'll get you some help." Thomas felt along the wall.

"Do you know what's happening, sir?" Raney said.

"The power went out."

"But why?"

"I don't know."

"Just where are you, sir?"

"Halfway across the room. I think this door's to the supply room." Thomas turned the knob. "Hello?"

"Ah, Thomas! You've also been detained in this desolate darkness?"

Thomas slammed the door.

"Wrong room."

"You mind if I have a seat on the throne? My leg's going numb."

"Go ahead."

A light cracked at the end of the throne room as another guard came through the entrance.

"'Ello?" He cried, "Is anyone in there?"

"Hold the door!" Thomas said.

"There you are, sir," the second guard said. "The crowd's getting rather cross."

"Crowd?" Thomas said, making his way to the light.

"More of a mob really, sir."

"Where?"

"The front gate."

"How many?"

"About fifty. They're sore that their power's gone out."

"The power's out around us, too?"

"Can't see a light anywhere, sir."

"Sir?" Raney called from the shadows.

"Oh! Sorry. We need a medidroid," Thomas said.

"Right away, sir," the second guard said. He tapped his intercom. "Strange."

"What?"

"I can't get a signal."

"That's impossible," Thomas said.

"Not really, sir. If the short-range antenna was knocked out, too, then..."

"Sir?"

"What is it, Raney?"

"I think I'll be passing out now."

"Raney?"

There was no reply.

"Look," Thomas told the other guard. "I need you to get on the videophone and round up my engineers."

"But the phone line's gone dead, too."

"All right," Thomas said. "I'll send a letter with you to Progress. You can use the royal air car."

"I believe they're all on holiday, sir. Their last session ended last week."

Thomas fumed and racked his brain.

"Shall I scrounge up some flashlights then, sir?"

Kirby sifted through the glass in his display case and pulled out a broken model. The *Ordway* had had its bridge blown off. He found one of its aft thrusters. He held the piece to the splintered model, then set the wreckage down.

"Excuse me, sir?"

Kirby turned around. "Yes?"

"I saw your door was open."

"You have news, Ditko?"

"Yes, sir. The other caveman, Duck, has trashed his room again."

"Move him to Engineering, then."

"But that's where Betty is."

"The crew can keep on eye on him. And take his weapon this time."

"Yes, sir," Ditko said. "If I may, sir, I've been thinking. Maybe we should land the ship."

"What? Whatever for?"

"It's just that, we don't have a reason to keep the natives anymore. I think we should let them go."

"We've compromised our location enough. I will not land this ship."

"But you shot at their leader, sir."

"I wasn't aiming for him. Besides," Kirby said, "I need Crow's help to find these dinosaurs."

"What if we released the others, then?"

"Very well." Kirby winced.

"Are you all right, Commander?"

"I was hit by a hideous headache."

"Maybe you should rest now," Ditko said.

"An excellent idea."

Morrison watched the stars streak by the *Giffen's* bridge viewport.

"We're about to drop out of hyperspace, sir," Ensign Neary said.

"Very good."

Neary pushed a lever, and the streaks turned back into stars. Unfortunately, it was hard to see them through all of the asteroids.

The bridge took on a crimson tint as sirens wailed everywhere. "Shields!"

Morrison shouted. His ship had become the cue ball in a game of galactic billiards.

"What happened?" he said, stumbling to Neary.

"I guess it was a two."

"What?"

"Those coordinates I typed in the nav computer. I guess that three was a two."

"Sod it," Morrison said. The *Giffen's* shields were getting pounded. "Ellis! Get us out of here."

"You want me to fly through that?"

"Sir, one of our engines is failing."

Then everyone shut up. There was a rock the size of Gibraltar lazily spinning their way.

"Neary. Jump to hyperspace."

"What are our coordinates, sir?"

"The same as last time." Morrison gaped at the viewport. "But change the three to a two."

"All right." Neary pecked at his keyboard.

"Sometime today would be nice."

"Sorry sir, I typed a wrong number."

"Sir, the rock's gravity is pulling us in."

"Almost," said Neary, watching the cursor blink backwards on his screen. He deleted an eight he had mistyped and entered a nine instead. "Ready, sir!"

"Engage!" Morrison said.

"What was that, sir?"

"Just pull the bloody lever!"

The crew gripped the edge of their consoles as the asteroids turned into streaks.

Lightle sat in his corner of engineering and studied the schematics. The mineral detector was almost done. As far as he could tell. He turned the gizmo in his hands. It looked like the drawing, at least.

Professor Duck had just moved in. He shared Betty's strip of lawn. He wasn't as loud as Lightle was led to believe, but boy did these natives smell. He had turned on the exhaust fans just to try to get some air.

Duck sat on the grass while Betty chewed a piece of cud. He had finished his bowl of protein paste, which left him rather parched. Duck eyed the bowl, then looked at Betty. He glanced around the room. The snake-legs to the side of them was busy with his work. Duck set the bowl under Betty's udder and tried to act casual. McFarlane slithered in and stopped at Lightle's station.

"Hey. How's the thingamajobbie comin'?"

"Good," Lightle said. "Almost done."

"Then it must be yer lucky day. I'm taking the aliens off of yer hands."

"Are you moving them somewhere else?"

"Nah, we're dumpin' them back on their planet."

"That's a relief," Lightle said. "I was...gross!"

"What is it?" McFarlane said.

"That savage is goosing the cow!"

McFarlane turned to see Duck milking Betty. Duck froze. He dropped the bowl.

"I heard they actually drink that stuff," Lightle said, eyeing the spill.

"There's no accounting fer taste," McFarlane said. "All right, you two. Break it up."

Peanuts made his way through the *Eisner's* ventilation shaft. He was above an empty room when he caught the scent of food. Peanuts removed the ceiling panel and dropped down to the floor.

The room had a refrigerator, a table and cabinets. Peanuts hopped on the counter. To the side of the sink was a strange-looking panel set in the countertop, with a tempting button on the outlet behind it. Peanuts gave it a push. The countertop panel slid away, revealing another sink. But this one was crisscrossed with blue laser beams a few inches down its basin.

"Warning. The waste atomizer has now been activated," a sultry computer voice said. "Please keep all appendages away from the intake chute."

Peanuts was spooked by the phantom voice. He hopped back to the floor. He tugged at the refrigerator until he got it open. The shelves were lined with glass jars with some kind of plants in them. Peanuts tipped one. It broke on the floor. He picked a stalk from the glass. He sniffed the plant, took a bite of it, and tossed it over his shoulder.

A sudden zap behind him made Peanuts leap across the room. The commotion had come from the countertop, but he didn't see anything. There was only the smell of something burning. He jumped back on the counter. The curious monkey inspected the lasers and reached out his hand to them. The waste disposal singed his finger. Peanuts flung a bowl at it. The bowl hit the lasers and vaporized. He clapped and tried a cup.

The cup was nice, but he wanted to try to disintegrate something bigger. Peanuts hopped to the floor, opened the fridge and removed a jar of plants. It disappeared in the atomizer with a most delightful zap. Peanuts lined the counter with jars of Busiek plants and shoveled them in the disposal.

Ensign Bagley was walking by when he heard the atomizer. *That's strange,* he thought. *The autochef must have whipped up a bad batch of paste.* Then he heard the breaking glass and a peculiar shriek.

"Hey!" he said as the kitchen door parted, revealing the chaotic scene, a phrase he repeated as the long-tailed alien heaved a jar his way. Bagley dodged with his phaser drawn. His wild shot stunned Peanuts. The chimp staggered toward the atomizer as Bagley reached out his hands.

"Hey, look out for that--"

Poof.

"Oh, shoot," Bagley said, taking inventory. The crew's supply of Busiek plants was down to a handful of jars. Bagley dreaded telling Kirby. His antenna strayed to the floor. There were two more bunches of Busiek plants from the jar the monkey threw.

He glanced around, broke off a stalk, and stuffed it in his mouth.

Dog led Sprang to the foot of a hut as the sun set on the village. "Snake god stay here," Dog told him. "Am most good hut in village."

"But this am Ugh's hut," Sprang said.

"Ugh? No, him stay somewhere else."

"Me live here with Ugh family."

"Okay," Dog said. "You in charge."

So Sprang moved into the same hut he had already been sharing as It. He slithered through its primitive rooms, waiting for his family. He turned to see Shirt in the doorway.

"Hello, Shirt," Sprang said.

Shirt stared at the green man's reptilian skin, his tentacles rippling like waves. By all rights, he should have been petrified. But something inside him said,

"It?"

"Yes," Sprang said. "Am me."

Shirt thought of the cause of It's transformation.

"Am my fault you am snake?"

"No, no," Sprang said soothingly. "It am just bad magic."

They watched the sunset for a moment.

"Am you change back soon?"

"Soon," Sprang told his foster brother. *If I can fix the Chameleon 3000.*

"Me hope so," Shirt told his friend. "Me think mom come home soon."

"Where's the Commander?" Bagley said, hurrying onto the bridge.

"The Commander's resting," Ditko said. "I'm overseeing the landing."

"Landing?"

"We're setting down on the planet."

"What for?" Bagley said.

"We're dumping the natives," Gruenwald said.

"Whose idea was that?"

"Mine," Ditko said. "Mine and the Commander's."

"Kirby put you in charge?"

"I am the first mate."

"Whatever," Bagley said. "Is Kirby around?"

"I told you, he's resting," Ditko said. "Is there something you want to tell me?"

"No, I guess it can wait," Bagley said.

"Oh, so I'm not good enough."

"All right!" Bagley snapped. "I vaporized one of the aliens. Happy now?"

The bridge screeched to a halt.

"Which one?" Ditko choked.

"The one with the tail."

"The monkey?"

"He fell in the food disposal."

"Well." Ditko swallowed. "I don't think this is going to sit well with the Starlins."

"Who's to know?" Bagley said. "They're five systems away. Besides, it was an accident."

"That may be so, but our treaty clearly--"

"Treaty? Give me a break. The Starlins ate our last diplomat, and you're worried about some treaty?"

"He's got a point," Gruenwald said. "I think we should keep this to ourselves."

"All right," Ditko said with a hint of contempt. "Is there anything else I should know?"

"Yeah. The monkey atomized almost all of our Busiek plants."

"Jeez," Gruenwald told Bagley. "You want to crash the *Eisner* next?"

"Well," Ditko said, feeling out of his league. "There's nothing we can do about that now. Ensign Gruenwald."

"Yes?"

"Take us down."

Ugh didn't know what to make of the snake god who'd taken over his hut, the one who spoke in his stepson's voice. He decided to go with the flow. The sun had set and Rock still wasn't back. Dog showed up at his door.

"Ugh, get snake god," the chief said. "Am time for sacrifice."

"But me no want sacrifice," Sprang said as his entourage walked to the square.

"Snake god am too humble," Dog said.

The village was out in force. They stood in a ring holding torches with a pile of wood in the middle. Sprang made out a shape in the flickering light. He and Ugh came to a stop.

"Why am mom tied to stick?" Shirt said.

Rock was to be the main course.

"Snake god no am pleased?" Dog said. "This am woman you strike down."

"Let her go," Sprang said, pale green.

"But her attack snake god."

Sprang tried to make his voice sound boomy. "Me say let her go."

Dog was disappointed in the snake god's fickle behavior. He was not only ruining his chance to spite Rock for choosing Ugh over him, but he was also depriving Dog's people of some quality entertainment. Everyone loved a good cookout. But the snake god had spoken. Chief Dog signaled to one of his flunkies.

"Let woman go."

"Look there," Ditko said, as the *Eisner* passed over a circle of lights on the ground.

"It looks like the landing strip Crow made," Gruenwald said.

"Set down inside of it," Ditko said. "But make sure we stay cloaked."

Gruenwald worked the guidance controls. "Approaching one hundred feet."

"Uh, Ditko?"

"*Commander* Ditko."

"Okay, Commander," Gruenwald said. "The circle's full of natives. I don't think we can land in there."

"Magnify," Ditko said. The crew's antenna perked up when they saw Rock tied to the stake.

"What's going on here?" Ditko said.

"Maybe some kind of primitive play?"

"Ditko," Gruenwald said. "Where do you want me to land this thing?"

"We have another problem," Bagley said. "The landing gear is stuck."

"What do you mean, it's stuck?"

"I mean it's stuck, 'Commander.'"

Ditko's face curdled. "You're all out to get me."

"Get over yourself," Gruenwald said. "Should I take her back up or squish the natives?"

Ditko tapped his pin. "McFarlane."

"Aye?"

"This is First Mate Ditko."

"I know who ye are."

"There's been a change of plans."

"That's a shocker," McFarlane said.

"Do you have all the natives rounded up?"

"Aye, but the hairy one's down."

"What?" Ditko said. "What happened?"

"He tried nickin' me intercom."

"Please tell me the gorilla's still breathing."

"The furball's just a bit knackered, is all."

"Thank goodness," Ditko said. "I want you to take him and hook him up to the end of a winch."

"What'd ye say?"

"Our landing gear isn't functioning. We're going to have to use a winch to lower the natives to the ground."

"Ye're off your trolley," McFarlane said.

"Just do it," Ditko said.

"Aye. But if I pop the hatch an' I spy me a beastie, I'm tossin' him yer cow."

Rock's head swam as she shrugged off the effects of Sprang's stun blast. She opened her eyes and saw that she was tied to a hunk of wood.

"Hello, Hairy," she said to the caveman trying to untie her. "Am this dream?"

"No, am real," Hairy assured her. "We am going to torch you, but then snake god change him mind."

"Him," Rock said, snapping into focus at the thought of Sprang. "Him am one who take boy, It. Untie me so me can smash."

Hairy quit fussing with the knot. "Me no think am good idea." Dog approached, holding a torch.

"Why her no untie?"

"Rock say she want to smash snake god," Hairy informed his chief.

"Snake god show mercy," Dog told Rock. "Yet you want to hit with club?"

"Him take son."

"Shirt over there."

"No, take other son."

"Her confused," Dog said to Hairy.

"You want untie her now?"

Dog thought for a moment.

"No. Maybe us cook her after all. Me go and ask snake god."

But before Chief Dog could do so, a door opened in the sky. And out of that door came a gorilla hooked to the end of a cable.

Dog and Hairy backed away as McFarlane lowered the ape. The winch unclamped the unconscious gorilla, setting him down beside Rock. Duck came next, understandably panicked as he held on for dear life. The townspeople gaped at the gift dispenser as it went back in the door in the sky. Then they caught a glimpse of another snake god peering over the edge.

"What are ye lookin' at?" McFarlane snapped, dangling a cow over them. Dog dropped his torch at the edge of the wood pile. Rock and Duck watched it ignite.

"Moo," Betty said, suspended in space.

The flames were spreading fast.

Lightle placed the mineral detector on his desk. He had managed to find the instruction manual for the one that was destroyed, and he flipped to the introduction.

Thank you for purchasing the Excelsior Series Mineral Analyzer. This equipment complies with the limits of a Class C spectral device, subject to subsection V of the ICC convention. Operation of this device may interfere with certain subspace and intraplanetary communications. To avoid the risk of electric shock--

"This doesn't help," Lightle said. He consulted the table of contents and turned to the section marked "calibration."

The Excelsior Series is capable of recognizing all organic and synthetic minerals on the Byrne-Austin Mineral Chart. To calibrate your analyzer, first turn the unit ON. Then set the FUNCTION switch to either ANALYZE or DETECT.

"That's easy," Lightle said.

If using in detect mode, first set the MINERAL TYPE indicator switch to ORGANIC or SYNTHETIC. Then turn the knob marked MINERAL NAME to the desired mineral.

Lightle set the switch to organic. He turned the dial until CALCIUM appeared in the window.

Test the calibration of the unit by pointing it at a substance known to contain the desired mineral. The selected mineral should now appear as a blip on the detection screen. A LED readout will show the approximate distance to the mineral.

Lightle took a Busiek plant from a drawer and placed it on his desk. He pointed the analyzer at it, crossed his fingers and looked at the screen.

Two blips.

The first blip read 1.3 bollands, the distance to the Busiek plant. The second blip was four kitsons away. About where the cow used to be.

Lightle got up from his desk and tracked the second blip. He watched the meter until it read 0. He looked down and saw a bowl. His eyes got wide as he remembered the alien's spilled milk. He looked around Engineering but there was no one else to tell. And the cow was scheduled to return to her planet! He tapped his intercom.

"Bridge, this is Lightle from Engineering."

"Lightle, this is Ensign Bagley."

"I need to speak to Commander Kirby."

"He's not here at the moment. Look, we're pretty busy right now. Is this something that can wait?"

Lightle heard voices raised in the background. "What's going on up there?"

"We have a situation here. I'm going to put you on hold."

Lightle's chest communicator piped elevator music. He set the detector down by the milk and bolted for the door.

"Would somebody give me a status report?" Ditko said, watching the screen.

"Okay," Bagley said. "We've just dropped two of the natives into some cannibals' barbecue."

"McFarlane, this is First Mate Ditko." Ditko waited for a reply. "Why am I hearing music?"

"Sorry about that," Bagley said. "I had an engineer on hold."

"Hang up on him."

"Okay."

"McFarlane," Ditko said, tapping his pin.

"Aye," McFarlane said.

"Tell me what you see down there."

"I see smoke, ya tosser."

"Is Betty...er, the cow okay?"

"So you got a girlfriend, eh? Well, your stupid moo is a wee bit nervous."

"Bring her back aboard."

"I'm tryin' to, ya git. She's a bit of a strain on the winch's motor."

"Just let me know when she's aboard."

Lightle burst onto the bridge.

"You have to save the cow!" he shouted.

"Yes, we know,' Ditko said.

"No, you don't understand," Lightle said. "The cow can save us all!"

The officers looked at one another.

"You're going to have to leave."

The fire fanned out, threatening to fence in Professor Duck and the ape. Duck dragged the gorilla to safety and patted down its smoldering hair. Ugh surged forward but found his way blocked by Dog and the chief's men.

"Ugh no go in fire," Dog said.

"But me must go and save mate."

"Fire take mate. Am sign from gods."

"Gods am wrong," Ugh said. But by then it was too late. Rock was surrounded by flames.

It took two cavemen to pound the stake Rock was tied to into the ground. She uprooted it herself. Suddenly top-heavy, Rock wobbled madly to keep from tipping over.

"Shouldn't we do something?" Bagley asked, watching from above.

"Bridge, McFarlane. Yer cow's secure."

"We could tractor beam her," Gruenwald said.

"No, no tractor beams," Ditko said. "We would have to drop our cloak."

"I'm pretty sure they know we're here already," Ensign Gruenwald said.

"But the Commander said--"

"Forget about Kirby. I thought you were in charge."

Rock stumbled around on her feet, the stake strapped to her back. She wished she could at least see her husband through the billowing smoke. Then all of a sudden, the door in the sky turned into a big green bowl, a brilliant disc that lit the village. Rock felt like she was falling. But she was used to falling down. Now she was falling up.

"We've got her," Bagley told First Mate Ditko.

"Bring her aboard," he said.

The tractor beam tugged at its prize stake-first, with Rock facing the ground. It was a strangely pleasant sensation until she smacked against the ship.

"What was that?" First Mate Ditko said.

"Bridge, this is McFarlane. Yer fine fair lass can't clear the hatch."

"She what?"

"The log's too long."

"But the cow fit," Ditko said.

"It wasn't tied to a bleedin' tree. The problem is, we picked her up sideways."

"Then turn her around."

"Ye can't turn someone in a tractor beam," McFarlane pointed out.

"Bagley, get down there and see if you can lend a hand," Ditko said.

"Uh, Commander?"

"What now?"

Gruenwald stared at the viewscreen.

"It's Sprang."

Sure enough there was their stranded shipmate lugging four buckets of water. He had one in each hand and two more in his tentacles. Sprang dropped them when he saw the *Eisner.*

"Big bowl back," Shirt whispered as he carried water behind Sprang. His eyes went up the tractor beam. "Why it taking mom?"

Sprang made a bee line for the craft, cutting through the crowd.

"He's alive," Ditko said, watching the screen. "McFarlane. Is the woman aboard?"

McFarlane used his phaser to disintegrate the top of Rock's stake. The tractor beam pulled her through the hatch and set her down beside Betty.

"She's in," McFarlane said.

"Gruenwald, get me over Sprang. Bagley, get me a lock."

The *Eisner* floated forward from its spot above the fire. The villagers parted, making way for Sprang to intercept it. He waved his arms and, looking up, almost ran Dog over.

"Snake god, where am you going?" Dog said. His lackeys restrained Ugh.

"Am going home."

"With other snake gods?"

"Yes."

"In big green bowl?"

"That's right," Sprang said.

Dog bonked Sprang over the head.

"Me think you stay here."

"They clubbed him," Gruenwald said, watching the scene from two stories above.

"Is he alive?"

"It's hard to tell."

"Let's fire our torpedoes."

Bagley's finger was on the button.

"Activate the cloak," Ditko said. "There's nothing we can do."

"I say we hold theirs hostage," Bagley said. "We've got two of them."

Ditko rubbed his aching antenna. "Just get us out of here."

The stars bled by the *Giffen* as it dropped from hyperspace. The crew held their breath, hoping not to materialize inside of something solid. Death by matter intrusion was quick. It was the anticipation that stunk.

Neary pushed the lever and the ship emerged in space. No black holes or meteor showers. Just stars and a big red planet.

"Neary," Captain Morrison said, scowling. "Does that look like Sol 3 to you?"

Neary consulted the nav computer. "I believe that's Sol 4, sir."

An explosion rocked the bridge.

"Stone me," Morrison said. "I suppose that was one of our engines."

"Complete overload," Ellis said.

The red planet loomed in the viewport. Its mountain range looked like a face.

"Get ready to take a field trip, boys. We're going to have to set down."

CHAPTER TWELVE

Cro was in his quarters during the *Eisner's* attempted landing, so he didn't expect it when Grell stopped by and said,

"We got a woman."

"What does she look like?" Cro asked as he followed Grell through the ship.

"Well I don't find her attractive, but she's only got two legs."

"Is she smart? Is she nice? Is she pretty?"

"Well from what I seen so far," Grell said, "I'm gonna go with feisty."

They stopped outside the quarantine bay. Cro swore he heard a "Moo."

"What was that?"

"The cow," Grell said.

"I thought you got a cavewoman."

"We got both. You want to see her or what?"

Betty was in the first cell, getting checked by a medidroid for signs of smoke inhalation. Next to her in a shimmering force field was Rock, still tied to her stake.

"Oh no," Cro said.

Rock had thought from the very beginning that Cro was after her family. And here he was, in cahoots with the snake men. She lifted her stake and charged.

"Augh!" Cro flinched, recalling Rock's previous bouts of ballistic behavior. She hit the semi-transparent field. It crackled and threw her back. Grell took in Rock's snarling as she bounced off the force field again.

"Classy broad."

Commander Kirby woke from his nap and focused on the clock.

"Blast!" he said as he threw back the sheets. He'd slept through active duty. He adjusted his uniform's medals as the door to his quarters breeped.

"Enter," Kirby said. Lightle snaked in, wringing his hands.

"Who are you?"

"I'm Lightle, sir."

"Ah yes, the engineer. You've had some progress, have you?"

"I've finished the mineral scanner, sir. But that's not why I'm here."

"Get on with it, then. I'm a busy squid."

"It's about the cow, Commander. I think she's the key to our calcium shortage."

"Preposterous," Kirby said. "That liquid-leaking lunatic couldn't be of use to us."

"I've analyzed that liquid, sir. It's rich in calcium."

"What?" Kirby said. "Are you sure?"

"Positive," Lightle said.

The Commander felt for his chair. "Why wasn't I informed of this? And where is Betty now?"

"She's still aboard the ship."

"Thank heavens," Kirby said. "That bovine's a glandular gold mine. Tell me, Lightle, how many of her kind do you think there are on this planet?"

"I have no idea, sir."

"No matter. We'll take them all."

"An entire species, sir?"

"I doubt that they'll be missed." Kirby's train of thought was derailed by a beep from his bookcase. "Excuse me, Lightle. It seems I have a message from Steranko."

"Would you like me to leave you, sir?"

"That won't be necessary. I'd like you to brief them on these cows." Kirby pushed a button on his desk and the bookcase slid away, revealing a screen set into the wall.

"Good fortune this wasn't shot up."

The screen danced with static until it formed an image of King Stanley.

"*GrRzZztings*, my cosmicpolitan colleague," Stanley's voice crackled. "Alas, this may *bZzZzT* last time that you hear my vociferous voice."

"I can barely see you," Kirby told the screen. "Is that a flashlight under your chin?"

The transmission dropped out, replaced by the royal seal and a scrolling message.

Please standby. We are experiencing technical difficulties.

"Lightle! You're the engineer," Kirby roared. "Fix this confounded contraption." Lightle fiddled with a knob. The signal kicked back in.

"...Chief Consulate Thomas speaking on behalf of King Stanley. One of our former *ZzZientisZztz* has conducted an unauthorized *expRzZment* which has *reZzzulted* in the destruction of Steranko's..."

The signal dropped out.

"...supply. We may *zZzZot* be able to *coMmzZrRcate* further after this *tRansMzzZn,* pending the.."

"...struction of our plan..."

"...I'm assured..."

"...all be finished within a month. Therefore, it is imperative that you..."

"...your mission on Sol 3. Once our people hear that..."

"...has been conquered, I'm sure that they'll all settle..."

"...get on with their lives."

The transmission cut itself off.

Commander Kirby was silent a moment. He sat in his chair and thought.

"Well, Lightle, it looks like these cows get to stay on Sol 3 after all."

"How's that, sir?" Lightle asked.

"It would be foolish to bring them to Steranko just as it's destroyed."

"Steranko destroyed?"

"On its last legs, you know."

"I didn't quite get that," Lightle said.

"Why, you heard it plain as day," Kirby said. "'The destruction of our planet.'"

"Well, the message was rather cryptic, sir. I..."

"Understood, soldier. I can see that you're in shock."

"Maybe if I could retrieve the message..."

"No time," Kirby said. "We've a planet to conquer."

"Conquer, sir?"

"You heard the king. Our people are settling on earth."

"Actually, that was the king's spokesman," Lightle said. "And I don't think..."

"It's time this pitiful planet partook of our military might!"

"Your antenna are trembling, sir."

"Anticipation!" Kirby said. "What a wondrous war we'll wage."

"Excuse me, sir, I have to go." Lightle inched toward the door. Kirby picked up a model spaceship and swooped it in the air.

"We'll build a fleet so ferocious even the Starlins will faint from fear!"

The Lake Village cavemen had no jail. They put Sprang in the next best thing. He woke up in the hospital, all six limbs tied to a bed. The guard saw Sprang's antenna open and hurried out of the hut.

The ape had the good sense to escape into the woods. But Duck was strapped to the bed beside Sprang, snoozing despite his confinement. Duck was a stranger whose dull wits resisted Dog's interrogation, but seeing as he dropped from the sky it was thought that he must have some value. Unless the snake gods just threw him away.

Sprang picked up his head and bent his antenna to take in his surroundings. The cavemen had done a thorough, if zealous, job of tying him down. His phaser was missing, but at least they let him keep his belt.

"Am snake god hungry?" a voice said from the door. Sprang turned his eyes. It was Dog. He was holding a plate of roasted something. Whatever it was, it smelled good. "Am sorry me club head so hard. Me glad you no am dead."

"How long was I out?" Sprang meant to say, but it came out a Sterankon shriek. Dog flinched as Sprang realized his translator was gone. Dog set the food on the floor.

"When snake god remember how to speak caveman, then maybe him can eat."

Sprang chafed his tentacles on his restraints as Chief Dog left the hut. He wished he'd taken the time to learn caveman instead of relying on his translator. He was sure he could manage to outwit Dog if he could speak his language. Plus, he had to tell his guards he had to relieve himself.

He could barely see the two guards as they stood outside the door, and he tried to make the caveman sound for the one he recognized. "Smath," Sprang said, trying to work his tongue like a caveman. "Smath." He rested his head back and then tried again.

"*Smath.*"

Smash thought the snake god called his name. Then he and Sprang heard a thunk. Smash's fellow guard teetered sideways, falling as straight as a tree. Smash had just enough time to get a look at the guard's assailant. The next moment, there was silence. The gorilla poked his head in the door.

The ape loped over to Duck's bed. The professor was still asleep. The gorilla sniffed him, snapped his ropes, and slung Duck over his shoulder. "What about me?" Sprang shrilled in Sterankon. The ape looked at him, perplexed. Then the gorilla turned to the door and told it, "ooh ooh eeeee."

"Ooh ooh eeeee," the door said back.

Well actually, it was Shirt.

The caveboy stepped over the napping guards, wearing Sprang's translator. "Ooh-ha ooh-ha," Shirt told his partner, who still had Duck over his shoulder. The gorilla pulled at Sprang's restraints and got him to his feet.

"Am It okay?" Shirt said.

Sprang recognized his caveman name and nodded. He felt for the edge of the bed. "Ooh eee-eee ahhh," Shirt said in gorilla. The ape, whose name was Larry, Shirt learned, slung Sprang over his free shoulder. Shirt checked for traffic and wondered how he would explain all this to his parents.

Captain Morrison met Ellis and Neary inside the *Giffen's* air lock. They wore quilted orange suits with fishbowl helmets. Morrison looked out a window.

"How's it look, sir?" Ellis said.

"Red. How's the atmosphere?"

"Neary says it's breathable."

"Good. Then he goes first."

"Me?" Ensign Neary hugged the walls.

"You're the one who got us here."

Neary swallowed. He pushed a button and stepped outside the ship. "We'll be right behind you," Morrison said. The door slid shut between them. Neary took a few tentative steps into the harsh terrain. He checked his suit's atmospheric readings and took his helmet off. The air was hot and bitter, but he gave the thumbs-up sign.

"Let's go," First Mate Ellis said.

"Hold it," Morrison said. "Look at his eyes."

Neary's antenna ballooned. His thumb swelled like a roasted marshmallow. He panicked and put his helmet on. His features deflated to normal.

"Ellis, when we're done here," Morrison said, "recalibrate the oxygen meter."

The officers sat at the conference table exchanging uncomfortable looks.

"You know what this is about?" Ensign Gruenwald asked Ditko.

"I have no idea." Ditko leapt from his seat when Kirby entered with Lightle, the engineer. "Ah, good afternoon, sir. I'm sure you're wondering about what happened last night."

"Sit down," Kirby said. "This is no time for snivelling. We're about to go to war." Bagley captured the mood of the room when he asked the

Commander,

"With who?"

"Whom, Ensign Bagley. Whom. Proper grammar is our first line of defense against an uncivilized enemy."

"Okay. Whom are we fighting. The Starlins?"

"All in good time, ensign. First, I'd advise you all to place your translators in your ear."

The door slid open again.

"Ah, Crow. Come in," Kirby said in English. "Well done, Grell. You're excused."

"I'll come back if I hear shots," Grell said. Cro put a few squid between himself and the Commander.

"Excellent timing," Kirby said. "I was just talking about you."

"Oh, really?" Cro said. "What about?"

"It appears I've just received orders to eradicate your race."

"My translator must be broken," Ditko said. "Did you say 'eradicate?'"

"One moment, Ditko," Kirby said. "I believe something's bothering Crow."

"I don't want you to wipe out my people," Cro said.

"Nonsense. They're savages."

"But that doesn't mean they should all be destroyed."

"Then we seem at a bit of an impasse. I must say, I'm disappointed."

"Who gave us these orders?" Gruenwald said.

"King Stanley himself."

The squid groaned.

"See here," Kirby scolded. "King Stanley speaks for Steranko."

"And what's Lightle doing here?"

"He's found a solution to our calcium problem. Lightle?"

"Cows," Lightle said.

"Cows?" Ditko said. "Like Betty?"

"Their milk is rich in calcium."

"So we're going to drink it?" Bagley said.

"That's right," Lightle said.

"Not me."

"Excuse me. Can we speak English again?" Cro asked.

"Sorry," Kirby said. "There's nothing more that concerns you here. Feel free to return to your room."

"What?" Cro said. "A minute ago, you declared war on my race."

"Nothing personal," Kirby said. "Every mammal has to go. Except for the cows, of course."

"I'd like to see these orders," Gruenwald said.

"Impossible. They were lost."

"So we're supposed to take your word for it?"

"Nonsense," Kirby said. "Lightle was there."

"And King Stanley said to level the planet?" Gruenwald asked Lightle.

"Not in so many words. Actually, his spokesman did most of the talking."

"Spokesman?" Gruenwald said. "Thomas?"

"I think that was his name."

Cro pounded the table. "ENGLISH!"

"Give him your earpiece," Kirby told Bagley.

"But I want to understand him."

"He's ranting, I assure you."

Bagley popped his translator out and slid it over to Cro. Cro fit it over his ear. In one ear, Cro heard Kirby shriek nonsensical Sterankon. But in his other ear, the translator said, "*There now. Can you understand me?*"

"Whoa," Cro said. "That's weird."

"Now then," Kirby said, "as a savage yourself, I'm sure you'll provide us with tactical advice."

"I'm still lost," Gruenwald said. "If we have the key to our calcium shortage, why don't we return to Steranko?"

"Because it bloody well won't be there." Kirby's eye twitched as the men gasped. "Our planet's about to explode, you see. We're to settle here on earth."

"What about the people back home?" Gruenwald said.

"They'll be joining us shortly," Kirby said. "I imagine they still have to pack."

"So we're colonizing earth?" Ditko said.

"Precisely," Kirby said. "Though I imagine a name change may be in order. Perhaps Steranko II."

"But why do you need to get rid of the humans?"

"Why Gruenwald, I'm surprised. I didn't take you for a flesh hugger."

"I'm just asking," Gruenwald said. "There's plenty of room for all of us."

"Yes," Kirby reflected. "I suppose we could use them as laborers until we rebuild the machines."

"I don't think any of this is going to sit well with the Starlins," Ditko said.

"They'll have an entire quadrant to themselves," Kirby said. "I imagine they'll be quite pleased."

"So let me get this straight," Cro said. "You're not going to wipe out my people?"

"Let's not jump to conclusions," Kirby said. "Perhaps you should meet with them first."

"Me?"

"Of course. They respect your opinion."

"No, they don't," Cro said.

"You'll be our ambassador," the Commander said. "Now tell me, who speaks for their people?"

"His name is Dog," Cro said.

The squids stifled their snickers.

"Curious name," Kirby said. "How do we contact this Dog?"

"I don't know," Cro told the Commander. "He's never far from the village."

"We'll land in the morning, then. I want you men to get your rest. We have a planet to conquer."

The men snaked down the hall in silence after Kirby's bewildering meeting. Gruenwald and Bagley caught up with Lightle. They each took one of his arms.

"We need to talk," Gruenwald said.

They herded him into the quarantine bay. Rock and Betty, still in their cells, paid the three squid little heed.

"Now tell us exactly what this message said."

"I told you," Lightle said. "It was really broken up."

"So reconstruct it," Gruenwald said.

"I don't know if I can. It was on Kirby's private channel."

They turned when they heard the door hiss. McFarlane slithered in.

"What are you doing here?" Gruenwald said.

"Is this a war meetin', then?"

"What are you talking about?"

"I heard the whole thing," McFarlane said. "I bugged the conference room."

"Get him out of here," Bagley said.

"No. He may be useful. You're good at decryption," Gruenwald told McFarlane. "I'll have you work with Lightle."

"Moo."

"What was that?"

"The cow," Lightle said. "I think she needs to be milked."

"Well I'm not touching her," Bagley said.

"Have you tried drinking it yet?"

"You can't drink it straight from the source," Lightle said. "It has to be processed first. I prefer mine two percent."

"It still sounds disgusting," Bagley said.

"If you chill it first, it's delicious."

They stared at the bucket in Betty's cell. McFarlane stepped up to the plate.

"What are you doing?" Lightle said.

"Come on, then. I'll give it a go."

Ellis welded a panel on the *Giffen's* ailing thruster.

"How's it coming?" Morrison said.

"It's awful hot in here."

"Take your helmet off, then," Morrison said.

"Very wry of you, sir."

"You wire that crossover yet?"

"Excuse me, sir?" Neary held up a part. "Do you know where this goes?"

"Bloody hell." Morrison's intercom beeped.

"Excuse me, Captain?"

"What?"

"You've got a call," the chest pin said.

"Who is it?"

"It's Steranko."

"Take a message," Morrison said. "I can't move in this bloody suit."

"You'll really want to hear this, sir."

Morrison sighed. "All right."

Morrison lumbered onto the bridge still wearing his space gear. "I'm warning you, Hitch, this better not be another one of your pranks."

"Take a look at the screen," Hitch said. He adjusted the vertical hold. "Greetings, Captain Morrison," a snowy Thomas said. "I hope that you can hear me. Steranko has experienced a temporary flux in our planet's power grid. This may be the last time I'm able to communicate with you for some time. Therefore, it is imperative you continue your mission and assist the *Eisner* on Sol 3. The calcium shortage is still our biggest concern, and--"

"Where's the rest?" Morrison said.

"It took me all morning to piece that together," Hitch said.

"A power flux," Morrison said. "I bet it's that wanker, Liefeld."

"What do we do?"

"We're not going anywhere on one good thruster," Captain Morrison said.

"I've been picking up something else," Hitch said. "The signal's pretty weak, but I think it's one of ours."

"One of our what?"

"A communicator, sir."

"On this planet? Where?"

"About four clicks to the south," Hitch said.

"What the devil is it doing here?"

"You've got me, sir."

"Then suit up, Hitch," Morrison said. "We're taking a little stroll."

"You can put me down now," Sprang told Larry from over the ape's shoulder. They were sitting around their camp in the woods.

"Ooo eee haa," Shirt said. Larry put Sprang back on his tentacles.

"Am It okay?" the caveboy asked.

"You learned Sterankon? Oh, that's right. You have my translator," Sprang said. "Do you mind if I take it back?"

"Okay." Shirt removed the earpiece. Larry growled something in ape.

"You keep it," Sprang said, backing off. Larry simmered down. "So what's the plan?"

"Us get mom back," Shirt said.

"Okay," Sprang said. "Good plan." He rubbed the bump Chief Dog gave him. "What happened to your friend?"

"Duck say him go get some grubs. Me think him am lost."

"How'd it go?" Grell said from the doorway to Cro's cell.

"They want to take over earth," Cro said.

Grell nodded. "Yeah, I heard."

"How'd you know?"

"Us janitors hear things."

Cro plopped down in a seat.

"Hey, cheer up." Grell patted Cro's back. "You'd think it's the end of the world."

"Are we bloody there yet?" Morrison said as he trudged through the martian landscape.

"Almost," Hitch said. He watched his tracker. "It looks like it should be right here."

The sun beat down on their pressure suits. Red mountains flanked their path. Morrison nudged a rock aside and spied a glint in the dust. "I've got it," he said, extracting the rusty communicator pin.

"How do you suppose it got there?" Hitch said.

"The *Eisner* must have been here."

"But why would they have left it behind?"

"Dunno," Morrison said. His antenna were sore from being scrunched in his helmet. "Let's get back to the ship." He bent down and picked up the fist-sized rock.

"What are you doing, sir?"

"I promised a friend a souvenir." He zipped the rock up in his suit.

"Sir?"

"What is it?"

"I've got an idea why they left their pin behind."

"Well share with me, Hitch."

"I imagine they were running for their lives."

Morrison followed Hitch's stare. The mountain behind him blinked.

"Oh, bugger." Morrison's vest pocket squirmed. "I think their boy wants out." He unzipped the spacesuit compartment and gently set the rock at his feet. It scooted up to the base of the mountain.

"Shall we start the running, sir?"

Duck sat on a log near the edge of the forest and tried to concentrate. He was jumpy around the snake-legs, whose screeches rattled him more than Big Teeth's, and he'd rather be gathering berries alone than trapped in the bowl in the sky. The woods were thick with bugs homing in on Duck's distinctive smell. That was the problem with prehistory. The mosquitoes were super-sized.

Rex didn't mind the bugs so much. They had a hard time piercing his hide. Plus, their buzzing was a nice distraction for the hairy man. It amazed Rex that the stubby creature would come here all alone. *I mean really, just look at him*, Rex thought as he pounced.

He's a sitting duck.

Morrison screamed in his communicator as he raced from a mobile mountain. "*Giffen*! Do you have a lock on us yet?"

"Sorry, sir," Neary's voice said. "We're getting a lot of interference from the rock formations."

"So are we," Captain Morrison snapped, daring a look over his shoulder. The rock creatures moved like snails. But speed was relative when the snail in question was several stories tall. "They're looking at us like we're biscuits, Neary. Where's my bloody lock?"

"Sir, I'm cramping."

"Stay with me, Hitch." Hitch shimmered and faded away. Morrison cursed just as he felt the tingly sensation himself.

"So you ported Hitch out first?" he said as he stormed onto the bridge.

"Sorry," First Mate Ellis said. "I thought the captain always goes last."

"Not bloody likely," Morrison said. "Do we have full thrusters yet?"

"Why? I'm not picking up any movement."

"Trust me. The hills have eyes."

A hologram of earth spun slowly over Kirby's desk. His first mate's nerves were more frayed than usual as Ditko approached the Commander.

"A daunting task, eh, Ditko?"

"What's that, sir?" Ditko said.

"Our taming this planet. We have the technology, mind you. But we may lose some fine squid."

"I thought we were going to talk to Crow's people."

"Harrumph. That never works. It's merely a chance to study our enemy inside their perimeter."

"I have to say, sir, I still have reservations about these new commands."

"So tell me, Ditko, which part of the planet would you like to oversee?"

"Excuse me, sir?"

"It's a bloody big planet," Kirby said. "I'm sure the king won't mind."

Ditko looked at the globe's soft glow.

"Ditkoville," he said. "Growing up, I always dreamed they'd name a town after me."

"Town?" Kirby scoffed. "Think bigger, lad. You'll have your own continent."

"I kind of like this one," Ditko said, eyeing Australia.

"These are trying times," the Commander said. "I need a squid I can trust."

"I thought you didn't like me, sir."

"Rubbish," Kirby said. "I've only chided you in the past because I saw potential."

"You mean it, sir?"

"Of course." Kirby put his hand on his shoulder. "I'm not a sentimental man, but I think of you as a son."

"Well, ah, sir, it's just that..."

"Yes?"

"I don't want to be eaten like Englehart."

"We're commanding officers," Kirby said. "We never go into battle."

Ditko gazed at his continent.

"In that case, sir, I'm in."

Morrison leaned over Neary's chair and watched the *Giffen* leave warp.

"There she is. Sol 3," the weary navigator said.

"Neary," Morrison said, steaming. "Since when does Sol 3 have four moons?"

"Oh," Neary said.

"Care to try it again?"

Neary gulped.

"Uh-huh."

Ugh dozed off and fell on his spear. This happened a number of times. He had the sense to stand vigil where the flying bowl took Rock, but not to point his weapon away now that fatigue set in. He rubbed his forehead and watched the stars in case the bowl returned.

He had not seen his son all day, leaving Shirt to his own devices, not knowing that included harboring a fugitive snake god. Ugh's first priority was getting Rock back. He needed someone to make dinner.

Ugh fell asleep facedown in the sand. He stayed that way until morning. He would have slept later had it not been for the spaceship that tried to set down on his head.

CHAPTER THIRTEEN

It was Cro's first time on the bridge of the *Eisner*. He felt like a five-year-old.

"What does this do?" he asked the Commander, gazing at the nearest console.

"That's our teleport station," Kirby said. "Not that the bloody thing works."

"What about that?"

"Navigation, my boy."

"And that."

"That's our cloaking device."

"Ah, excuse me, sir," Ditko said. "Do you think it's wise sharing information with a potentially hostile race?"

"Nonsense. Crow's one of us," Kirby said. "Aren't you, lad?"

"Uh, sure."

"There you have it. Now, how would you like to take her for a spin?"

"Seriously?" Cro said.

"Ha! Had you going there, didn't I? Gruenwald! Is the landing gear secure?"

Gruenwald thought, *I hope so*. But he answered with "Aye, sir."

"Excellent. Take us down. And remember, Crow," the Commander said, "our fate is in your hands."

"Right," Cro said. "So, I was just wondering...what am I going to say?"

"Tell your people we come in peace. Then we'll set up the forced labor camps."

"I don't know if they'll be too keen on that." The ground approached in the viewport. "What if we--PULL UP!"

It was then that Gruenwald noticed the caveman standing directly below them. "Sorry," he said, pumping the brakes. "He kind of blended in."

"Why doesn't he move?" Ensign Bagley said.

"He's sleeping," Cro said. "Look."

"Curious creature," Kirby said. "Gruenwald. Beep the horn."

The *Eisner* emitted a muted, short meep. Ugh slept right through it. This time the *Eisner* blarted a tone that sounded like twenty-two semis. Not only did Ugh scramble out from its descending shadow, the whole village looked up.

Dog assembled a welcoming party. They lined up, facing the ship. The men of the village steadied their weapons, trying not to panic.

Kirby slithered down a ramp, followed by Ditko and Gruenwald. They carried a table between them, set it up and lined it with chairs. Dog looked on, befuddled. Kirby tapped his pin.

"Bring her down."

McFarlane and Bagley followed Cro out the ship. The squid dragged Rock by her arms. Her hands and feet were tied behind her. Her mouth was likewise gagged. Ugh, still woozy from waking up, saw his wife in restraints and charged. Kirby produced his phaser and calmly dropped Ugh in his tracks. It had the effect that Kirby hoped for. Some of the natives clapped.

"Do you know that savage?" the Commander asked Cro, who had taken a seat beside him.

"That's his wife." Cro nodded toward Rock.

"An excitable chap," Kirby said. "McFarlane! Release the female, would you? But closer to her own kind." McFarlane and Bagley dragged Rock the distance between the squid and cavemen. Some of the warriors inched away, but Dog planted his club. The strain of Rock's weight showed on the squid's faces. They dumped her at Dog's feet.

"People of earth," Cro said as McFarlane and Bagley slithered back. "Please accept this generous gift on behalf of Commander Kirby."

The Lake People's warriors encircled Rock. Smash poked her with his spear. Her gag muffled Rock's violent response.

"Her okay," Smash said.

Cro held out his arms like Kirby instructed and continued with the script. "Now that you've seen our good intentions, Commander Kirby invites Chief Dog to join him at our table."

"Why you speak for snake gods?" Dog said. Cro glanced at the Commander.

"The...ah, snake gods have not decided if you're worthy to speak to themselves." The squid listened through their communicators.

"Oh, he's good," Bagley said.

"And how come Crow hold arms like that? Him want to give Chief Dog hug?"

A wave of snickers rolled over the crowd. Even some of the squid hid their faces. Cro's eyes pleaded with the Commander.

"Oh, very well," Kirby said.

"Chief Dog," he said in a commanding voice, standing as Cro took a seat. "I am Commander Kirby of the starship *Eisner* and the Sterankon Royal Fleet. I greet you in the name of King Stanley."

"You am chief of snake gods?"

"I am. Now be a good savage and come have a seat. I really don't like to shout."

Dog eyed the table suspiciously. "Me stay over here."

"Very well," Kirby said. "Now then, I take it you're duly authorized to speak on behalf of Earth?" Dog was slow with his reply.

"Me no like big words."

"What the snake god asked," Cro interjected, "was do you speak for your people?"

"Me speak for Lake Village," Chief Dog said.

"But not for Earth?" Kirby asked.

"What am earth?"

"This planet."

"Oh." Another pause. "What am planet?"

"This could be a problem," Ditko said to Kirby in Sterankon. Then to Cro, in English: "don't you people have some kind of leader?"

"Dog is their leader," Cro said.

"I meant a leader for the earth."

"We don't have one of those," Cro said.

"Why didn't you tell us that?"

"Tiny steps, Ditko," Kirby said. "So tell me, Chief Dog, do the Lake People have any enemies?"

"Us no like Swamp People so good. And then there am Big Teeth."

"Ah yes," Kirby said. "Tell me, how would you like if I destroyed this Big Teeth for you?"

"That be nice," Dog said.

"And all I'd ask in return is, oh, your land and all your men."

At first, Dog thought the snake god was joking. "That no am good deal."

"Then you leave me no other choice," Kirby said. "Ditko, disintegrate him."

"Ah, sir, this wasn't what we discussed."

"The time for talk has passed! This savage's sowing of insurrection could lead to languid labor!"

"What?" Ditko said.

"Commander, I object!" Gruenwald said, springing from his seat.

"Ditko, you have your orders!" Kirby bellowed, twitching wildly.

"Ditko," Cro said, his voice trembling as much as the First Mate's phaser. "I think this is a bad idea."

"You're not the Commander."

"Ditko, I need you to listen to me," Gruenwald said.

"Shut up!" Ditko said. "You never even liked me. Ow."

The threat to his chief had overcome Smash's primal fear for a second, long enough to hurl his spear. It lodged in Ditko's shoulder. As instants went, it was a long one. Many thoughts flew through both sides' heads. Among them was the realization that even a snake god could bleed. An oozy green liquid that bubbled, but still. Dog raised his club and roared.

"To arms!" Kirby said, overturning the table to intercept the onslaught of spears. "Weapons on disintegrate, men! We'll show them--bloody hell!" He was the only squid beside Ditko who wasn't slithering back up the ship. Cro retreated with them.

"Go on without me, sir," Ditko said, leaning against the table.

"Never surrender," Kirby barked. He peaked a twitching eye over their cover. "Can you get to the ship?"

"I think so, sir."

"Good lad. I'll cover you. Go!" As Ditko broke for the *Eisner*, Kirby raised an antenna again. He poked a tentacle over the table and squeezed the phaser trigger. Dog fell over. Stunned, not vaporized.

"Rot!" Kirby made for the ramp. A spear punctured one of his tentacles. The savages pounded on the hull as the *Eisner's* hatch retracted.

No one noticed the stray snake god who was trying to flag down his ship. Sprang had been out with Shirt and Larry searching for Professor Duck. He had gotten back to town too late.

"Rats."

Sprang returned to the woods.

"Unhand me!"

"But, sir. Your tentacle."

"I'm aware of that," Kirby said. "McFarlane, call a droid for Ditko. Then take Gruenwald to the brig."

"Me?" Gruenwald said. "What for?"

"Insurrection," Kirby roared. "Now take him away."

Kirby pushed the spearhead through his leg, then snapped it off its shaft. "Are you all right, sir?" Bagley asked.

"All right? Good lord, we're at war!"

"You didn't give them much of a chance," Cro told the Commander.

"If I were you, I'd remember that some of those spears were meant for you."

Thomas looked out the palace window. Steranko was still in the dark. He halfway wished he hadn't shot his best engineers into space.

"Excuse me, sir?"

"Raney! How's the leg?"

"Still a bit stiff, sir."

"I'd offer you a Busiek plant, but I'm afraid we're almost out."

"Actually, sir, I was wondering if you'd come and address the mob."

"Are they violent?" Thomas said.

"No. Just testy, sir. One of them called me a name."

Thomas followed Raney to the front gate, expecting to find a crowd. Instead he found a half-dozen citizens languishing in the sun.

"You call this a mob?" Thomas asked Raney.

"There were a lot more earlier."

Thomas addressed the alleged protesters. "Excuse me, good people."

"Who are you?"

"I'm Thomas, King Stanley's chief advisor."

"Where's the king?"

"He's inside."

"I bet he's got air conditioning."

"Please," Thomas said. "I know this has been inconvenient, but we're all in the same boat."

"No we're not," a protester said.

"What?"

"Your boat's bigger."

"What are you talking about?"

"Well, look at this place," the protester said. "Your boat's more like a yacht."

"All right," Thomas said. "So maybe it wasn't the best analogy..."

"Let's go looting," an old man said.

"Why would you do that? No one pays for anything."

The squid stared at their tentacles.

"Why don't you people go back to your homes?"

"There's nothing on the tele."

"Don't you have hobbies?"

More tentacle staring.

"Now, really," Thomas said. "You're pathetic."

"A right fine mess you've gotten into," McFarlane told Gruenwald.

"You could let me escape."

"And tell Kirby what?"

"Tell him I overwhelmed you."

"No offense," McFarlane said, herding Gruenwald into the cell next to Betty. "But that doesn't sound likely now, does it?" McFarlane placed a tentacle on a sensor plate. The cell's stasis field dropped like a curtain. "Don't worry, boyo. I'm still on your side," McFarlane said. "For now."

"So, how'd it go?" Grell asked as he slithered into Cro's room.

"Terrible. The Commander tried shooting their chief."

"And the natives fought back? I heard. Your people are pretty good with them sticks."

"Thanks," Cro said. "But I'm afraid next time we're going to need a bigger stick."

"Too bad you can't hurry up and clone a lot more men," Grell said. "Or at least a few of that crazy broad, Rock. She could probably take out the whole ship."

"But it doesn't work that way. On Earth it takes nine months just to make a baby," Cro said.

"Man, you guys are slow."

"We don't make them in labs, remember?"

"Yeah," Grell said. "But nine months? That's a long time before you hatch."

"But our babies grow in the mother," Cro said.

"Right. She lays the egg."

"No, the baby stays in the mother."

"Where?"

"In her stomach," Cro said.

"Gah!" Grell wretched. "Then it bursts out her chest?"

"Are you all right? You look green. er."

"Go on without me," Grell said. "I think I'm gonna be sick."

"And how are we feeling?" the medidroid said as Kirby lay in bed. It probed his bandaged tentacle.

"Unhand me, you rattlebrained robot!"

"Now, now, Commander," the medidroid said in its artificially sweetened voice. "Someone's grumpy this morning."

"It's the afternoon, you twit."

"That attitude isn't helping, mister. I'm afraid you need more rest."

"Bagley!" the Commander bellowed, seeing the squid in his doorway. "Tell this infernal android to leave!"

"We're almost done," the medidroid said. "Now, since you've been a good boy, why don't I let you pick out a sticker?"

"BAGLEY!"

"This one has a smiley face, and this one's got a -- SKREEE!"

There was a whine of exploding machinery as Kirby shot his doctor. The medidroid's severed trunk whirred and sparked before it toppled over. Kirby set the phaser on the nightstand.

"Never did care for doctors."

"Was that necessary, sir?" Bagley asked.

"Its wires were clearly crossed. Now, what brings you here, Bagley?"

"Nothing, sir."

"What's that you're holding there?"

Bagley smiled nervously. "Maybe now's not a good time."

"Nonsense," Kirby said. "I'm feeling better now that I've mangled that machine. Now out with it, lad."

"Okay," Bagley said. "This is from the men." He handed Kirby the sheets of paper. The Commander scanned the names.

"Why, a get-well card. How thoughtful."

"Actually, it's a petition, sir."

Kirby flipped back to the front page. "A petition, you say? For what?"

"Well, sir, we've been talking and...we don't want to take over Earth."

"What?!" Kirby said, antenna bulging. "What is the meaning of this?"

"Well I know Crow's people have Sprang and all, but the way we see it, we started it."

"Insurrection! Conspiracy!"

"Yes, well," Bagley snatched the petition. "This was all just a practical joke."

"Skullduggery skippered by scoundrelous squid!"

"I'll leave you to rant then, sir."

Bagley was fortunate that the Commander's phaser was recharging.

McFarlane set a monitor on Lightle's desk in Engineering. He fiddled with a knob, trying to fill the screen with something other than static.

"You'll never pick up anything in here," Lightle said. "The walls are too thick."

"Move these around," McFarlane said.

"What for?"

"Just do it, boyo." Lightle grasped the antennae atop the set and halfheartedly gave it a go.

"This is stupid. This will never-hey!"

"Don't move," McFarlane said. A shadowy figure formed in the snow, the sound equally fuzzy.

"*GrRzZztings*, my *coZzRrRkpolitan* colleague."

"That's him!" Lightle said. "That's King Stanley." In his excitement, he nudged the antennae. The faint signal was gone. McFarlane took the loss in stride and reached into his toolbox. He removed a roll of tinfoil.

"What's that for?" Lightle said.

"Boosting the signal," McFarlane said. He tore off a sheet of foil. But instead of wrapping it around the set's antennae, he wound it around Lightle's.

"Hey!" Lightle said.

"Don't move, ya baby." McFarlane crimped the foil. Lightle's antennae were yanked around. McFarlane used him as a tuner.

"--Chief Consulate Thomas speaking on behalf of King Stanley."

The signal was crystal clear.

"Hold still," McFarlane told the squid. "I have ta hook up the recorder." Lightle's grasp on the rabbit ears tightened as he struggled to hold his eyes still.

"One of our former scientists has conducted an unauthorized experiment which has resulted in the destruction of Steranko's power supply."

"Are you getting this?" Lightle said.

"Aye."

"We may not be able to communicate further after this transmission, pending the planning and construction of our planet's new power grid. I'm assured by Progress these goals will all be finished within a month.

"Therefore, it is imperative that you continue your mission on Sol 3. Once our people have learned that our mineral shortage problem has been conquered, I'm sure that they'll all settle down and get on with their lives."

Thomas' image gave way to static. Lightle relaxed his antennae. McFarlane ejected the video disc.

"This changes things a bit now, don't it?"

Kirby's slither had a slight limp to it as he entered the bridge.

"Sir!" Bagley said. "You should be in bed."

"Balderdash," Kirby said. "Do you think those savages are resting while they plan their next attack?" Kirby took his seat and noticed the new squid on his crew. "Gibbons, what are you doing here?"

"I took over for Gruenwald, sir."

"Right," Kirby said. "Are you qualified?"

"I flew the *Eisner* this morning."

"But the ship was on autopilot."

"Yes. But I uh, turned it on."

"Very well," Kirby said. "Carry on."

The door heralded the arrival of McFarlane and Lightle.

"Ah, Lightle!" Kirby said. "Just the squid I was looking for. During my convalescence, I've had some thoughts on these cows of yours."

"Beggin' your pardon, cap'n, but we've got somethin' you oughtta see." McFarlane slid the data disc in without waiting for permission. The crew sighed in relief as they watched the unbroken transmission. But the Commander stood unfazed as the rebroadcast left the screen.

"I must say, that was a poor forgery."

Bagley's antennae sprung up. "What?"

"These savages don't know the first thing about a disinformation campaign."

"Are you saying Crow's people have the means to fake a subspace transmission?"

"Hmm," Kirby said. "You're right, Bagley. It probably was the Starlins."

"Cap'n, I made this disc meself."

"No need to apologize, McFarlane. I can see how a squid with an untrained eye could fall for this fakery."

"But sir," Bagley said, "our home's still there. This changes everything."

"Tut-tut," Kirby chided. "That's just what the Starlins would have us believe."

"But--"

"I'll have no more talk of this dubious disc. We've too much work to do."

Captain Morrison stared at the wretched ringed planet.

"Anything yet?" he said.

"Well, sir," Neary said, "as near as we can tell, we're looking at Sol 6."

"Sol 6. As in sixth from the sun."

"That's right."

"And we're looking for Sol 3. Ellis, bring her about," Morrison said. "And point us at the sun."

The *Giffen's* viewport panned until a bright glare filled the screen.

"Do you think you can manage to follow that?"

"I believe so, sir," Neary said.

"Good. We'll bloody hopscotch there one planet at a time."

Ditko tried to read a magazine, but his shoulder hurt too much. He set it aside when he had guests.

"How do you feel?" Bagley said. McFarlane trailed him in.

"I'm not sure. I haven't seen my medidroid since this morning."

"Listen, something's come up," Bagley said. "We decrypted the transmission."

"Have our orders changed?" Ditko said.

"That's the point. We were never told to invade in the first place."

"What did the Commander say?" Ditko reached for his medication.

"He wouldn't listen," Bagley said. "He said it must be a trick."

"And you saw the transmission?"

"I decrypted it meself," McFarlane said. "The cap'n's mad, he is."

"That's why we're here," Ensign Bagley said. "We're thinking about a coupe."

"A coupe?"

"We need you in on this. You're second in command."

"But to overthrow the Commander?"

"We wouldn't hurt him," Bagley said. "We'd just lock him up."

"Yeah, with Gruenwald."

Bagley glared at McFarlane. Ditko leaned back in bed and thought. "Would that make me Commander?" The other squid looked at each other.

"Sure," Bagley said. "You're first mate."

"All right, I'll do it," Ditko said.

"Good. We move tonight."

Gruenwald sat in the corner of his cell and stared at the soft blue force field. Betty, his neighbor, was a poor conversationalist, though she thought the same of him. He found after the first few hours he did not take well to confinement and wondered if McFarlane had even tried to contact Thomas for him.

Betty mooed, her usual reaction to company. Gruenwald stood as McFarlane entered.

"Here to milk your friend?"

"Quiet," McFarlane hissed. He rapped his phaser on the door. Ditko and Bagley slithered in.

"What's going on?" Gruenwald said. Ensign Bagley moved toward his cell.

"We're getting you out of here."

"What about the Commander?"

"He doesn't know," Bagley said. Ditko held back and McFarlane stood guard as Bagley lowered the force field. He handed Gruenwald a phaser.

"I have to admit," Gruenwald told Ditko, "I didn't think you'd do this."

"Actually, I'm not." Ditko drew his phaser. The squid froze in their tracks.

"What are you doing?" Bagley said.

"I'm stopping an insurrection."

"But you were in on this."

"I only pretended to be to see how far you'd go," Ditko said.

"Put that away," Gruenwald said. "I'm sure we can talk this over."

"Step back in your cell." Ditko motioned to Bagley. "You too."

"You wouldn't shoot."

"Maybe he wouldn't," McFarlane said. "But ye know I would."

Now Bagley and Gruenwald had two phasers on them.

"I knew Ditko was a weasel, but you?"

"I knew it," Gruenwald said.

"Sorry, lads, but I always side with a winner."

"But Kirby's insane," Bagley said.

"The Commander's a great man," Ditko objected.

"He almost got you killed twice."

"The first time was an accident."

Gruenwald tried to keep his composure.

"And what's your excuse?" Bagley asked McFarlane.

"The cap'n's mad, but he's got vision."

Gruenwald snapped.

"KIRBY'S A CLONE!"

The soft hum of the *Eisner's* engines was all that filled the room. Ditko got his color back.

"Is not," he said.

"I don't know what happened," Gruenwald said. "But the clone rot has set in. A few more days and you won't be able to tell him apart from King Stanley."

"How do you know?" Bagley asked Gruenwald.

"Thomas told me."

"It might have helped if you'd told us sooner."

"He's lying," Ditko said. Gruenwald snaked forward slowly, his hands in the air.

"Can we stop this nonsense, please?"

McFarlane kept his weapon drawn. He flashed a deadly grin.

"Ach, I hate ta tell ya, lads, but this just makes things sweeter. For when the cap'n falls apart, I guess I'll be in charge."

"What about me?" Ditko said.

"Whatever," McFarlane said. "Now you two there. Put your phasers on the floor and step into the hole."

Gruenwald and Bagley surrendered their weapons. They saw no other choice.

Cro had thoughts of mutiny himself as he wandered onto the bridge.

"Crow!" Kirby said. "Why are you here without a proper escort?"

"Actually, Commander, I was looking for Ditko or Bagley."

"They said they were feeling quite ill," Kirby said as McFarlane rushed through the door.

"Cap'n, we've got an emergency."

"State your business," Kirby said.

"Me n' Ditko just thwarted an act of treason," McFarlane said. "We caught Bagley tryin' to bust Gruenwald out of stir."

"Intolerable!" Kirby barked. "That mutinous malcontent!"

"We locked him up with Gruenwald. Ditko's restin' in his room."

"Well done, soldier," Kirby said. "It appears that I misjudged you."

"I've been thinking, maybe I should go back to my village," Cro said innocently.

"What about him?" McFarlane asked Kirby. "Shouldn't we lock him up, too?"

"Crow? He's harmless."

"I'm only a guest."

"I'm tellin' ye, I don't trust him."

"You can drop me back on Earth," Cro said.

"Now, now," Kirby said. "Perhaps we'll place you with Gruenwald and Bagley to gather intelligence. See if you can get them to talk, will you?"

"Just drop me off anywhere. I'll swim if I have to."

"McFarlane. Take him away."

Cro trudged to the makeshift prison in the quarantine bay. He saw that he'd have two cellmates.

"Can't you put me with the cow?"

"Nah," McFarlane said. "And I'll be takin' this." He removed Cro's translator. Cro joined the two squid at phaserpoint, then turned to them when they were alone.

"So, what are you in for?"

Gruenwald's indecipherable shriek made Cro jump out of his skin. He slumped against the wall of their cell.

"Moo," Betty said.

"Oh, shut up."

Neary's stomach was three jumps back as the *Giffen* faced a new planet.

"Well?" Captain Morrison said. Neary pecked at his keyboard.

"That's it," he said. "Sol 3."

"About bloody time. Ellis, find me the *Eisner*."

"Captain?"

"Yes?"

"I'm going to be sick."

"Not on the bridge, Neary." The queasy squid broke for the door.

"Captain?"

"Yes, Hitch?"

"I don't feel so good, either."

"Anyone else?"

Ellis raised his hand.

"Poncies," Morrison said.

"But we made four jumps in one day."

"All right, Ellis, you find me that ship?"

"She's on the far side, sir."

"What time is it there?"

"Late evening, captain."

"We'll rendezvous in the morning. And Hitch?"

"Aye, sir?"

"Find a mop. I just heard Neary chunder."

CHAPTER FOURTEEN

Red lights strobed the quarantine bay. Alarms rang through the ship. Cro and his cellmates were roused from their slumber.

"What's happening?" Cro said. One of the squid trilled something. Cro cursed their lack of translators. But he could tell by the way they chattered that things were not looking up.

Gibbons was a door repairman by trade, not an officer. He stared at the strange blip on his radar.

"Uh, Commander?"

"What is it, Gibbons?"

"That's what I was wondering." The blip was coming their way. Kirby snaked over and took a look.

"What the devil is that?"

"It's one of ours," McFarlane said, manning Bagley's station.

"Impossible," the Commander said.

The *Giffen* flew into view.

"Commander," Ditko said in wonder.

"They're hailing us, cap'n."

"Shields up."

"Sir?"

"They could be hostile, Ditko. McFarlane, put them on-screen."

"This is Captain Morrison of the *Giffen*. We're here to lend a hand."

"Close the channel," Kirby said. His counterpart blinked off the screen. "A terrible ruse. The real *Giffen* was lost in Levitz Bay."

"Umm, Commander?" Gibbons said. "Isn't it possible they salvaged it?"

"Hmm. Good thinking, Ensign. Fire a warning shot at their bow."

The green recruit scanned his controls.

"The red button, Ensign Gibbons."

Sweat beaded Gibbon's antennae.

"How do you aim it, sir?"

On the *Giffen's* bridge, they were at a loss.

"They cut us off," Ellis said.

"Hail them again," Captain Morrison told him.

"Aye, sir."

"Bugger me!"

The *Eisner* had turned and fired on them. The crew stared in disbelief.

"Shields!"

The shot splashed wide of the *Giffen*. Captain Morrison gripped his chair.

"Neary, ready two photon torpedoes. Ellis, open that channel!"

The hailing frequency beeped. Morrison stood and faced the screen.

"Commander Kirby, this is Captain Morrison. Stand down or we will return fire."

"My apologies, Captain Morrison," the strangely friendly image replied. "I was merely trying to determine if you are who you said you were."

Morrison turned to First Mate Ellis, who shrugged *don't look at me*.

"Now then," Kirby continued, "we have a great deal to discuss. Why don't you and your men beam aboard the *Eisner*?"

"Is Ensign Gruenwald there?"

"Gruenwald is being held for treason. He's our prisoner."

"Uh-huh," Morrison said. "Let me put you on hold for a minute." Kirby's on-screen image froze. Morrison polled his men.

"What do you think?"

"He's looney."

"Nuts."

"I think he's kind of cool."

"Don't they know he's a clone?" Ellis said.

"I think only Gruenwald knew. Suggestions?" Morrison said.

"We could beam Kirby to isolation and put his crew in charge."

"We don't know what influence he has on his men. They may retaliate."

"They're going to need an answer, sir."

Morrison took Kirby off hold.

"With all due respect," he told the Commander, "why don't you come here instead?"

Morrison and his men stood at attention, watching the teleport disc. It shimmered with dancing molecules as Kirby beamed aboard.

"Welcome aboard the *Giffen*," Morrison said once Kirby was whole. The Commander stepped off the platform, taking in his surroundings.

"So you're Morrison, eh? I don't recall hearing that name when I was on the Fleet."

Their conversation was interrupted by another incoming arrival.

"And this is McFarlane, my head of security."

"Is this all of your men, Commander?"

"My First Mate, Ditko, is manning the ship along with Ensign Gibbons."

"I see," Captain Morrison said. "And what about Ensign Bagley?"

"Bagley?" Kirby said. "That spineless squid tried joining the insurrection."

"Would you like something before we begin?" Morrison asked the Commander. They settled into the conference room, the two crews facing each other.

"Could I trouble you for a Busiek plant? I'm afraid we're running low."

"Of course, Commander."

"I wouldn't mind a stalk meself."

"Yes, I'm afraid that a small simian has squandered our supply."

"Simian?" Morrison said.

"The savages call them 'monkeys.' Bloody thing took a bite of my finger."

Morrison tried to switch Kirby's train back onto its track.

"So I understand you've made progress toward solving our mineral shortage."

"Progress? Why, we've solved the problem." Kirby leaned in. "Cows, you see."

The *Giffen* contingent was dumfounded.

"Can you run that by me again?"

"Cows, Captain Morrison. A four-legged mammal with horns that produces a frothy white beverage."

"And that's..."

"Chock full of calcium, naturally. The beasts squirt it right from their glands. A brood of breeding bovines will make our problem a thing of the past."

Captain Morrison sat back in his chair.

"So you've accomplished our mission, then."

"You must be joking, Captain. We're to colonize Sol 3."

"I'm sorry." Morrison's crew was aghast. "Why would we do that?"

"To relocate our fellow Sterankons," Commander Kirby said. "There's been a tragedy back home."

"Yes, the planet's power went out. But that doesn't affect our mission."

"Ah, I see you've fallen for the Starlin's little ruse."

"Excuse me?" Morrison said.

"Yes, we received the transmission ourselves," Commander Kirby said. "Naturally, I saw through it."

"Ensign McFarlane, could you shed a little more light on this for me?"

"Aye," McFarlane said. "A few days ago we received a transmission from King Stanley himself. He said there'd been a catastrophe and Steranko's days were numbered. Then we decrypted another transmission that said it wasn't so."

"And what do you believe?"

"Well, cap'n, I believe my king. And I stand by my Commander."

Morrison looked down his row of men. He shifted in his seat. "I have to say, we just received a transmission from Steranko ourselves. It didn't say anything about colonization."

"Now, now, Captain," Kirby said. "You're starting to sound like Gruenwald."

"And you say he was charged with mutiny?"

"It shames me to admit it. He's a discredit to his race."

"So tell me, Commander," Morrison said. "What was the nature of Gruenwald's charges?"

"He undermined my authority while I tried to make peace on Sol 3."

"So you've made contact with the natives?"

"Naturally," Kirby said. "One of them ate my away team. And my officer Sprang is AWOL."

"And after this native...ate your men, you tried to negotiate?"

Kirby chuckled. "Not with the dinosaur, naturally. But with the cavemen, yes."

"I see," Captain Morrison said. "And what are these cavemen like?"

"Savages," the Commander said. "Except perhaps for Crow. I'm confident he'll come around when he's released from the brig."

"Wait a minute," Ellis said. "You've got a native aboard your ship?"

"Two of them, if you count the cow," Commander Kirby said.

It was getting hard to keep up.

"I'd like to speak to this 'Crow,' Commander," Captain Morrison said.

"Of course. I'll also send a tape along I used to learn his language."

"Beggin' your pardon," McFarlane said, "but I don't agree with the Commander. I fear Cro may have been compromised by those traitors Gruenwald and Bagley."

Excellent, Captain Morrison thought. He liked these cavemen already.

"So what do we do now?" Ellis asked, glad to be back on the bridge.

"We humor them," Morrison said. "I can handle a crackpot clone. It's McFarlane we have to watch. Hitch, is this 'Crow' aboard yet?"

"I have to get a fix on him, sir. Their teleport bay is broken, so I'm doing this the hard way."

"Captain, I have an idea."

"Share it with us, Neary."

"I've been thinking about this Ensign Sprang that Kirby stranded on Earth. I may have a way to find him."

"How?"

"Totleben, sir," Neary said. "This planet is pre-industrial, right? They don't have synthesized metal. And totleben is a synthetic metal."

"I'm with you so far."

"Our translators and Chameleon 3000's are both made of totleben. So if Sprang's wearing either one of them, we could track him down that way."

"How?" Captain Morrison said.

"We could convert a short-range scanner into a mineral detector. If we find any trace of totleben, it's got to be Ensign Sprang."

"I like it," Morrison said.

"Captain, Crow's ready to beam aboard."

"Send him right here, Hitch. I don't feel like going out of my way."

"Aye, sir. Here he comes."

The air in front of Morrison blurred. Cro's scream formed along with his body. Their guest wailed like a banshee even after he was whole.

"First time, huh?" Morrison said in caveman, having listened to Grell's English tape. Cro stared mutely at his hands.

"I'm Captain Morrison."

The room spun. "Where am I?"

"You're aboard the bridge of the *Giffen*. We just arrived on earth. Didn't Kirby tell you where you were going?"

"Just, 'no sudden moves,'" Cro said. He smiled before his eyes rolled back and everything went black.

Cro came to his senses lying on the conference room floor. Morrison was the only squid with him.

"What happened?" Cro said.

"You fainted."

"No, before that." Cro got to this feet.

"We call it teleportation."

"Tell a poor tation?"

"Your physical form was broken down and reassembled here."

"Oh." Cro felt for the back of a chair. "Let's not do that again."

"Can I get you something?"

"A glass of water?"

"Here you go," Morrison said.

"Your water tastes funny."

"It's bottled. Listen, Crow, you seem like a reasonable..."

"Human?"

"...so let me get right to the point. The man who's in charge of the ship you're on is, how should I put this..."

"Insane?"

"Right." Morrison grinned. "So I was looking for someone on the inside who could help me save your people."

"I'd like to," Cro said. "But I don't see how I can help if Kirby keeps me locked up."

"I was under the impression that Kirby liked you."

"He almost shot me twice."

"Do you know Gruenwald?" Morrison said.

"Gruenwald?" Cro said. "Yeah. He's one of the, uh, aliens I'm trapped in that room with."

"Can you give a message to him?"

"Not really," Cro said. "They took away those things that make us understand each other, so now when I try to talk to them, I just hear" he mimicked their shrieks.

"I see," Captain Morrison said. "Is there anyone on the outside you can trust?"

Cro thought it over. "There's Grell."

"Grell? I don't think I've heard of him."

"He's a janitor."

"Excuse me, sir," Ellis said at the door.

"Can this wait? I'm talking to Crow."

"I don't think so, sir."

"What is it?" Morrison said.

"Do you remember that meteor shower the first time that we jumped?"

"Of course I do."

"Well I just picked it up on my long-range scanner," First Mate Ellis said. "It looks like it's following us."

"Okay," Morrison said, "so we stay on Sol 3 till it's passed."

"That's the problem. This planet we're on? It's kind of in the way."

At least Cro knew what was happening the next time he teleported. But no one had bothered to tell his stomach.

"Good lord, man!" Kirby said. "You look ill!"

"Captain Morrison wants you to call him," Cro told the Commander. "Now can I be excused?"

"Nonsense. You've not been properly debriefed." Cro threw up on Kirby's chair.

"McFarlane, take him back to his cell. Then find that bloody janitor."

Kirby had Ditko hail the *Giffen* while Cro was led away.

"Hello, Commander," Morrison said. "Did Crow get back okay?"

"He appears to be a bit squeamish."

"Teleportation doesn't agree with him. Anyway, I'm glad you called. Have you checked your long-range scanners lately?"

"Good lord! Steranko's gone?"

"Ah, no," Morrison said. "I was referring to the mass of objects near this planet's moon."

"Ditko, bring up that quadrant, will you?"

"Right away, Commander." Ditko cycled through empty screens until he said, "oh my."

"What is it?"

"Meteors, sir."

"We've seen this storm first-hand. Just one of these rocks could leave a crater ten times the size of your ship."

"Well then," Kirby told Morrison, "it appears our course is clear."

"I'm glad to hear that, Commander."

"We let these meteors pummel this planet while we lie low in space."

"But the humans would suffer horribly."

"They're savages, Morrison. SAVAGES!" The Commander foamed at the mouth.

"Right," Morrison said. "You know what? I'm getting another call. I'll have to get back to you, then."

"Commander?" Ditko said meekly as the hailing channel closed.

"What is it now?" Kirby said.

"We're not really going to do it, are we? Let Cro's people die?"

"What would you have me do, Ditko? Use the *Eisner* as an ark?" Kirby chuckled at the thought.

"It just seems cruel, that's all."

"Gibbons, what are your thoughts on this?"

"I don't know how to answer that, sir. This isn't the kind of thing I dealt with when I was fixing doors."

"Chin up, men. We won't be beat by a spot of space debris."

But there seemed no point to Ditkoville if it was one big crater.

"Who thought that went well?" Morrison asked his crew. "Put your hand down, Hitch."

"Why don't we just leave Kirby here, grab some cows, and go home?"

"First off, Ellis, we're not going anywhere until we free Gruenwald. Second, I don't like the idea of leaving Cro's people behind."

"We don't know what will happen. The meteors could miss this continent or burn up in reentry."

"That's true," Morrison said. "But the way this mission's going so far, who thinks we'll get lucky?"

Even Hitch kept his hand down.

"Hail the *Eisner*," Morrison said. "I want to meet with Crow. Neary, how's your project coming?"

"I think I've found him, sir. I'm picking up some totleben metal in the village below."

"Beam him up then," Morrison said. "It's time we saved this squid."

But what materialized a minute later looked like a small version of Cro. At least he wasn't screaming. He just backed away in fear. Morrison looked the caveboy over.

"Hello. What have we here?"

Minutes earlier, Shirt was playing quietly in his room. He heard a sound at his window and stuck his head out to investigate. There was an ape and an alien poking out of the shrubbery.

"You not supposed to be here!"

"I tried to stop him," Sprang told the boy. "He doesn't listen to me."

"You have to go back now," Shirt said in ape. "Mom no can see you here."

"Ooo ooo ooo eee ahh."

"Shirt, why you in window?" Rock said from the kitchen. She waved a plate. "Come eat."

"Ooo oo ooo!"

"What that?"

"That am long tail," Shirt said, thinking quick.

"Why am it by window?"

"Maybe it smell food," Shirt said.

"Shirt no play with long tail," Rock said. "Me hear him bite can make you sick."

"Him gone now, mom!" Shirt called. Sprang tried to pull Larry away, but the ape had his mind set on food.

"Me make sure him gone," Rock said as she approached the window. She froze when her son turned transparent.

"Shirt!"

Outside, Larry shrieked.

"Come on," Sprang said, tugging the ape. Then Rock leaned out the window. She locked eyes with the alien. The same one who had made It vanish.

"*You.*"

Larry and Sprang grinned sheepishly. And then they ran for their lives.

"Neary, I have to tell you, this doesn't look like a Sprang to me."

"But he's wearing a translator, sir."

"I see that," Morrison said. He bent down to look Shirt in the eye. "Can you understand me?"

Shirt looked around, nervous, but nodded slowly.

"What's your name?"

"Shirt."

"Shirt, I'm Captain Morrison. Do you know where you are?"

"In bowl."

Morrison shared a smile with Ellis. "That's right," he said. "In bowl. And do you know why we brought you here?"

"So you can make Shirt a snake-legs, too?"

"No, Shirt," Captain Morrison said. "We're not going to hurt you."

"But you make It a snake god," Shirt said.

"What did we make a snake god?"

"It."

"It what?" Morrison said.

"Excuse me, sir," Ellis said. "I think It's a person."

"What's a person?"

"Not What, sir. It."

"Bugger me," Morrison said. He turned back to the boy. "Shirt, is It a friend of yours?"

"It am friend," Shirt said. "First him am a caveboy but then him turn into snake."

"I see," Morrison said. "Do you know where It is now?"

"Him and Larry come get food before me go in bowl."

"Neary, are you picking up life forms near the spot you beamed up Shirt?"

Neary worked his instruments. "I'm reading three of them, sir."

"Can you tell me if one of them has four legs?"

"Sorry, sir," Neary said.

"Pick one," Morrison said. "Shirt, I need you to stand over here. We're going to find your friend. Ellis, Hitch. Set your phasers on stun in case Neary surprises us."

Sure enough, what materialized next was a hyperactive ape. Larry charged but was promptly stunned.

"Neary."

"Sorry, sir."

Another form took shape next to Larry. This one was a squid. He was in duck-and-cover mode until he realized the screaming had stopped. Morrison smirked at the cowardly entrance.

"You must be Sprang."

Cro had a surprise waiting back in his cell.

"Where were you?" Gruenwald said.

"You learned English."

"I took a nap while you were gone and listened to this tape."

"I met with Captain Morrison," Cro said.

"Morrison's here? We're saved."

"He said that there's a meteor shower that could destroy the Earth."

"Hey, some of us don't understand English," Bagley snidely shrieked. Gruenwald ignored him.

"Does Kirby know?"

"He's excited about it," Cro said.

Gruenwald felt the walls of their cell. "We've got to get out of here."

At which point Cro disappeared. The next thing he knew he materialized on the bridge of the *Giffen*.

"Would you warn me before you do that?" Cro snapped.

"Sorry," Morrison said.

Cro saw Larry slumped in a corner. "What happened to him?"

"We shot him."

"Huh," Cro said. "He's used to it." He noticed another guest. "Shirt!"

"You two know each other?" Morrison said.

"Sure. I've been to his house."

"Do you remember me?" Sprang asked.

"How do I know that voice?"

"I'm It," Sprang said.

"Wait," Cro said. "The caveboy?"

"I was incognito."

"No kidding!" Cro beamed. "That was you?"

"It's a small world after all," Morrison said. "Now let's get down to business."

CHAPTER FIFTEEN

Dog stood with his men on the outskirts of town, squinting at the cliff. They knew the sentry was up there, but the bright morning sun hurt their eyes.

"Me think him wave right arm," Smash said, using his hand as a visor.

"Am sure?" Dog said.

"Me sure," Smash nodded.

"Then that mean guard see fire."

"Me thought left arm mean fire," Ugh said.

"Left arm mean big lizard."

"Two arms mean big lizard," Smash said, correcting his chief.

"Then what do left arm mean?" Dog said.

The cavemen scratched their heads.

The villagers were expecting one of the catastrophes they had prepared for. But the elders were too busy squabbling over what the signal meant.

"Am fire," Dog said.

"Am swamp people."

"Am big lizard," Ugh insisted.

"At least big cloud block out sun."

They all agreed on that. In fact, the shadow had grown quite large. At which point, Ugh looked up.

"Uh-oh," he said.

The early warning detection system had no signal for flying bowls. The lookout had not been waving so much as pointing at the sky.

"Snake gods," Chief Dog said. The *Giffen* hovered overhead.

"What do now?"

"Me no am afraid. Them scared of pointy sticks." Dog realized he only had a club. "Ugh, give me stick."

"Me need it for fight," Ugh said. "What if snake gods have boy?"

"If them have Shirt, then Rock will fight."

Ugh handed Dog his spear.

The villagers gathered around their chief, expecting the big bowl to land. They were thrown a bit when the air shimmered and Cro formed out of it. He stood directly beneath the *Giffen*, a few yards from the Lake People, and seemed a bit preoccupied with his peculiar-looking belt.

"People of Lake Village," Cro said. His microphone wasn't on.

"Sorry," Morrison said in his earpiece. "Take it from the top."

"People of Lake Village," Cro said. This time his voice thundered, amplified by a voice modulator and piped through the *Giffen's* speakers. "I come on behalf of the snake gods with a message for you all."

"Good," Captain Morrison coached in Cro's ear. "They're not throwing anything yet."

"You have made the snake gods angry," Cro boomed, "by attacking their mighty chief. As punishment, they have decided to destroy all of your homes."

"Why Crow talk so loud?" Dog said. "And how him grow from air?"

"The snake gods gave me great power," Cro's stomach-rumbling voice replied.

"Me think pointy sticks scare snake gods, so them send Crow instead."

"Your words make the snake gods angry," Cro warned.

"Them no hurt us," Dog said.

"Perhaps you need a lesson," Cro said. "Behold the snake gods' wrath."

"What am wrath?" Dog said.

"It's anger."

"Then why use stupid word?"

Cro sighed.

"Just watch, okay?"

Cro gestured dramatically. Nothing came of it.

"Stall them," Morrison said. "We have to make sure the target's empty."

"Snake gods' wrath am not so bad," Dog said. His people laughed. Then the big bowl spat a ray of light that blew up one of their huts.

"Now you see the snake gods' power," Cro roared as the townspeople gasped. "The rest of your village will be destroyed by fire from the sky." Cro paused to let the fear set in. Plus, he was enjoying himself. It was Smash's wife, Petal, who broke down first.

"Save us," she begged from the crowd.

"The snake gods will not save your homes," Cro said. "But they may spare your lives." The *Giffen's* speaker system squeaked. Cro and the villagers winced.

"Keep going," Morrison said.

"The snake gods will spare anyone who comes to live in their bowl."

The villagers were mulling it over. "Am them good cooks?" one asked.

"Real good," Cro replied. He could hear a few pleased *ooh's*.

"Big bowl no am home," Dog said, hushing the congregation. "This am home. No leave."

"But snake gods say us must go," a caveman said from the crowd.

"Me am chief, not snake gods," Dog said. "Me say us stay here."

"But you'll die here," Cro said, his voice breaking. The amplifier squealed again. Dog held his spear over his head to calm his people down.

"You come here and make big noise. Hurt ears with lights and tricks. But me say you am enemy, so you am one must die." Dog took a few steps forward and hurled his spear with brutish force. The crowd watched in dread anticipation as it flew straight for Cro's heart. Cro reached for a switch on his belt and prayed the gizmo worked. The spear halted and fell to the ground two feet in front of him. Smash made the most insightful comment.

"Pointy stick no hurt."

Cro bent down to pick up the spear. His force field got in the way. He flipped it off, picked up the shaft, and snapped it over his knee.

"Me think me change mind," Dog said. "Big bowl sound okay."

Cro beamed back aboard the bridge of the *Giffen*. The crew met him with applause.

"Well done," Morrison said.

"Thanks." Cro removed his force field belt. "I'm glad that this thing worked."

"So am I. I kind of whipped it together. So Dog's addressing his people?"

"He's having a problem grasping why he can't come aboard right away."

"We're drawing too much attention already," Captain Morrison said.

"Incoming message, sir," Ellis said.

"Speak of the devil." Morrison turned to face the screen. "Hello, Commander."

"Captain," Kirby's image said.

"I take it you'd like some answers."

"Quite. I saw that display just now. Why wasn't I informed?"

"I thought I was within my rights, Commander. We were gathering intelligence."

"We already attempted to use Crow for that. Those savages punctured my leg."

"I wasn't aware of that," Morrison said. "But Crow's a valuable asset. With your permission, I'd like to keep him under my command."

"Hmmm." Kirby narrowed his eyes. "I don't see how much use he can be. We'll deal with those savages soon enough."

"But there's more of them than we thought. Cro just informed me of another tribe that lives on the edge of the swamp."

The Commander arched an antenna. "I see your interrogation has unearthed new information."

"Yes, sir," Morrison said. "We'll be sending Crow to these Swamp People as soon as we're done here. Also, I'd like permission to beam a few supplies to your ship."

"Supplies?" Kirby said. "Whatever for?"

"We've got a few crates of Busiek plants. I understand you're low. I'd also like to see if I can fix your teleport bay."

"Quite generous of you, Captain. Carry on." Kirby blinked off the screen. Captain Morrison turned to Cro.

"Ready for the matinee?"

Rock picked quite the morning to go for a walk alone in the woods. But she had already lost her foster son, It. She could not bear losing Shirt, too. Since Shirt had literally disappeared she had followed the tracks by his window, tracing them back to the woodsy retreat where Rex had eaten Duck. Rock found a scrap of Duck's clothing and was relieved it wasn't Shirt's. She spun around when the leaves rustled. Big Teeth showed himself.

Rex had been out for breakfast. He could not believe his luck. Another of the hairy people had come to the woods alone. This one had his back to him, and he decided to have some fun. Thinking he would scare his snack Rex bent down, pounced, and roared.

Rock whirled around and found herself facing the legendary beast. She swung her club as Rex was still rumbling, cutting him off mid-roar. Rex's head twisted a quarter turn. The rest of his body didn't, and his last conscious feeling was equally split between pain and embarrassment.

Rock watched Big Teeth's monstrous noggin come to rest on the ground. She was more irritated than anything else. He'd delayed her search for Shirt.

She was more irate when she got back to town and heard about what she'd missed.

McFarlane and Kirby stood at attention in the *Eisner's* teleport bay. Morrison and Neary had just beamed aboard, followed by two wooden crates. Each of them was identical, about the mass of a compacted squid. Kirby rapped on the lid of one of them.

"Is this all of them?" he asked.

"Yes, Commander," Morrison said.

Kirby nudged the crate. "Heavy bugger."

"It has most of my tools."

"So these must have the Busiek plants."

"That's right," Morrison said. "If you show Neary the way to your storage room, he'll help unpack the jars."

"McFarlane, give him a hand, will you? Then report back to the bridge."

"Aye, sir," McFarlane said. He and Neary loaded the crate on a hovering platform and followed it out the door.

"I'll let you get on with your work then, Captain. Call if you need anything." The door hissed behind the Commander. Morrison pried the lid off his crate. A pair of eyeballs poked out from an assortment of nuts and bolts.

"About time," Hitch said as his captain unpacked him.

"You have everything?" Morrison asked.

Hitch patted his bulky backpack. "Just make sure I have enough time."

"Don't worry," Morrison said. "I can run dozens of diagnostic tests that won't do a bloody thing."

Lightle hunched over a glass of cold milk at his desk in engineering. He jumped when he turned around.

"Ensign Lightle," Kirby said.

"I swear I didn't do it!"

"Do what?"

"Err, nothing," Lightle said. "I thought you were somebody else."

Kirby slithered across Lightle's lab and found a refrigerator. He opened it and removed one of its many vials of two percent milk.

"I can explain that," Lightle said.

"Hoarding supplies?" Kirby asked.

"I was going to share those with the crew."

"Indeed," the Commander said. He replaced the beverage on the shelf.

"Your secret's safe with me. I understand you've become somewhat of an authority on these cows."

"It's more of a hobby, really..."

"No need to be humble," Kirby said.

"Well," Lightle said, "I still think they're the answer to our problem."

"As do I," Kirby said. "Which brings me to the reason why I'm here. I have an assignment for you."

McFarlane and Neary barely spoke on their way to the *Eisner's* pantry, but as they unloaded the Busiek plants, McFarlane sprung his question.

"So, what do ye think of our cap'n?"

"He's...got quite the presence," Neary said, placing a jar in the refrigerator.

"You think he's mad, don't ye now?"

"Why would I think that?"

"I understand," McFarlane said. "Ye don't know me or trust me. But I'm out for the good of Steranko."

"Is that so?" Neary said.

"Aye. So I'm gonna tell ye somethin' that maybe I shouldn't. Do with it what ye will."

"Look, there's no need to be so dramatic. We're all on the same team, right?"

"Then I guess I shouldna had Gruenwald and Bagley gum up the teleport bay."

Neary looked McFarlane in the eye. He tried to decipher his game. It was obvious McFarlane was playing both sides, but not which one he was on.

"Why would you do that?" Neary said, stacking another jar.

"I was the only one left from our first away team. I didna want to go back."

"That sounds like mutiny," Neary said.

"Self-preservation, I call it."

"By telling me this, I'm obligated to report you to Captain Morrison."

"Aye, ye do that," McFarlane said. "Then tell me what ye've really got planned."

Bagley eyed Gruenwald's protein paste. "Are you gonna finish that?"

"Go ahead."

Bagley took his bowl. "This prison food isn't bad."

"It's the same thing we've had since we left Steranko."

"Nah, I think they flavor it here."

The quarantine bay door opened. Grell entered with his cleaning supplies. He took a look to either side and spoke into his pin.

"All clear."

"Why are you whispering?" Bagley said.

A screw bounced off of his head. The squid looked up and saw a strange face peer through the overhead vent.

"Who are you?" Gruenwald said.

"Keep it down." Three more screws plinked to the floor. Hitch removed a ceiling panel and set up a motorized winch. But instead of hoisting the prisoners up, he lowered himself to them.

"What are you doing?"

"You go first." Hitch attached the cable to Gruenwald. He pressed a button on the remote, and Gruenwald was winched through the ceiling. Bagley followed while Hitch unpacked his duffel bag below.

"Come on," Bagley said.

"I have to cover our tracks first." Hitch placed two small metal devices at intervals on the floor.

"Holovid projectors?" Gruenwald said.

"AIB's," Hitch told him.

"What does that stand for?"

Hitch flipped the switch on the first projector. Out popped a life-sized Gruenwald.

"It's just a hologram," Gruenwald said.

Virtual Gruenwald looked up at the real one. "Somebody bring me a mirror. Do I really look that bad?"

"Gruenwald," Hitch said, "meet AIB Gruenwald."

"Is that what we're calling us?" the AIB said.

"Artificially Intelligent Beings. What's wrong with that?" Hitch said.

"It makes us sound fake."

"You are fake," Hitch told it.

"Can we get on with it?" the real Gruenwald said.

"Oh, looks who thinks he's so superior just because he's solid."

Hitch activated the Bagley hologram.

"What's going on?" it said.

"Those two bozos are breaking out and leaving us behind."

AIB Bagley looked up at the real one, then out at his cell. "That stinks."

"It's what you were programmed for," Hitch said.

"In that case, I'm shutting me off."

"Good luck with that," AIB Gruenwald said. "You can't touch anything."

"I love these guys," the real Bagley said.

"Hurry up," Grell said by the door. "We won't be alone forever."

"What if they tell Kirby?" Gruenwald asked.

"They're programmed not to," Hitch said.

"What if they see the projectors, then?"

"Their tentacles cover them up."

"Would you stop talking about us like we're not standing right here?"

"Sorry," Hitch told the bogus Bagley.

"Holograms have feelings, too."

Neary rendezvoused with Morrison in the *Eisner's* teleport bay. Neary set his crate aside.

"How'd it go?" Morrison said.

"McFarlane's onto us."

"That dodgy squid. What did he say?"

"He said he was the one who had Gruenwald and Bagley sabotage the teleport bay."

"What did you say to that?"

"I told him I'd have to report it to you," Neary said.

"And so you did."

"Do we tell the Commander?"

"And have him throw McFarlane in the cell with the AIB's?"

"Good point." Neary mulled it over. "I could knock him out and take his place with a Chameleon 3000."

"Can you do his accent?" Morrison said. Neary cleared his throat.

"Ach, now, cap'n, surely it can't be that tricky, now."

"That's woeful."

"So we leave him alone, then."

"We'll be gone soon enough," Morrison said. They heard a muffled sound overhead.

"Psst. Is it safe?"

"It took you long enough."

"We crawled through half the ship," Hitch said, lowering himself to the floor. The two escaped squid followed.

"Glad you could make it," Gruenwald told Morrison, shaking his old friend's hand.

"Thanks. Now pick a crate."

"Traveling in style, huh?" Gruenwald said, squeezing into a box. Bagley did the same.

"What about me?" Hitch said.

The color drained from Morrison's face. "Brilliant. Who counted the boxes?"

"I have to go the same way I came," Hitch said. "Kirby doesn't know that I'm here."

"Share one with Bagley," Morrison said. Bagley shook his head.

"There's not enough room. And I don't want my molecules getting scrambled with his."

"That's an old wives' tale," Hitch told Bagley, who closed his crate's lid.

"Get your own."

"I'm afraid there's no other choice," Captain Morrison told Hitch. "You have to stay here for now."

"Just teleport me without a box."

"Can't do it," Morrison said. "They're expecting us to do four transfers. They'd know if we did five."

"Then make Neary stay. Or one of them. This isn't my ship."

"You know your way around in the vents. It's only for a day."

"I'm claustrophobic."

Morrison smirked. "You came here packed in a box."

"All right," Hitch sighed. He hoisted himself back up through the ceiling and closed the panel behind him.

The *Giffen's* hangar was being transformed into a caveman village. The floor was covered with grass and dirt beamed up from remote locations. Trees were anchored with steel-enforced trunks beneath a hologram sky. And a dozen squid struggled with carpentry as another hut collapsed.

"How's it coming?" Morrison asked Ellis, surveying the work.

"We can't get the houses right."

"I see that," Morrison said. "I'll work up some schematics."

"How'd it go on Kirby's ship?"

"Brilliant," Morrison said. "Until we botched the sodding crates and had to leave Hitch behind. How about you? Did Crow convince these Swamp People to come aboard?"

"He has history with their chief," Ellis said. "But they were impressed when we blew up their hut."

"Good," Captain Morrison said. "I want this ready for guests by sundown."

"Aren't we going to a lot of trouble just to make them feel at home?"

"I think it's in both our interests to try and keep Crow's people calm. And that reminds me," Morrison said. "I want clubs and spears checked at the door."

"All right," Ellis said. "Just don't make me say I told you so when Kirby shoots us down."

Commander Kirby checked on his prisoners as the sun set behind Earth.

"Look who's here. It's Commander Clone!" the bogus Bagley said.

"Did you come here to surrender?" AIB Gruenwald said.

"Behave yourselves!" Kirby bellowed. Betty mooed from her cell next door.

"Your girlfriend wants out," the fake Bagley teased.

"Enough!" Kirby said. "You soldiers are a bloody disgrace to Steranko. I've half a mind to cut off your meals."

"He's got half a mind, all right."

"We didn't eat dinner anyway," AIB Gruenwald said.

"Intolerable!" Kirby said. The rowdy holograms whooped it up as Kirby slithered away.

Betty sighed. If only the Commander had been wearing his translator.

Chief Dog went to sleep all snug in his hut, with his son Fight snoring beside him. When Dog felt something tingle, he woke up in a foreign land.

He was lying in the grass. At first he thought he sleepwalked again. But the village didn't look right. It was close, but the huts were half-finished. The stars didn't look right, either. They seemed to be closer, somehow. And the whole place had a detached sound, a distant, foreign hum.

Instinctively, Dog dug in the grass. He flinched at what he found. A hard, shiny surface just under the dirt. He scrambled to his feet. He didn't see a nearby shrubbery turn into a door.

"Dog!" Cro said, hurrying into the hangar. "It's okay. It's me."

"Crow?" the bewildered caveman said.

"It's me. You're in the bowl."

Dog's dull eyes took in his surroundings. "This no look like bowl."

"The snake gods made it look like home."

"It no smell as bad," Dog said. "Where am Fight and other caveman?"

"They'll all be here soon," Cro said. "Why don't you try to get some sleep?" The air glittered beside them. Fight appeared, still snoring.

"Where boy come from?" Dog said.

"The snake gods' power brought him here."

"How come him no move? Him dead?"

"He's sleeping," Cro said, adding under his voice, "like you were supposed to be."

Ugh was beamed up next. The caveman village was growing.

Morrison rubbed his antenna's eyes. He leaned over Ellis' station. "How many aboard?"

"Thirty-five," First Mate Ellis said. "We're almost halfway there."

"Let me know if there's any sign of activity aboard the *Eisner*," Morrison said.

"Are we beaming up any animals?" Neary asked. "Besides the cows, I mean."

"Six dozen humans are more than enough. How's Crow holding up?"

"Still on crowd control," Ellis said. "He seems to have things under control."

"We finish relocating his town tonight. Tomorrow we work on the Swamp People."

"That may be cutting it tight," Neary said.

"Why do you say that?"

"The meteor shower is closing in fast. It may hit earth by then."

"I thought you said we had two days," Captain Morrison scowled.

"How am I supposed to know how long it takes a rock to fly through space?"

"Stone me," Morrison said. "Ellis, keep up the teleports. I have to make a call."

The *Eisner's* ventilation shafts were not designed for comfort. Hitch tossed and turned in his hiding place, but could not get to sleep. His chest pin beeped. He tapped it.

"Captain?"

"How are you?" Morrison said.

"Just wishing I had a pillow, sir."

"I don't want to stay on this channel too long. Can you make it there another day?"

"I guess so, sir," Hitch said.

"I want you to be my eyes and ears. Things are about to get hairy."

"Okay," Hitch said. "But I get your quarters for a week when I get back to the ship."

"Fair enough. Call me first thing in the morning," Morrison said.

Hitch closed his eyes in the foreign craft and listened to it hum.

CHAPTER SIXTEEN

Rex was out prowling at the crack of dawn. He inventoried his wounds. First an axe, then a spear, to his head. Then the snake-legs shot off his arm. But nothing was more of a pride remover than being knocked out by the female. He followed Rock's scent back to her village, looking for payback.

But there was no one home. Normally if he strolled into town, there'd be spears flying everywhere. But this morning, not so much as a peep. *That's funny*, Rex thought. He decided to hike to the swamp village to try his luck there.

Morrison was bleary-eyed as he slumped in his captain's chair. He spent the night supervising the transfer of the Lake People onto his ship and was in no mood for a page from Ellis.

"Sir, you'd better come down here. The natives are getting restless."

He walked into pandemonium in the caveman reservation. There were humans on top of the unfinished huts and hanging from the trees, digging up grass and flinging gooey glops of protein paste.

"What's the meaning of this?" Morrison barked in English.

"Where am snake god chief?" Dog said.

"I am the chief," Morrison said.

"You no chief me see last time."

Morrison remembered how Dog had had an ill-fated meeting with Kirby. "The chief you talked to last time is from a different snake god tribe. I am the chief of this village."

"Then me want gooder food," Dog said.

"I gave you the same food the snake gods eat."

"Then let snake gods eat mush. Me want roast oink or burnt fuzzy-tail."

"I'll see what I can do," Morrison said.

"And how come us no can go in huts? Me want to sleep in bed."

"The huts should be done by tonight, Chief Dog. Now will you calm your people down?"

Dog waved his hands, unconcerned by the chaos. "Them just cranky," he said.

For the first time since he left Steranko, Morrison wished he was home.

"Thomas?" King Stanley said, wandering out of his room.

"Hello, your highness." Thomas struggled to remove himself from his boss' throne.

"I see you fixed the power problem that's plagued the populace."

"Actually, it's daylight, sir."

"Ah. So the power's still out."

"I'm afraid so, sir," Thomas said.

"A world left wanting by waning wattage!"

"Very poetically put." Thomas freed himself from the throne. "Can I help you back to your room?"

King Stanley collected his thoughts.

"Say, is that my crown you're wearing?"

"I don't believe so, sir."

"And do you hear those volatile voices?"

"It's only a demonstration, your highness. I was just going to check on them."

"Be careful, Thomas!" King Stanley said. "These times are ripe for rampant rebellion!"

Thomas escorted him back to his room and headed for the front gate.

The smattering of squid outside the palace had swelled into a mob. There were placards that read DON'T KEEP ME IN THE DARK and POWER TO THE PEOPLE, squids with bullhorns leading chants and flyers denouncing King Stanley. Raney the guard intercepted Thomas.

"Good to see you, sir. Can you address the mob again? They've gotten a bit cheeky."

"There were only a handful before," Thomas said.

"They've gotten organized."

"Do they have a leader?"

"There he is," Raney said. Thomas did a double take when he saw

"Grandpa Shuster?"

"He's had them worked up since morning. The old codger."

Thomas approached the gate. Grandpa Shuster went to meet him.

"What are you doing here?" Thomas said.

"I'm tired of being cooped up with your grandma."

"You could have called," Thomas said.

"No, I couldn't. The lines are still down."

"You're embarrassing me," Thomas told Grandpa. "Can we talk about this inside?"

"I haven't seen you in years," Grandpa said.

"I'm sorry. I've been busy."

"Look, it's the king!" a protester shouted.

"I'm not the king," Thomas said.

"You look like him."

"I assure you, I'm not."

"Then why are you wearing his crown?"

"Looks like somebody's gotten too big for his britches," Grandpa Shuster said.

"Good people, please," Thomas told the crowd. "Go back to your homes."

"First, you have to read our demands." Grandpa Shuster produced a scroll. Thomas unrolled it, eyed Grandpa warily, and began to read.

"One. Restore the planet's power. That's reasonable," Thomas said. "Two. Provide us with discs of all the holovids we missed." He looked up at the crowd. "Oh, come on."

"Just the good ones," someone said.

"Like my soaps," another squid added.

"And edit out the commercials."

"I can't do that," Thomas said.

"Then we want to elect a new king," Grandpa said.

"You didn't elect this one."

"Can we at least speak to the king?" someone said.

"The king is indisposed."

"I bet he killed him!" a woman cried.

"Let's storm the castle!"

The crowd roared.

"All right, I'll get him," Thomas said. He figure they deserved each other.

Cro, Shirt and Larry were out for a stroll in the *Giffen's* caveman village. The natives had calmed after eating a batch of doctored protein paste. It was laced with a mild meat flavor and enough sedative to knock out a rhino. Even Rock was feeling mellow. She waved dopily at her son.

"So how do you like it here?" Cro asked Shirt, who had passed on the tainted paste.

"Am okay," the boy said. "But why am Fight here, too?"

"Dog's boy? Is he bothering you?"

"No," Shirt said. "Him leave me alone. No want him head bashed in." Larry patted his human friend. Shirt was still the only one that he would listen to, and even though Shirt kept his translator on he was beginning to learn ape on his own.

"Don't worry," Cro said. "You won't have to share a hut with Fight."

"Me just glad snake gods am friends," Shirt said as his tribesman dozed off.

"Me too," Cro said. Though he knew from experience that not all of the 'snake-gods' were.

Chief Snake slept in a few hours despite the excitement in the swamp. His thoughts raced to the day before when the big bowl dropped from the sky. Snake was upset that his old rival Crow had been chosen to speak for the snake gods. He feared Crow would take his people aboard and leave him behind, though Cro assured him the snake gods would have room for everyone. Still, Snake felt a strange unease as he walked out of his hut.

It was 90 degrees and dry that day, with an 80 percent chance of panic. When Big Teeth came roaring into town, that pushed things over the top. "Us anger snake gods!" a cavewoman screamed. Snake had the same idea.

The Swamp Village wasn't empty like the one across the lake. But Rex's careful reconnaissance showed that there weren't many warriors around. He knew nothing of the monkey fever that wiped out most of the town but was about to make the most of it when a flying green bowl arrived.

That's new, Rex thought as the *Giffen* uncloaked and hovered over him. He deferred to its superior size and skulked back into the swamp.

"Should we fire, sir?" Ellis asked from his station, tracking the beast from above.

"It appears we drove him off." Morrison asked Cro, "friend of yours?"

"That would be Big Teeth."

"Lovely fellow."

"Not up close," Cro said.

"Well, his interference has made your people scamper all over the swamp. We'll have a devil of a time getting teleport fixes." Morrison turned to his crew. "Ellis, how long till the meteors strike?"

"Look out the viewport, sir."

There were scores of shadows against the sun.

"Blimey," Morrison said. The bridge's hailing frequency beeped.

"It's the *Eisner*, sir," Ellis said.

"Captain," Commander Kirby said, "what the devil is going on?"

"We've had a bit of an incident involving the Swamp People," Morrison said.

"Do you require our aid?"

"No thank you, Commander."

"It's also come to my attention that Crow's village is abandoned. Not a bloody savage in sight."

"Yes, we noticed that ourselves," Captain Morrison said. "But Crow tells me it's normal."

"Is that him behind you?" Kirby said. "Let me speak to the lad."

Cro took his place on center screen. "Hello, Commander."

"Now what's this about your people leaving? I thought you had them whipped into shape."

"I'm afraid I may have scared them too much," Cro said. "They're highly nomadic, you see. Whenever they think they're in danger, they'll just find a new home overnight."

"Hmmm," Kirby said. "No matter. They won't get far enough. I only wish I could see those savages' faces when they're maimed by meteors."

"Uh, right on," Cro said.

"Captain Morrison, I trust you'll be joining us on the far side of the planet?"

"We're having some issues with our starboard thruster. I'd like to address that first."

"And how goes your quest for cows?"

"Not too well, I'm afraid to say." He wasn't lying about that part.

"There'll be ample time to build a bovine bulwark," Kirby said. "Now, join me for tea when we rendezvous. We'll watch the storm together."

"Sounds delightful," Morrison said. "We'll be there as soon as we can."

"And be a good chap and bring Crow along," the Commander said. "I'd like his thoughts on subjugating Sol 3's sole survivors."

"I'm sure he's looking forward to it."

"It's a historic day, Morrison. We'll show these savages how advanced we are if we have to crush every last one of them. Now if you'll excuse me, I have a pressing engagement elsewhere," Kirby said.

Morrison turned away from the screen once Kirby signed off.

"Neary, plot a course for Steranko. And check your figures this time. Ellis, I want you to comb the swamp. Save everyone you can."

"What about Hitch?" Ellis said. "He's still on Kirby's ship."

"I'm aware of that," Captain Morrison said. "I'll leave no squid behind."

Rex had a snack on his way from the swamp, but the goat was an appetizer. Then he stumbled upon a triceratops, which were always picking fights. But the beast mistook the axe in Rex's forehead for a horn. He let Rex pass unmolested, like they belonged to a club or something.

As Rex lumbered along the lake, he saw the green bowl depart. Or at least vanish. Either one was good enough for him. Something that big was bound to flush out all kinds of panicky food. Rex figured he'd camp at the edge of the swamp and see what came his way.

Kirby stood by the door to the conference room in full military dress. He nodded solemnly to each of the squid as they filed in. There was Ditko, McFarlane and Gibbons, followed by Lightle, the engineer. Kirby stopped Lightle and took him aside.

"How's our project coming, soldier?"

"It's almost ready to be deployed, sir."

"Excellent. Keep me informed."

Kirby slithered to the head of the table, which was bare except for a projector.

"Within the hour, we strike a blow for the future of Steranko, a planet we've all come to call our home," Commander Kirby said. "But alas, it is no more. Now fate and superior firepower have delivered a new home. Therefore, it is with great pride I present Steranko II."

The projector hummed, beaming Kirby's 3-D vision for the Earth. Its landmasses were color-coded and pocked by smoking craters. The holographic globe spun slowly, allowing each squid a view.

"Sir, I requested a different continent," First Mate Ditko said.

"That's prime real estate I've given you."

"Ah, yes, but it's smoking, sir."

"Consider it a challenge, Ditko," the Commander said.

"And what's with this woeful location you've given me?" McFarlane complained.

"It's surrounded by water."

"It's surrounded by icebergs. Ye'd freeze your bullocks off."

"Have a care, soldier," Kirby said.

"All right, then. Thanks for the glacier."

"Enough!" Kirby pounded his fists on the table. The hologram globe jumped. The squid looked in their Commander's eyes and saw a new level of crazy.

The meteors out the viewport looked close enough for Cro to touch. For all his supposed intellect, he was feeling rather small. Morrison and his officers seemed to take armageddon in stride, but Cro was humbled by his place in the world, even though he was floating above it.

"I've found another one, Captain," Ellis said from his controls.

"How many Swamp People does that make?" Morrison asked.

"Twenty-two."

Morrison snapped Cro from his thoughts. "How many are missing?"

"We counted seventeen yesterday," Cro said. "Plus the ten that were out on the hunt."

The horizon glowed with trailing embers, meteors burned by re-entry. But the largest of them were getting through. "I'm sorry," Morrison said. "We've done all that we can."

"I understand," Cro said.

"Neary, set a course for the *Eisner*."

"What about Kirby, sir?" Ellis said. "We can't fool him much longer."

"I think it may be time for some good old-fashioned sabotage," Morrison said. "I have to go back anyway to smuggle poor Hitch out."

"We should nick their cow, too," Neary said. "We never found one of our own."

"Right." Captain Morrison thought it over. "I'll need a bigger box."

Hitch was aching from his long night in the ventilation shaft. His stomach growled as he followed what he thought was the duct to the bridge. But he took a wrong turn somewhere and wound up back in the quarantine bay. He was about to try calling Morrison when he heard voices below.

"Ah, look who's here," the fake Bagley said. Hitch crawled to the AIBs' cell. He peered through the slats of an air vent but couldn't see who else was there.

"He came for the cow's new orders," the holographic Gruenwald cracked.

"Don't listen to them," Lightle said, carrying a hefty toolbox. He lowered the force field to Betty's cell and unpacked his equipment.

"Mooo," Betty said. Or more accurately, "I have to tell you something."

"I know," Lightle said. "We're going to get you out of here soon enough."

"I'm afraid the cow's been spoken for. She's Kirby's pet," Bagley said. Hitch tried not to laugh from his lookout above. These AIB's were a hoot.

"Moooo," Betty said. Or, "hey genius, those squid next to me aren't real."

"You're awful chatty," Lightle said, fitting the cow with a harness.

"Mooo," she protested.

"Easy, girl. This is going to make your life easier."

"What's going on there?" Gruenwald said.

"He's fitting her for a nice dress."

Lightle ignored the obnoxious squid as McFarlane slithered in. He was carrying a bucket and seemed surprised he had company.

"What are you doing here?" Lightle said.

"I was thirsty," McFarlane said. "Do ye mind if I give it a go?"

"You could at least have brought her flowers."

"Careful," McFarlane told Gruenwald.

"He's a lover, not a fighter."

The AIB's cracked up.

"That's enough out of you two," McFarlane said, snaking toward their cell. Betty mooed furiously.

"You're upsetting your mother."

"That's it," McFarlane said. He rolled up his sleeves, set down his bucket and lowered the squids' force field.

"What are you doing?" Lightle said.

"Cover me," McFarlane said, glaring at Gruenwald and Bagley. But before McFarlane snaked forward, there was a crash from overhead.

The *Eisner's* air vents weren't designed to support the weight of a squid, much less the three squid who trod upon them during the great escape. Hitch came crashing down and fell right through AIB Bagley. The hologram projector was crushed. Bagley switched off like a TV. AIB Gruenwald feigned ignorance as McFarlane stepped into the cell.

"Just let me say, I had no idea Bagley wasn't real."

"Shut your gob," McFarlane said. He reached under Gruenwald's tentacles. With the flick of a switch Gruenwald disappeared, revealing another projector. A part of McFarlane admired how Morrison had strung them along, but the other part was furious. He looked up.

"We've been had."

Cro and Sprang chatted on the bridge of the *Giffen*, catching up on old times.

"So this made you look like a caveman?" Cro said, holding a Chameleon 3000.

"Right. Want to try it on?"

"Sprang, get off the bridge," Captain Morrison interrupted. "We're about to hail the Commander. I don't think you want him seeing you here."

"Excuse me, sir," Ellis said. "We've got the Eisner in view."

Sprang slithered into the hallway. "Open hailing frequencies," Morrison said. "It's time we...bloody hell!"

The *Eisner* was facing them, floating in space. And it had fired two shots.

"Shields!" Morrison screamed.

"Another warning shot?" Ellis said.

They had their answer when the *Giffen* was rocked by the first photon's explosion.

"Status!"

"Direct hit," Neary said. "Shields are almost down."

The second volley hit. The power blinked on and off on the bridge.

"Prepare to fire!" Morrison said, picking himself off the floor.

"Weapons aren't responding, sir." The *Giffen* rocked again.

"Stone me!" Captain Morrison said. "We get the bloody point!"

"We're a sitting duck, sir," Neary said. Cro climbed into Hitch's chair.

"Sir, we've got an incoming message."

"Let me hear it." Morrison said. He straightened his tunic and took a breath as sparks showered the bridge.

"So you thought you could fool an old space squid, did you?" Commander Kirby said.

"I don't know what you're talking about," Captain Morrison said.

"Stowing away savages! Conspiring with Crow! Holographic hooligans masquerading as my men!"

"Oh, that," Morrison said.

"I trust you've learned your lesson. Or shall I make my point again?"

"That won't be necessary," Morrison said. "I hereby surrender my ship." He kept his eyes on the screen so he wouldn't have to look at his men.

"Excellent," Kirby said. "I take it your teleporter's still in order?"

"Ellis?" Morrison said.

"It appears to be working, sir."

"Very well," Kirby said. "Then I'll accept your surrender personally when you beam aboard my bridge."

"I'd like to bring someone else with me. A token of our good will."

Kirby arched an antennae. "Oh?"

Morrison looked off-screen. "Bring the prisoner here," he said. His men offered a round of blank looks.

"Oh!" Ellis said under his breath. "Yes, sir, right away." He went out the door, where Sprang was hiding.

"Play along," Ellis said.

"Sprang!" Kirby said as Ellis marched his long-lost squid into view.

"He's been our prisoner," Morrison said. "I'm turning him over to you."

"Bloody barbarians," Kirby said. "Have they mistreated you, soldier?"

Cro jumped into view before Sprang had a chance to reply. "He's been on a hunger strike," Cro said. "It's not our fault he can't speak."

"This is a matter for Sterankons only," Commander Kirby said.

"But this was all my idea," Cro said. "I was trying to save my people."

"You?" Kirby said. "You're a savage."

"I think you know better than that."

"Morrison, am I to believe this creature was the mind behind all this?"

"It's okay," Cro told Morrison firmly. Morrison played along.

"I wouldn't call him a mastermind. But he had a hand in it."

"Then let him suffer the consequences," Commander Kirby said. "Bring him along with Sprang. And if you or Crow have phasers drawn, I'll have you shot on sight."

"Just give me time to set the coordinates," Captain Morrison said.

"Very well." Kirby signed off. Morrison turned to Cro.

"I take it you have a plan?"

CHAPTER SEVENTEEN

The *Giffen* floated helplessly out the *Eisner's* front viewport, but Kirby had his back to it as his antennae twitched. He was flanked by McFarlane on one side and Gibbons on the other. Ditko was at his station, lowering the *Eisner's* shields to allow the *Giffen's* men to teleport in. They all watched the same empty spot on the bridge.

"Phasers on stun," Kirby said.

The air shimmered in front of them. Kirby's men leveled their weapons. McFarlane frisked Captain Morrison once he materialized.

"He's clean."

The Commander locked eyes with his vanquished foe, but Kirby did not gloat. He would allow Morrison his dignity in the short time the traitor had left.

The space beside Morrison shimmered and was shortly displaced by Cro. Cro struggled to rein his stomach in as McFarlane patted him down. Sprang appeared to Morrison's other side, scared out of his wits. McFarlane went to search the squid.

"Keep your hands off him," Kirby said.

"But cap'n," McFarlane objected.

"Can't you see that soldier's in shock? Come over here, m'boy."

Sprang gave Kirby a blank look.

"Go on," Morrison said.

Sprang hesitated, but slithered forward and stood in front of Kirby. Kirby raised his hand as if to shake Sprang's, but then saluted instead.

"Welcome back, soldier."

Sprang sniffed the Commander.

"Good lord," Kirby said.

"I'm sure we can bring him back to us, sir," Ditko said.

"Quite right. At ease, soldier," Kirby said. Sprang took his place by McFarlane.

"Now then, Captain Morrison, I demand you explain yourself."

"Actually," Cro interjected, "there's someone else who should be here."

"Poppycock," Kirby said.

"The Swamp People have a new chief."

"I see no reason to negotiate with a few stray savages."

"I can help make the peace if you let me live," Cro said.

"Turncoat," Morrison muttered.

"Hmm," Commander Kirby said. "Ditko, hail the *Giffen*."

"Yes, sir." Ditko got Ellis on-screen.

"I'm looking for a savage named Shirt," Kirby said. "Send him to my bridge."

"It's all right, Ellis," Morrison said.

"He's on his way." Ellis signed off. The tension on the bridge was heightened when the door opened again. A cleaning droid rolled through, followed by Grell in his work clothes.

"What the devil are you doing here?" Kirby said.

"Sorry, sir. I didn't know you had company."

"Get that bloody thing off of my bridge."

Grell fumbled with the remote to his cleaning droid as the space beside Morrison shimmered. Shirt materialized next to the captain and Cro.

"This is Shirt?" Kirby said. "He's a boy."

"He inherited the role from his father," Cro said.

"What's that curious belt he's wearing?"

"Morrison made it for him. We bought his people's support with junk."

"Clever," Kirby said. "Is that why this savage has a translator?"

"No, it isn't," Cro said. "He wanted to understand you if you spoke in the snake gods' tongue."

"Marvelous," Kirby grinned. "So tell me, Chief Shirt," he addressed the boy. "What do you have to say for yourself?"

Shirt looked at Kirby, then turned to Cro. Cro nodded.

"Ooo ooo eeeee."

"It's a--HURK!" McFarlane choked as Sprang yanked him off his feet. Sprang heaved the squid at a nearby console as Gibbons got off a shot. The phaser blast hit Sprang dead-on but did not fell a squid. Instead, it shorted his Chameleon 3000, revealing an unconscious ape.

Grell pushed a button on his remote. His cleaning droid ejected three phasers. He tossed two to Cro and Morrison. Grell aimed the third at Kirby but Ditko stunned the janitor first.

Morrison caught his weapon and dodged a blast in one smooth rolling motion. Cro fumbled his and picked it up. Shirt flipped the switch on his belt.

Commander Kirby assessed the battle. McFarlane was dazed but stirring. Gibbons, Morrison, Ditko and Cro had phasers trained on each other.

"Bravo," Kirby told Morrison. "An excellent attempt. But I expected treachery." He tapped his chest communicator. "Activate Plan B."

The wait for Kirby's countermeasure was suitably ominous. The combatants maintained their tense standoff as the door to the bridge slid away. Morrison was the first to react.

"No, really. A cow?"

"Mooo," Betty said, glaring through a laser-sighted monocle. At her command her simple harness whirred, clicked and transformed, encasing her in metal plates and horn-mounted missile launchers.

"Take cover!" Captain Morrison said as Betty launched her attack, scattering cavemen and squid alike with her indiscriminate aim.

"Lightle! Your bionic bovine's gone mad!" Kirby roared into his pin.

"She's not listening to me," Lightle's voice said. "I'm afraid we've unleashed the beast."

As First Mate, Ellis was acting captain with Morrison away. He combatted his anxiety by barking at his men.

"Neary! Put that fire out!"

"Aye, sir," Neary said. He unhooked a fresh extinguisher from beneath a NO SMOKING sign.

"Bagley, how are our shields?" Ellis said.

"Still down," the squid replied.

"Keep on it. And let me know the second that the *Eisner's* shields go down. Gruenwald, how are you doing?"

"Reinforcements are standing by."

"Good," Ellis said. "Have they been briefed?"

"Such as it is," Gruenwald said. "Sprang...uh, the real one...is coaching them now. He's trying to use small words."

"And you're okay with the controls?" Ellis asked.

Gruenwald did a quick scan of his station. "No problem. They're just like they were on the *Eisner*."

"Stand by," Ellis said.

The two squids' antenna turned to the viewport.

"It must be going well."

"What makes you say that?" Gruenwald asked.

"Because," Ellis said. "We're still here."

Betty's harness was sprouting new weapons. Laser trails scorched the bridge floor. She decided to concentrate on the two hairy men. It was their race she had the most grievances with. The snake-legs would have to wait.

"Bugger me!" Morrison huddled by Cro. "That's one vindictive cow."

"I still don't like having Shirt up here," Cro told him.

"Neither do I. But the bloody gorilla wouldn't listen to you."

Cro poked his head up. "Shirt!"

Shirt was huddled one station away. He hurried across the gap. A volley of blasts bounced off the caveboy's energy barrier.

"Cover me," Morrison told Cro.

He crawled across the room.

"Sir, your phaser isn't on stun," Ditko told the Commander.

"I'm aware of that, Ditko," Kirby said.

"But you're shooting up your own bridge."

"Nothing that can't be replaced," Kirby said, waiting for his gun to recharge. A phaser blast sailed over his shoulder. Cro was getting the hang of his aim.

Morrison crawled undetected and snaked a tentacle over his goal. He pulled a lever on Ditko's console, which caused a pleasant hum.

"They've dropped the shields!" Ensign Gibbons said. The *Eisner's* crew surged forward. Morrison stunned Gibbons before he was hit himself. He slumped to the floor, unconscious.

"Get that bloody shield back up," Commander Kirby bellowed. Lightle entered through the door as Ditko restored the controls. Cro popped up from behind his cover. His shot sailed wide of its mark.

"Am snake chief dead?" Shirt asked, doe-eyed, as Cro ducked down beside him.

"No, he's just sleeping," Cro told the boy. It seemed the right thing to say. Without Morrison, Cro doubted that they would hold out much longer.

"Listen to me," Cro told Shirt. "I want you to run for the door."

"But me want to stay with Crow," Shirt said.

"I'll catch up with you, okay?"

The caveboy's eyes were welling up.

"Okay," Shirt sniffed.

Cro took a deep breath and popped back up.

"Go!"

Shirt broke for the door. He scampered behind the nearest console as Cro aimed carefully. His blast stunned Ditko, who fell forward, pushing the shield controls.

"Destroy them!" Kirby bellowed. Lightle, McFarlane and Betty pinned Cro down with wild shots. Then the space in front of their target was occupied by Chief Dog.

Dog took poorly to teleportation and promptly doubled over. But as soon as Dog was stunned, another caveman took his place. Ugh beamed aboard next to his son. He knelt down beside Shirt.

"Am boy okay?" Ugh said. Shirt nodded. A shot passed over their heads. Ugh popped up, hurled his spear, and pinned Lightle's sleeve to the wall. Kirby, McFarlane and Betty split up, fanning out over the bridge.

"Crow need help," Shirt told his father.

"Okay. Boy stay here." Ugh was smart enough to keep his head down as he made his way toward Cro.

Smash beamed aboard by Morrison and picked up the unconscious squid's phaser. He sniffed it, turned it in his hand, and threw it at Lightle. When that didn't work, he clubbed the squid with much better results.

The battle shifted for good once Rock, the cleanup hitter, arrived.

"Ach, not her," McFarlane said as Rock charged into battle. He decided to slither away and fight another day. But as he triggered the door a chunk of debris whizzed over his shoulder. He turned around and there was Shirt clutching a fistful of rubble. The boy dropped his force field in order to throw, but he was not afraid.

"So that was you, eh, boyo?" McFarlane said, amused. "I'll make ye a deal, then. You leave me be, and I won't have to shoot."

Shirt cocked his throwing arm.

"All right, then," McFarlane said. "I'm sick of the lot of ye." He switched his phaser to displace and leveled it at the boy. Shirt hurled his hunk of metal faster than McFarlane could shoot. McFarlane said, "guh," and his last conscious act was to squeeze his phaser's trigger. Shirt disappeared, beamed to safety aboard the *Giffen's* bridge.

"At last," Gruenwald said. "We couldn't get through that little shield of yours."

Shirt got his bearings, looked out the viewport, and worried for his family and friends.

Smash was trying his best to not get blown to bits by a cow. Betty was unloading at will and having the time of her life. One of her blasts sailed over Smash and brought the ceiling down. He was pinned under a pile of rubble. Betty moved in for the kill.

"Stupid moo, face me," someone said. Betty looked over her shoulder. A hairy creature was facing her down from several yards away.

Rock stood her ground. She kept her club shouldered. It was a straight shot between them. Betty snorted, trained her sight and shot a single rocket. Rock strode forward, swung her club, and batted the rocket away.

Betty fired a second missile. Rock swatted it aside. Her look of calm ferocity made Betty break out in a sweat. Her armor produced twin shoulder canons which fired concussion grenades. Rock strode right between the blasts. She did not blink an eye.

Betty took a few steps back as Rock bridge the gap between them. They studied each other. Betty swallowed hard and prepared herself for the business end of a club. Instead, Rock set her weapon aside and knelt in front of the cow. She took Betty by the horns and headbutted her right through her armor.

Betty blinked slowly. She tipped over. And that was the end of that.

Cro looked at all the unconscious bodies strewn around the bridge. He tried to remember who was left. Then he found himself facing a phaser.

"Surrender and I'll grant you a merciful death," Commander Kirby said. "That's more than a savage deserves." There was a thud. The Commander flopped forward, revealing Ugh behind him.

"Thanks for the save," Cro said.

Ugh smiled and patted his club. There was nothing like the classics.

Neary beamed aboard just in time to miss the entire fight. He ducked under a swishing club.

"Hey! I'm on your side."

"Sorry," Ugh said. He helped Neary up. "Snake gods all look same."

Neary took in the stunned and clubbed bodies. The bridge was shot to pieces.

"What's wrong?" Cro asked him. "We won."

"I'm just thinking about what Morrison's going to say when he wakes up and has to fix this."

Snake wondered why he hadn't run into any of his people. Surely some of them must have fled the same direction as he. But he had searched the swamp for hours and not seen anyone.

Smoke choked the air. The sky was dark and blotted out the sun. Snake worried that his people might blame this whole mishap on him. He parted a tall grass thicket.

He was no longer alone.

Rex didn't smell the hairy man coming, but he didn't waste any time. Chief Snake studied Big Teeth's tonsils. Rex snapped him up and reared back. The dark clouds parted long enough to reveal a really big rock. It was like the ground had been turned upside down and was falling from the sky.

If Rex could speak, and his mouth wasn't full, he would have probably said something like, "Rats."

CHAPTER EIGHTEEN

The *Giffen* floated beside the *Eisner* over the newly cratered Earth. Cro entered the *Giffen's* engine room, where Morrison was making repairs.

"You wanted to see me?"

"Yeah," Morrison said. "You want to hand me that?"

Cro assumed he was referring to the gizmo by his feet. He passed it to Morrison. "How are you feeling?"

"Bloody sore," Morrison said. "I must have been stepped on while I was out."

"That was probably Smash," Cro said.

"But you made a good call, sending your people in instead of us to fight."

"Well, we've got more experience bludgeoning things," Cro told Morrison.

"I mean it, I'm impressed. Kirby may be a lunatic, but he was a pretty tough squid in the end."

"What can I say? I'm ahead of my time."

"I've been thinking about that," Morrison said. "What if I told you I could send you someplace where there were a lot more people like you?"

"You could do that?" Cro said.

"It involves some bending the rules," Morrison said. "And also time and space. But I think I could pull it off."

"What about all of you?" Cro said.

"Well, my ship is bolloxed up. But I'm scavenging parts from the *Eisner*. She'll be spaceworthy in a week or two."

"Then what will you do with the *Eisner*?"

"We're going to tow it," Morrison said.

"How?"

"With tractor beams."

"Oh," Cro said, trying to picture it. "And you're bringing Betty, too?"

"That's right," Morrison said. "She's deadly, but we need her milk."

"And what about my people?"

"They can stay aboard until the dust clouds settle down a bit on Earth. It may be cold, but that'll make those nasty lizards bugger off."

"I just want to thank you for all of your help," Cro said.

"No, I want to thank you. And I will if you let me," Morrison said.

"All right. Tell me more."

An honor guard of squid and cavemen turned out to say good-bye. Cro was moved as he stepped on the bridge. He never realized he had friends.

"Am Crow leaving now?" Shirt said, stepping forward. Cro knelt in front of the boy.

"I guess so," Cro said.

"Why you no stay here?"

"Because I don't belong."

"But Crow am friend," Shirt said.

"Don't worry. Larry will take care of you." He gave Shirt a hug. Cro moved on to Ugh and Rock. He eyed Rock warily. To his surprise Rock blinked back tears and gave him a bear hug.

"Crow am mighty warrior," she said. "Him help keep son safe."

"You're welcome," Cro said warmly. "And thanks for not crushing my skull." He shook Ugh's hand. "Thanks for saving me."

Ugh handed him his club. "Here. You take. This am best club. It help keep Cro safe."

Cro's eyes welled up. He thought of his father.

"Thank you," he said.

"I'm gonna miss you," Grell said next.

"Thanks. I heard you got a promotion."

"Yeah," Grell said. "I'm warden now. I get to make Kirby clean."

"Nice working with you," Sprang told Cro. Cro shook hands with Morrison's men. He congratulated Daisy and Leech on expecting their first child. Finally, he came to Chief Dog.

"Take good care of our people," Cro said. Dog nodded solemnly.

"It's time," Captain Morrison said.

Cro took his place away from the crowd and looked down the line of faces.

"Remember," Captain Morrison said as he worked the controls at his station, "we only have enough power to do this once. Are you sure you're ready to go?"

It was too late for second thoughts.

"Yes," Cro said. "I'm ready."

Morrison pulled a lever and the lights dimmed on the bridge. The cavemen in line shied away but Cro knew what was coming. A point of light formed near the floor and etched a door in front of him. Cro lingered a moment, smiled at Shirt, and stepped through the portal.

The Lake People had a rough go of it after Chief Dog passed away. Many of them died from exposure or poor leadership. They were contemplating eating Chief Fight when the bears got to him first. Things looked up when they merged with the Swamp People and appointed Shirt their new chief. He was a great warrior, a fair and just leader, and wise beyond his years. Not that anyone would have argued with him. His right-hand man was an ape.

Shirt saw his tribe, now dubbed the Cave People, through the long winter that coated Earth. But his greatest achievement was, in fact, the adoption of the wheel. Shirt saw it on the snake gods' ship and thought it came in handy. So the wheel wasn't invented as much as backwards-engineered.

As time passed, the dinosaurs died out from the unseasonable cold. As for the snake gods, their legend faded from caveman history.

Though the cave paintings of flying bowls would haunt archeologists for years.

The crew of the *Giffen* were greeted as heroes when they returned to Steranko. Morrison restored the planet's power and became its first president. Unfortunately, his second term was cut short by a coup.

Betty had been cloned multiple times to provide enough milk for the planet. The process accelerated the otherwise-leisurely rate of evolution. By the fifth year a batch of test tube cows stood up and placed guns in their hands, and the Daughters of Betty trampled the planet under their iron hooves. Eventually the squid of Steranko came to accept the bovine rule, and the races lived in harmony as long as there was free TV.

Cro stepped out of the dimensional doorway and into a brave new world. Except that it looked an awful lot like the one he left behind.

The idea was for Morrison to send him forward in time to an era where the cavemen had evolved as much as Cro. But looking around, Cro feared that he had not been sent far enough. The cavemen he saw gathered around a fire could have come from his former tribe. They were no less slouched, uncivilized, or conversationally challenged. They may even have regressed.

But then a girl came into view, carrying firewood. Unlike the others, she walked upright. She knelt beside the fire. Her eyes caught Cro's as she piled the sticks. She stood and walked toward him.

She was the most beautiful women he had ever seen. Cro felt like he had seen her before. She reminded him of

"Daisy?"

A look crossed her face, surprise mixed with interest. "How do you know that name?"

"You, uh, look like a Daisy I know."

"My grandmother's name was Daisy."

"Lucky guess," Cro smiled. Small world.

"You're not from around here, are you?"

"I used to be," Cro said. "But lately I've been...traveling."

"I thought so," she said. "My people aren't known for complex sentences."

"So what's your name?" Cro said. "Is it Daisy?"

"No," she said. "It's Violet."

"Violet. That's a pretty name."

"Thanks," she said. "What's yours?"

"Cro," he said, bracing himself for the usual response.

"Oh, as in Cro-Magnon man?"

"Exactly," Cro beamed.

"Would you like to take a walk with me, Cro?"

It was a beautiful day.